HALLOWEIRD

HALLOWEIRD

CLASSIC STORIES FROM THE SEASON of SAMHAIN

Edited by Johnny Mains

THE·BRITISH·LIBRARY

This collection first published in 2024 by
The British Library
96 Euston Road
London NW1 2DB

Selection, introduction and notes © 2024 Johnny Mains
Volume copyright © 2024 The British Library Board

"When Hell Laughed" © 1928 The Estate of Christine
Campbell Thomson. Licensed by the Marsh Agency.
"The New House" © 1965 The Estate of Elizabeth Walter.
Reproduced by permission of A. M. Heath Literary Agents.

Every effort has been made to trace copyright holders and to obtain their permission for the
use of copyright material. The publisher apologises for any errors or omissions and would
be pleased to be notified of any corrections to be incorporated in reprints or future editions.

Cataloguing in Publication Data
A catalogue record for this publication is available from the British Library

ISBN 978 0 7123 5502 5

Frontispiece illustration by Denslow from *The Pearl and
the Pumpkin* (T. Fisher Unwin, 1904).
Cover design by Mauricio Villamayor with illustration by Mag
Ruhig. Original interior ornaments by Mag Ruhig.
Text design and typesetting by Tetragon, London

Printed in Wales by Gomer Press Ltd.

CONTENTS

Introduction: A Brief History of Early Halloween   vii
A Note from the Publisher   xv

POEMS

Hallowe'en
  John Mayne   3

Halloween
  Robert Burns   9

Hallowe'en: Or, A Tale of Terror
  Revi   21

'Twas the Night of All Hallows
  Geraldine   25

TALES

Vermudyn's Fate: A Tale of Halloween
  R. Fryer   33

Out of the Night
  Elizabeth Phipps Train   53

The Face in the Glass
  Letitia Virginia Douglas   71

'Struther Kannock's Halloween
  Edgar L. Wakeman   85

The Phantom Ride: A Hallowe'en Ghost Story
  Lyllian Huntley   105

The Vow on Hallowe'en
  Lyllian Huntley Harris   115

The Banshee's Halloween
    Herminie Templeton Kavanagh   121

The Graveyard
    Alphonse Courlander   145

All Souls' Night
    Eleanor Fitzgerald   155

The Sword
    Rachel Swete Macnamara   163

Cockrow Inn
    Tod Robbins   171

When Hell Laughed
    Flavia Richardson   195

All Souls'
    Edith Wharton   207

Moonlight-Starlight
    Virginia Layefsky   235

The New House
    Elizabeth Walter   249

The Grove
    Mary Williams   283

Acknowledgements   299

INTRODUCTION

A Brief History of Early Halloween

But ah! What a miserable relic of olden times—a mere
shadow of the Halloween of the past, is our degenerate festival.

JOHN O' GROAT JOURNAL, 31 OCTOBER 1845

My earliest memory of Halloween haunts me still. We lived in deep countryside and it was so dark the stars were too afraid to come out. Someone
knocked at the door; I opened it, forgetting to turn the hall light on. There
stood a girl around the same age as me (seven, or so) dressed as a witch,
holding a neepie* on a string. It had stabbed-in een† and a coarsely cut
wound of a mooth.‡ It was one of the most frightening things I had ever
seen, the flame of the candle dancing inside, throwing weird light out of
its eyes and maw, with the rim of the lid glowing…

If I close my eyes, I can still see that hellish image.

As an adult, I'm quite hesitant to go near them when in the supermar-
ket; I'm only at my happiest when they are boiled and mashed and have
a nice knob of butter mixed into them. And pumpkins are much easier
to carve…

Back in the mists of time, prehistoric Ireland and Britain's year was split in
half by the great pagan fire-festivals, Beltane/May Day, which marked the

---

* turnip

† eyes

‡ mouth

beginning of summer and Samhain (once a seven day event) which marks the beginning of winter. These were both druidic magic ceremonies, but as Sir James George Frazer notes in his rather immense work, *The Golden Bough: A Study in Magic and Religion* (1890), the dates had little to do with solstices or equinoxes and more to do with moving livestock:

> When May Day comes, the seed has long been committed to the earth; and when November opens, the harvest has long been reaped and gar-nered, the fields lie bare, the fruit-trees are stripped, and even the yellow leaves are fast fluttering to the ground. Yet the first of May and the first of November mark turning-points of the year in Europe [...] they do deeply concern the European herdsman; for it is on the approach of summer that he drives his cattle out into the open to crop the fresh grass and it is on the approach of winter that he leads them back to the safety of the stall. Accordingly it seems not improbable that the Celtic bisec-tion of the year in two halves at the beginning of May and the beginning of November dates from a time when the Celts were mainly a pastoral people [...] clearly traced in the popularity, on the one hand, of May Day and its Eve (Walpurgis Night) and, on the other hand, of the Feast of All Souls at the beginning of November, which under a thin Christian cloak conceals an ancient pagan festival of the dead.

History shows that the main celebrations of Hallowe'en were purely druidical, the calling together of wicked souls.[*] In time these druidic ceremonies were grafted with some of the characteristics of the Roman festival in honour of Pomona held about the first of November, in which nuts and apples, representing the winter store of fruits, played an impor-tant part.

---

[*] There is extensive online writing on Saman, lord of the dead—however this was a fabrication by General Charles Vallancey in his 1786 book *A Vindication of the Ancient History of Ireland*. No character of this description is found in mediaeval Irish literature.

The Christianisation of these pagan festivals began in 610CE, when the church decided that there were far too many saints for whom to have a day and a festival and "All Hallows" or "Hallowemass" was instigated in memory of the martyrs—this took place on the first of May. It was changed in 834CE with a new date, that of November 1st. It was a commemoration of all the saints, so there was the new name, "All Saints' Day". All Saints Eve/All-hallowmass/ Hallow Eve, became the night when superstition and the mystery of existence ran riot.

Bobbing for apples can be seen on the Luttrell Psalter (an illuminated volume containing the Book of Psalms and other devotional material and liturgical calendars). The Psalter, which was created between 1320 and 1340, shows a presumably older or ancient tradition of a person with their hands tied behind their back trying to catch the apple with their teeth. Shakespeare mentions "Hallowmass" in several of his works, including *The Two Gentlemen of Verona* (written between 1589 and 1593): "to speak pulling, like a beggar at Hallowmass". In 1667, the Hallowmass Fair of Beauly saw a remarkable price for cattle "which brought a great deal of money to the country and the Highlanders went home well pleased."

In 1780, the printer, journalist and poet John Mayne of Dumfries, wrote the twelve stanza poem "Hallowe'en", published in *Ruddiman's Weekly Magazine*. Five years later, Robert Burns, influenced greatly by Mayne's work, presented his own "Halloween", twenty-eight stanzas long and clearly a dry run for one of his most celebrated work which would appear in 1790, the epic that out-Halloweens "Halloween"—"Tam O' Shanter". But with "Halloween" we see not only a celebration, but a valuable historical document of the rituals and games of the time. It wouldn't be long before everyone was offering their own take—such as "Halloween" in the *Poetical Works of Jane Little, the Scotch Milkmaid* (1792). The mimicry of Burns in this is excellent and I can only imagine how tiring but lucrative it must have been as a publisher to have yet another Burns-style poem come along! English poet Charles Graydon decoded

Burn's poem for English readers with his own take, "On Nuts Burning, Allhallows Eve" (1801), and in doing so created an evocative piece in its own right.

1809 saw the publishing of *British Georgics*, an epic work by the Scottish poet James Grahame (1765–1811) which detailed the beauty that happened in the British Isle over the course of the year. His poem saw that the Burns fanboying had yet to dissipate even though Burns had been in the ground thirteen years. It does however have moments of its own *real* power, such as the following lines on the religious politics that happened *specifically* during Hallowe'en:

A few dim candles in derision shine
Of Romish rites, now happily forgot

The above alludes to the mockery of Catholic torch processions by first reformers. In 1818, tragedy befell Dumfries, when "some foolish clown" wrapped himself in a white sheet and knocked on the door of a cottage in Maxwelltown (west of the River Nith, which forms the historic boundary between Kirkcudbrightshire and Dumfriesshire) and screamed at the person who opened the door. Unfortunately the recipient was a pregnant woman and before the night was over she had delivered a dead child. The culprit was never found. In 1820, Walter Scott's novel *The Monastery* dealt with an infant daughter, born on Halloween and consequently gifted with the power of seeing the invisible world. And just imagine, being in the crowd at the Theatre Royal, Perth on 16 October 1820, to see Scott's *The Heart of Midlothian*, the "popular new Drama of Halloween", alongside *Hallowe'en, or, The Vampire and the Water Kelpie* and a new "melo Drama" called *Meg Murnoch, The Mountain Hag*.

In 1822, Hallowmass gets a mention in a novelette called *The Haunted Ships* by Allan Cunningham in *Traditional Tales of the English and Scottish Peasantry*, where on the Scottish side of the Solway Firth, "infernal shallops" (coastal fishing vessels) with those on board full of laughter and song vanish during a "certain night" with "the drowning shriek of mortals" heard. This is an expansion of his poem "Rhyme Legend of Richard Faulder, Mariner: Voyage in the Spectre Shallop" which was published in 1821 in *The London Magazine* and reprinted in *Twenty Scottish Songs* in 1822. And if H. P. Lovecraft wasn't aware of "Richard Faulder" (maybe he came across it in an old copy of *The New-York Literary Gazette and American Athenaeum, Volume 2*, where it was also reprinted) I'll eat my cthulhu plush.

In 1824, a gentleman wrote to the *Fife Herald* (he also mentions that he remembered the year of the great meteor, forty-one years before) who recalled "with infinite delight" his childhood during which efforts were made to catch an apple, affixed to one end of a stick, balanced and suspended by a string, whilst to the other end a burning candle was attached as a counterprize. This refers to "Snap Apple" and the game was so popular in the 18th and 19th centuries that Halloween was often referred to as Snap Apple Night. Candles and apples are hung from the ceiling and the goal is to get a bit of apple without consuming any wax or getting burned. This game, with its direct lineage to the Luttrell Psalter, saw at that time five-hundred years of apple bobbing. As of today, we've reached seven hundred years trying to drown ourselves for pleasure.

In 1827, David Lyndsay wrote "The Three Damsels: A Tale of Halloween" for *Forget Me Not; A Christmas, New Year's and Birthday Present for 1827*, a slight love story, but certainly a fun one. *The Knickerbocker*, in 1833, published an observance titled "All Saint's Eve; or, A Recollection of the Irish Peasantry by an American in Ireland" which mentions the Pookah, "an imaginary monster, supposed to be all powerful on All Saint's Night." Also mentioned is the beautiful saying, "my corpse to the devil"—and the gift of a pig at a wedding festival. By the time we get to 1844, we have Arthur Cleveland Coxe's *Halloween; A Romaunt, With Lays, Meditative and Devotional*—an overindulgent piece that could only have been written during that unconventional period.

"Hallowe'en" (1870) by Helen Elliott was published in *Godey's Lady's Book and Magazine* and is a key text in the history of America's love affair with Halloween and Halloween parties. Clinton Scollard's "A Ballad of Hallowmass" was published in *Lyrics of the Dawn* (1902). Scollard, a minor poet, nevertheless gives his best when:

> It happened at the time of Halloween, when the dead may walk abroad,
> That the wraith of Ralph of the peaceful heart, went back to the courts of God.

The American periodical *The Judge*, in 1912, had this write up on the evening, an almost pre-*Purge* take on things: "In smaller towns the evenings bring terror […] if citizens are not routed out by fires in their domiciles, they awake in the morning of All Saints' Day to wonder why the saints had not during the night prevailed over deviltry."

With this book I've leant more heavily on tales and poems published before 1924 and *Halloweird* covers just under two-hundred years of Halloween writing. Beginning with John Mayne's (regardless of how his surname is spelt, I'm claiming him as a relative!) toe-dip into pleasing terrors and then blowing our minds with Burns's brilliance, I really wanted to create an anthology with a sense of time, yet have stories that feel timeless when you read them. All dashed with horror and fun. One of the biggest surprises when researching and putting this book together was when I discovered the prose poem "Hallowe'en, or, A Tale of Terror" by the mysterious "Revi". I genuinely believe it's a lost classic of Halloween writing and should be used by every editor for the next two hundred years until anthology collectors get sick of using it. It's also a privilege to use a story by Lyllian Huntley Harris, only known for having one story in *Weird Tales* and not only using that, but another story by her that's never been reprinted in one hundred and twenty-three years.

This book, while seasonal, can be read all year round, preferably at night, using only candlelight to illuminate the page. Treat yourself. Trick yourself. Because for me, at least, *every* day is Halloween.

JOHNNY MAINS, 2024

A NOTE FROM THE PUBLISHER

The original short stories reprinted in the British Library classic fiction series were written and published in a period ranging across the nineteenth and twentieth centuries. There are many elements of these stories which continue to entertain modern readers; however, in some cases there are also uses of language, instances of stereotyping and some attitudes expressed by narrators or characters which may not be endorsed by the publishing standards of today. We acknowledge therefore that some elements in the stories selected for reprinting may continue to make uncomfortable reading for some of our audience. With this series British Library Publishing aims to offer a new readership a chance to read some of the rare material of the British Library's collections in an affordable format, to enjoy their merits and to look back into the worlds of the past two centuries as portrayed by their writers. It is not possible to separate these stories from the history of their writing and as such the following stories are presented as they were originally published with minor edits only made for consistency of style and sense. We welcome feedback from our readers, which can be sent to the following address:

British Library Publishing
The British Library
96 Euston Road
London, N W I 2 D B
United Kingdom

At the time o' Halloween
Strange unchancy things are seen

"HALLOWE'EN" BY E. B. SINCLAIR,
EDINBURGH EVENING NEWS,
31 OCTOBER 1949

Poems

HALLOWE'EN

John Mayne

Published in Ruddiman's Weekly Magazine, *November 1780*

John Mayne (1759–1836) was a Scottish printer, journalist and poet, born in Dumfries. He left home at an early age and worked with the famous Foulis brothers at their publishing business in Glasgow. He was intimately acquainted with Robert Burns, who did him the honour of homaging Mayne's "Hallowe'en" and also adapting two lines of "Logan Braes" into his own song of "Logan Water", avowing that he did so. Sir Walter Scott, in allusion to Mayne's most-celebrated poem "The Siller Gun" (based on the Dumfries custom of shooting for the "siller gun", a supposed gift from James the Sixth) said it surpassed the efforts of Robert Ferguson and came near to those of Burns. Mayne died on 14 March 1836, of "advancing age".

Things unattempted yet in prose or rhime.

Of a' the festivals we hear,
Frae Handsel-Monday till New Year,
There's few in Scotland held mair dear
For mirth, I ween,
Or yet can boast o' better cheer,
Than Hallowe'en.

Langsyne indeed, as now in climes
Where priests for siller pardon crimes,
The kintry 'round in Popish rhymes
Did pray and graen;
But customs vary wi' the times
At Hallowe'en.

Ranged round a bleezing ingleside,
Where nowther cauld nor hunger bide,
The farmer's house, wi' secret pride,
Will a' convene;
For that day's wark is thrawn aside
At Hallowe'en.

Placed at their head the gudewife sits,
And deals round apples, pears, and nits;
Syne tells her guests, how, at sic bits
Where she has been,
Bogle's ha'e gart folk tyne their wits
At Hallowe'en.

Grieved, she recounts how, by mischance,
Puir pussy's forced a' night to prance
Wi' fairies, wha in thousands dance
Upon the green,
Or sail wi' witches over to France
At Hallowe'en.

Syne, issued frae the gardy-chair,
For that's the seat of empire there,
To co'er the table wi' what's rare,
Commands are gi'en;
That a' fu' daintily may fare
At Hallowe'en.

And when they've toomed ilk heapit plate,
And a' things are laid out o' gate,
To ken their matrimonial mate,
The youngsters keen
Search a' the dark decrees o' fate
At Hallowe'en.

A' things prepared in order due,
Gosh guide's! what fearfu' pranks ensue!
Some i' the kiln-pat thraw a clew,
At whilk, bedene,
Their sweethearts by the far end pu'
At Hallowe'en.

Ithers, wi' some uncanny gift,
In an auld barn a riddle lift,
Where, thrice pretending corn to sift,
Wi' charms between,
Their joe appears, as white as drift,
At Hallowe'en.

But 'twere a langsome tale to tell
The gates o' ilka charm and spell.
Ance, gaen to saw hampseed himsel,
Puir Jock Maclean,
Plump in a filthy peat-pot fell
At Hallowe'en.

Half filled wi' fear, and droukit weel,
He frae the mire dught hardly speel;
But frae that time the silly chiel
Did never grien
To cast his cantrips wi' the Deil
At Hallowe'en.

O Scotland! famed for scenes like this,
That thy sons walk where wisdom is,
Till death in everlasting bliss
Shall steek their e'en,
Will ever be the constant wish of
Jockie Mein.

HALLOWEEN

Robert Burns

Published in Poems, Chiefly in the Scottish Dialect, *The Kilmarnock Edition (1786)*

Robert ("Rabbie") Burns (1759–1796) is regarded as the national poet of Scotland. Living in abject poverty, in Alloway, Ayrshire, he was taught to read and write by his father. Robert was smart enough to leave the home and get a job in the "liberal professions", but the poverty the family suffered meant that Robert was only allowed to work as a hired plough-boy or shepherd. But in the breaks between the two jobs he was able to go to Parish school, and it was there that his passion for books began, and he turned his hand to writing poetry. Of course, his first effort was a love poem, and it was this passion (or weakness) for the other sex that would run through most of his life's work.

After Burns's father died penniless in 1784, Burns saw himself entwined with several women and tried to leave the country for Jamaica. To try and get enough money to go he arranged publication of some of his work in nearby Kilmarnock. *Poems, Chiefly in the Scottish Dialect* (1786) brought him considerable acclaim. This volume includes "Halloween", and he "communicates" with John Mayne's poem through it. Burns died only ten years after its publication, aged 37. His death has been stated (from several sources) to be from either rheumatic fever, a bacterial condition from a tooth abscess or an overindulgence of alcohol. Years after his death, Burns's skull was removed by John McDiarmid and several phrenologists, along with a plasterer called James Fraser, made casts of it.

Yes! let the Rich deride, the Proud disdain,
The simple pleasures of the lowly train;
To me more dear, congenial to my heart,
One native charm, than all the gloss of art.

GOLDSMITH

Upon that night, when fairies light,
   On Cassilis Downans dance,
Or owre the lays, in splendid blaze,
   On sprightly coursers prance;
Or for Colean, the rout is taen,
   Beneath the moon's pale beams;
There, up the Cove, to stray an' rove,
   Amang the rocks an' streams
          To sport that night.

Amang the bonie, winding banks,
   Where Doon rins, wimplin, clear,
Where Bruce ance rul'd the martial ranks,
   An' shook his Carrick spear;
Some merry, friendly, countra-folks
   Together did convene,
To burn their nits, an' pou their stocks,
   An' haud their Halloween
          Fu' blythe that night.

The lasses feat, an' cleanly neat,
   Mair braw than when they're fine;
Their faces blythe, fu' sweetly kythe,
   Hearts leal, an' warm, an' kin':
The lads sae trig, wi' wooer-babs,
   Weel knotted on their garten;
Some unco blate, an' some wi' gabs,
   Gar lasses' hearts gang startin
              Whiles fast at night.

Then, first an' foremost, thro' the kail,
   Their stocks maun a' be sought ance;
They steek their een, and grape an' wale
   For muckle anes, an' straught anes.
Poor hav'rel Will fell aff the drift,
   An' wandered thro' the bow-kail,
An' pow't for want o' better shift,
   A runt was like a sow-tail
              Sae bow't that night.

Then, straught or crooked, yird or nane,
   They roar an' cry a' throu'ther;
The vera wee-things, toddlan, rin,
   Wi' stocks out owre their shouther:
An' gif the custock's sweet or sour,
   Wi' joctelegs they taste them;
Syne coziely, aboon the door,
   Wi' cannie care, they've plac'd them
              To lye that night.

The lasses staw frae 'mang them a',
   To pou their stalks o' corn;

But Rab slips out, an' jinks about,
    Behint the muckle thorn:
He grippet Nelly hard and fast;
    Loud skirl'd a' the lasses;
But her tap-pickle maist was lost,
    When kiutlin in the fause-house
              Wi' him that night.

The auld Guidwife's weel-hoordet nits
    Are round an' round divided,
An' mony lads an' lasses' fates
    Are there that night decided:
Some kindle, couthie, side by side,
    And burn thegither trimly;
Some start awa, wi' saucy pride,
    An' jump out owre the chimlie
              Fu' high that night.

Jean slips in twa, wi' tentie e'e;
    Wha 'twas, she wadna tell;
But this is Jock, an' this is me,
    She says in to hersel':
He bleez'd owre her, an' she owre him,
    As they wad never mair part,
Till fuff! he started up the lum,
    An' Jean had e'en a fair heart
              To see't that night.

Poor Willie, wi' his bow-kail runt,
    Was brunt wi' primsie Mallie;
An' Mary, nae doubt, took the drunt,
    To be compar'd to Willie:

Mall's nit lap out, wi' pridefu' fling,
 An' her ain fit, it brunt it;
While Willie lap, and swore by jing,
 'Twas just the way he wanted
    To be that night.

Nell had the fause-house in her min',
 She pits hersel an' Rob in;
In loving bleeze they sweetly join,
 Till white in ase they're sobbin:
Nell's heart was dancin at the view;
 She whisper'd Rob to leuk for't:
Rob, stownlins, prie'd her bonnie mou,
 Fu' cozie in the neuk for't,
    Unseen that night.

But Merran sat behint their backs,
 Her thoughts on Andrew Bell:
She lea'es them gashin at their cracks,
 An' slips out-by hersel':
She thro' the yard the nearest taks,
 An' for the kiln she goes then,
An' darklins grapit for the bauks,
 And in the blue-clue throws then,
    Right fear't that night.

An' ay she win't, an' ay she swat—
 I wat she made nae jaukin;
Till something held within the pat,
 Good Lord! but she was quaukin!
But whether 'twas the Deil himsel,
 Or whether 'twas a bauk-en',
Or whether it was Andrew Bell,

14

She did na wait on talkin
     To spier that night.

Wee Jenny to her Graunie says,
   "Will ye go wi' me Graunie?
I'll eat the apple at the glass,
   I gat frae uncle Johnie:"
She fuff't her pipe wi' sic a lunt,
   In wrath she was sae vap'rin,
She notic't na, an aizle brunt
   Her braw, new, worset apron
      Out thro' that night.

"Ye little skelpie-limmer's-face!
   I daur you try sic sportin,
As seek the foul Thief ony place,
   For him to spae your fortune:
Nae doubt but ye may get a sight!
   Great cause ye hae to fear it;
For mony a ane has gotten a fright,
   An' liv'd an' died deleerit,
      On sic a night.

"Ae hairst afore the Sherra-moor,
   I mind't as weel's yestreen,
I was a gilpey then, I'm sure,
   I was na past fyfteen:
The Simmer had been cauld an' wat,
   An' stuff was unco green;
An' ay a rantin kirn we gat,
   An' just on Halloween
      It fell that night.

"Our stibble-rig was Rab M'Graen,
    A clever, sturdy fallow;
His sin gat Eppie Sim wi' wean,
    That lived in Achmacalla:
He gat hemp-seed, I mind it weel,
    An' he made unco light o't;
But mony a day was by himsel',
    He was sae fairly frighted
                That vera night."

Then up gat fechtin Jamie Fleck,
    An' he swoor by his conscience,
That he could saw hemp-seed a peck;
    For it was a' but nonsense:
The auld guidman raught down the pock,
    An' out a handfu' gied him;
Syne bad him slip frae 'mang the folk,
    Sometime when nae ane see'd him,
                An' try't that night.

He marches thro' amang the stacks,
    Tho' he was something sturtin;
The graip he for a harrow taks,
    An' haurls at his curpin:
And ev'ry now an' then, he says,
    "Hemp-seed I saw thee,
An' her that is to be my lass,
    Come after me an' draw thee
                As fast this night."

He wistl'd up Lord Lennox' March,
    To keep his courage cheary;

Altho' his hair began to arch,
 He was sae fley'd an' eerie:
Till presently he hears a squeak,
 An' then a grane an' gruntle;
He by his shouther gae a keek,
 An' tumbled wi' a wintle
    Out-owre that night.

He roar'd a horrid murder-shout,
 In dreadfu' desperation!
An' young an' auld come rinnin out,
 An' hear the sad narration:
He swoor 'twas hilchin Jean M'Craw,
 Or crouchie Merran Humphie,
Till stop! she trotted thro' them a';
 And wha was it but Grumphie
    Asteer that night?

Meg fain wad to the Barn gaen,
 To winn three wechts o' naething;
But for to meet the Deil her lane,
 She pat but little faith in:
She gies the Herd a pickle nits,
 An' twa red cheekit apples,
To watch, while for the Barn she sets,
 In hopes to see Tam Kipples
    That vera night.

She turns the key, wi' cannie thraw,
 An'owre the threshold ventures;
But first on Sawnie gies a ca',
 Syne bauldly in she enters:

A ratton rattl'd up the wa',
　　An' she cry'd, Lord preserve her!
An' ran thro' midden-hole an' a',
　　An' pray'd wi' zeal and fervour,
　　　　　　Fu' fast that night.

They hoy't out Will, wi' fair advice;
　　They hecht him some fine braw ane;
It chanc'd the Stack he faddom't thrice,
　　Was timmer-propt for thrawin:
He taks a swirlie, auld moss-oak,
　　For some black, grousome Carlin;
An' loot a winze, an' drew a stroke,
　　Till skin in blypes cam haurlin
　　　　　　Aff's nieves that night.

A wanton widow Leezie was,
　　As cantie as a kittlen;
But Och! that night, amang the shaws,
　　She gat a fearfu' settlin!
She thro' the whins, an' by the cairn,
　　An' owre the hill gaed scrievin,
Whare three Lairds' lan's met at a burn,
　　To dip her left sark-sleeve in,
　　　　　　Was bent that night.

Whiles owre a linn the burnie plays,
　　As thro' the glen it wimpl't;
Whiles round a rocky scar it strays;
　　Whiles in a wiel it dimpl't;
Whiles glitter'd to the nightly rays,
　　Wi' bickerin', dancin' dazzle;
Whiles cookit undeneath the braes,

Below the spreading hazel
      Unseen that night.

Amang the brachens, on the brae,
    Between her an' the moon,
The Deil, or else an outler Quey,
    Gat up an' ga'e a croon:
Poor Leezie's heart maist lap the hool;
    Near lav'rock-height she jumpit,
But mist a fit, an' in the pool,
    Out owre the lugs she plumpit,
        Wi' a plunge that night.

In order, on the clean hearth-stane,
    The Luggies three are ranged;
An' ev'ry time great care is ta'en,
    To see them duly changed:
Auld, uncle John, wha wedlock's joys,
    Sin' Mar's-year did desire,
Because he gat the toom dish thrice,
    He heav'd them on the fire,
        In wrath that night.

Wi' merry sangs, an' friendly cracks,
    I wat they did na weary;
And unco tales, an' funnie jokes,
    Their sports were cheap an' cheery:
Till butter'd so'ns, wi' fragrant lunt,
    Set a' their gabs a-steerin;
Syne, wi' a social glass o' strunt,
    They parted aff careerin
        Fu' blythe that night.

HALLOWE'EN:
OR, A TALE OF TERROR

Revi

Published in Belfast Commercial
Chronicle, *18 November 1807*

The following poem was written under a pseudonym, like many poems published in the local papers of the early 1800s, and I haven't been able to trace the true identity of "Revi". While the identity may never be known, "Hallowe'en: Or, A Tale of Terror" is one of my favourite pieces of this whole book. It is "proper" horror and I think it would have thrilled those who were told it senseless! It appears here for the first time since its initial publication.

The night it was gloomy, the Croghan it lour'd,
As MAC UILIN traversed the Banks of the Mourne;
In torrents the rain, rude and pitiless, pour'd
As by Hallowe'en Fancy, his footsteps were borne.

For his heart was the prey of sad joyless despair,
Since CELIA his passion insulting reprov'd,
And he swore he'd lose all in the magical sphere,
To force to his bosom the fair that he lov'd.

Tho' the tempest was howling, and starless the sky,
He dreaded no dangers, he fear'd not the storm;
But he silently pray'd that his gloom piercing eye
Might soon have a glimpse of her fanciful form.

Near the mouldering walls of an Abbey he strayed,
There, thrice he invok'd the foul demon of Air;
Then a flowerless sod o'er his shoulder he laid,
And seal'd with his blood the unsanctified prayer.

His rites scarce had ceased, when lo, in the gloom
On the ivy clad walls a blue flame he descried;
He trembled as down by the ash coloured broom,
A pale ghastly phantom towards him did glide.

'Twas not the sweet phantom of CELIA was nigh;
But a Gnomon of Hell met his horror-struck view;
"I come," cried the Fiend, with a heart-rending cry,
"Invoked by your spells to be wedded to you.

Long and sad was I chain'd in the venomous dell,
Till, thrice you invoked the Spirit of Air;
And your blood on the parchment confirmed the spell,
Now with me you'll fly to the Gulph of Despair."

Then the merciless Fangs close encircled his arms,
And she told him a tale which no mortal could tell;
How his Hallowe'en freaks and his magical charms,
Had doom'd him fore'er to the cavern of Hell.

Then ghastly she smil'd, "never more shall we sunder,
Ne'er again to the world shall your footsteps return."
Then she tore out his heart with a yell loud as thunder,
And headlong both plunged into dark-rolling Mourne.

STRABANE, NOV 10, 1807

24

'TWAS THE NIGHT OF ALL HALLOWS

Geraldine

Published in The Brooklyn Daily Eagle, *31 October 1865*

As frustrating as Mr. and Mrs. "Anonymous" always are—there's not much we can glean about "Geraldine". They appear to be American, wrote for *Oliver Optic's Magazine* ("the best magazine in the world or *anywhere else*") in 1872, which was edited by William Taylor Adams until its demise in 1875. There is mention of their poetry being "crowded out" in the *Grant County Herald* (Wisconsin) in 1878 and two poems published in the *Seward Independent* (Kansas) in April 1890 were reprinted (in the *Mulvane Record*, Kansas) the year after. There *was* a "Rose Geraldine" writing poetry in *Peterson's Magazine* in 1873. It could be that Rose's first poems were written under a loose pen name until she became more confident in her work, or simply due to domestic issues of the day. Another poet, Geraldine Meyrick from Santa Cruz was briefly in contention, until I discovered that she wasn't writing until the late 1890s and was a young teenager.

'Twas the night of All Hallows, when goblin and sprite,
Were to roam, it is said, on that terrible night;
For Tradition had whispered, and who could deny,
That this night the Good People their influence ply;
Each youth then with heart, bounding wild with delight,
In frolic, would brave fiercest terror or fright;
Each maiden, unconscious of evil or harm,
Would timidly venture some portent or charm.
All was gladness and joy, faces beaming with mirth,
While closer, and closer, each drew round the hearth;
The wind whistled louder, and fearfully shrill,
And louder it grew, over mountain and hill,
'Twas a deed that was worthy of notice, remark,
On Halloween Night, to go forth after dark;
For 'tis said such enchantments, on this night, were wrought,
That those who would venture, were sorely distraught.

The hours passed so heedless: long stories were told,
Of dreamers, who've dreamed, of large vessels of gold;
The listeners were many, some laughed and some sang,
Till louder, yet louder, the merriment rang;
When one of the maidens, sprang up with a scream,
"My Linen, my Linen, I laid by the stream!"
All sprang to their feet, looking stern and amazed,
While the Maiden far into the pitchy gloom gazed,
"In mercy, I pray you, oh! follow me not;"
And before they could speak, she sprang from the spot.

The joyous festivities quickly were hushed,
And stories forgotten to their minds at once rushed;
On swiftly she rushed; the fast deepening gloom
O'ershadowed, encircled her as a dark tomb;
She hastens quick onward, and looks not around;
She fancied she heard there a queer stealthy sound;
Her strength is now failing—'twill shortly be spent—
Too late for remorse, too late to repent.
She moves not, she breathes not, her heart ceased to beat;
Oh, horrors! she certainly hears coming feet;
At length she returns, with step weak and slow;
Her sad heart is weary and brimful of woe;
She essays to call; ere her words have been said,
She feels that two hands on her shoulders are laid.

Oh, night of sad horrors! of dismal despair!
Which called for a strength superhuman to bear;
No kind hand to help her—so helpless and frail;
No loved voice to cheer her, or hear her deep wail.
With tottering step, she arrives at the door;
It quickly is opened—she falls on the floor.
Those locks that were raven, are frosty and white.
Through the terrors and woes of that horrible night;
Those cheeks, once so beauteous, their roses have paled,
And her buoyant young spirit with terror is quailed;
She lies there, but lo! most amazing to note,
Encircling her neck was a FROLICSOME GOAT.

You may look for those scenes, but 'twill soon be in vain;
They are passing away—they return not again;
The people who heard them in childhood and youth,
Deemed them the strongest assertions of truth;

Through long years of sorrow they came as a balm,
As oil on the troubled waves, bringing a calm;
When thraldom, oppression, their country had wrung,
They poured o'er the legends their loved bards had sung;
As a sunbeam they shone on their suffering path,
Assuaging their sorrows, appeasing their wrath;
But they too are gliding; this joy will not last;
And stories and legends be dreams of the past.

Tales

VERMUDYN'S FATE
A TALE OF HALLOWEEN

R. Fryer

Published in Chambers's Journal of Popular
Literature, Science, and Art, *Fifth Series, vol. 1,
nos. 34 (23 August) and 35 (30 August), 1884*

This story was originally presented as "anonymous" when I first came across its publication in a newspaper—until I tracked it to its original publication. Using my bibliographical aids for *Chambers's Magazine*, I discovered the author to be "R. Fryer." That's where the trail runs cold, so, as with other authors I may have been unable to find in previous books, answers on a postcard, please!

I

A LITTLE knot of miners were gathered round the fire in Pat Murphy's drinking-saloon, situated in that delightful locality known to diggers as Rattlesnake Gulch. They were listening eagerly to the details of a story related by Gentleman Jack, a member of their fraternity who had recently visited San Francisco. He had gone there with the twofold object of having what was facetiously termed a "fling," just to relieve the monotony of existence, and also with the intention of exchanging the gold he had accumulated during the past six months for notes and coin. He had likewise in some mysterious way contrived to get rid of the burden of his wealth, and now returned almost penniless to the bosom of his friends; but this fact in nowise diminished the cheerfulness with which the wanderer greeted his mates, or disturbed the equanimity with which he recounted his adventures since their last meeting. He had just ended his narration with the account of a curious discovery of which he had heard the details that morning on his way back to the Gulch.

"A mighty queer story, anyhow," observed Pat, alias "Flash" Murphy, as he emptied his glass.

"Mighty queer!" repeated the chorus, following suit.

"Spin out that yarn again, mate!" demanded a gentleman who rejoiced in the sobriquet of Old Grizzly. This personage had only entered the "bar" in time to catch the concluding words of the narrative. "Let's have it, Jack!" he repeated impatiently.

Thus invited or encouraged, the young man rejoined carelessly: "It was nothing much, only the finding of a man—all that was left of him at least—in a place they call the Devil's Panniken, when they were blasting the rock for the new railroad between Sandy Bar and 'Frisco—"

"I know the place—travelled that road years afore they ever thought of running cars through it," interposed Old Grizzly. "But what about the man?"

"Well, that's the queer part of the story; not that they found a man, but that they should have found him where they did, and with so much gold on him too," answered Gentleman Jack with his slow languid drawl.

"Say!" ejaculated Old Grizzly, who was listening with a curiously eager excited face to the indifferent, careless utterances of the younger man. "Cut it short, mate, and tell us how they found him."

"Well, they were blasting a big rock, and as it broke, it disclosed a cave right in the heart of the limestone; but there must once have been an entrance to it, for the skeleton of a man lay there. All his clothes had fallen to dust; but there was a ring on one finger, and about seventeen ounces of gold lay in a little heap under him. It had evidently been in his pockets once; but the bag that held it, and the skeleton's clothing, were alike a heap of dry light dust. There was nothing to identify him, nothing to show how long he had been there. The very ring he wore was of such a queer outlandish fashion that the fellows who found him could make nothing of it."

"Was that all?" demanded the elder man.

"All that I can recollect.—Stay! I think he had a rusty knife somewhere near him, but nothing more. It's a queer story altogether. How he got there, if he died in the cave, and by what means it was afterwards closed up—these are all mysteries."

Old Grizzly smoked in silence for some time; and the miners had resumed the usual occupations of their idle hours, drinking, smoking, playing poker, and quarrelling, which amiable amusements had been momentarily suspended in order to welcome the return of the "Wanderer" with due *empressement*, when suddenly the deep voice of Old Grizzly was heard above the babel of tongues, saying: "This story of Jack's about the Devil's Panniken and the man they found there puts me in mind of what befell me and a mate of mine when we were riding through that same place one October night hard upon twenty years ago. His Satanic Majesty had a hand in that job, if ever he had in anything."

"Spin us your yarn, old chap!" shouted a dozen voices; and passing the word for a fresh supply of whisky, they gathered closer round the log-fire, filled their pipes, and prepared to listen with the keen interest of men who lead an isolated and monotonous life far from the stir and life of big cities, and are therefore ever ready and eager to hail the smallest incident with pleasure; while a good story-teller is regarded with universal respect. Rattlesnake Gulch was at that period a comparatively new Claim, on the very outskirts of civilization, and news from the cities was long in reaching the denizens of this locality.

"What I am now going to tell you, boys, has never crossed my lips from that day to this, and most likely never would, if I hadn't chanced to come along just now as Jack was speaking about the body those navvies found in the Devil's Panniken."

Being politely requested by his hearers to "Shell it out!" Old Grizzly continued: "Whether you believe what I'm going to say is no matter now. *I* believe it, though I can't understand how it all came about. Well, as I said before, the time was hard on twenty years ago, and the night was the last in October."

"Bedad, and it's that same night now!" put in Murphy.

"So it is!" acquiesced Old Grizzly; "but I never thought of it till this minute; and now the whole thing comes round again on All-Halloween, of all nights in the year. Those of you boys who've been raised in the old country will know what folks believe, in most villages and country places, of Halloween, and the strange things that happen then to men abroad at midnight, and to lads and lasses who try the Halloween spells for wives and husbands."

"Sure everybody knows them things," agreed Murphy, casting an uneasy glance over his shoulder as he spoke.

"Well, true or false, I for one thought little enough of them when I was young; but as luck or fate would have it, I rode through the Devil's

Panniken on the 31st of October, that special night I'm going to tell you of. I wasn't alone either; perhaps, if I had been, I shouldn't have felt so jolly; for, not to speak of the loneliness of the place, with its great black rocks towering up on either side of you, and almost shutting out the sky, except for a narrow strip overhead, the place had an ill name both with the Injuns and with miners. Many a queer tale was told round camp-fires, and folks said the place was haunted; that miners had lost their way there many a time, and had never been seen or heard of again.

"I'd been working all that season at a Claim—a new un then, but worked out and forgotten now—which we used to call Cherokee Dick's, because a Cherokee Injun first showed us the place. There was perhaps a dozen of us all told; but I chummed and worked from the first along with a chap they called the 'Flying Dutchman.' When we had been together a goodish bit, he told me his real name was Cornelius Vermudyn; and I acquainted him with mine and where I hailed from. He was a Dutchman, sure enough, but had travelled half over the world, I used to think from his talk; and he could speak as good English as you or me—or any here."

A dubious smile hovered for an instant on Gentleman Jack's lips at this naïve statement, but nobody observed him; they were all intent on Old Grizzly and his yarn, and that worthy continued: "We began to find our Claim about cleaned out, and we—that's me and Vermudyn—reckoned to make tracks before the winter, and get down 'Frisco-way. Well, we each had a good horse and a nice bit of gold, and we was sworn mates—come what might—so we started, riding as far as we could by day and camping out at night, if we weren't able to reach a settlement or diggings by nightfall.

"On this night, it seemed as if we'd no luck from the beginning. We lost our way for a goodish bit, and were some time finding the track again; after that, night seemed to come on us suddenly like. We'd rode and rode that day without ever a sign of man or beast, and when we came to this place, Vermudyn says: 'This must be the famous Devil's Panniken, old boy.' I had been almost falling asleep on my horse's neck; but I woke with a start, and answered all in a hurry: 'Of course it is.' It seemed somehow as if I knew that place well, and I began to ride on quickly.

"'Stop!' hollered Vermudyn, 'unless you want to lame your horse or break his knees among those rocks.' As he came up with me, he put his hand on my arm, and I drew rein.

"'Anyhow,' I said, 'let's get out of this, and then we'll camp for the night. I'm as tired as a dog, and can hardly stick in my saddle.'

"'Why not camp here?' says Vermudyn with a laugh. 'Who's afraid?'

"'I'm not—if that's what you mean,' I answered; 'but I'd rather camp outside.'

"'A good two miles of bad riding,' said he quietly. 'Why shouldn't we content ourselves with a snug corner of the rocks, where we can shelter from the wind? As far as I can make out, there's brush and litter enough for a fire, and we've got a bait for our horses.'

"While he talked and argued, I grew more and more tired, exactly as if I had ridden a hundred miles without drawing rein. It seemed then as if I didn't care what came next, so long as I could roll myself up in my blanket and snooze, so I answered short enough: 'Have your own way. The place is ours, I reckon, as much as it is other folks's.'

"'The pixies and demons, you mean,' laughed Vermudyn. 'I know all the miners' tales! Never fear. I dare wager we shall see nothing worse than ourselves, if we stop for a month of Sundays.—Did you ever hear,' he went on, 'of the White Witch of the Panniken? She should meet us here-abouts, if all tales be true. She waits for lonely travellers, and shows them gold in the rock where gold never was in daylight; and if a man is tempted, for the gold's sake or hers, to spend the night with her, he's never seen or heard of in this world again. She feasts him with the sight of big nuggets and her own beauty, while she sucks his heart's blood like the vampyre; and when his body is drained to the last drop, he is flung aside among the rocks or dropped in some dark gully; and she comes back to watch the road for a fresh prey.'

"'I've heard of the White Witch many a time; but I never knew the rights of the story until tonight,' said I. 'But witch or no witch, we'll have to stop; the road grows harder, and my horse seems to stumble at every step. It's so dark, too, I can hardly see my hand before my face; yet it seemed almost daylight when we rode into the gorge.'

"'The pair of us will be too many for the White Witch, anyhow,' said Vermudyn. 'Too much human society don't agree with her ghostly constitution.'

"We had stopped together, and I was just going to get off my horse, when Vermudyn sang out in a hurry: 'I see a light!—there to the left. Let's ride up. We may find a party forced to camp out like ourselves; or they may be Injuns; and any company is better than none tonight.'

"'Right enough,' says I, rubbing my eyes. 'There is a light, and a pretty strong one too; a steady light, mate, and not a Will-o'-the-wisp. I never heard before of white man or Injun daring to camp in the Devil's Panniken.'

"'Well, we must go up quietly till we can see our company,' said my mate. 'We don't want to drop on a gang of freebooters, who'll ease us of the dust, and then leave us with a bullet through our heads, as a parting gift.'

"After this, we rode forward in silence for what seemed a quarter of a mile; but we went at a foot's pace, on account of picking our way among the rocks that lay thick in the road. Then, as we turned a sharp corner, we saw all at once that the light came not from a camp-fire, but from a house!

"'Well,' says I, 'in all the years I've worked in these parts, man and boy, and tramped from claim to claim, I've never heard that there was a hut or shanty in this place.'

"'Nor I neither,' returns Vermudyn; 'but perhaps it's a new spec; though what folks could want with a house where there's neither gold to find nor land to farm is more than I can tell. We may thank our luck we've tumbled across it.'

"He jumped off his horse as we drew rein at the door of the queerest old house I ever saw. It was a tumble-down sort of a place, half-stone, half-wood; and the woodwork was fast going to decay, though we could see plainly enough that time and money had once been spent over it. The stone was pretty rough; but the house was all pointed gable-ends and queer-shaped long windows. The high-peaked overhanging roof and the diamond panes reminded me of houses I'd seen in England when I was a young un. The pointed gables were faced with carved oak; and heavy oaken beams, black with age, formed the framework of the upper stories; while the spaces between were roughcast with shingle and plaster. The wickedest old faces were grinning and leering at us from the carvings above the windows; and we could see the whole place, every stick and stone about it, as plain as daylight. We had been riding in darkness through the Devil's Panniken, a darkness that grew blacker as we went on; and the light from this house fairly dazed us at first. Every window flamed as though there were jolly fires in each room, and hundreds of candles. The place seemed all aflame inside and out; the walls were as bright as if the moon was shining her clearest and strongest full on the house; yet,' said Old Grizzly, dropping his voice impressively, 'there was no moon at all that night! We stopped and looked at one another in wonder, and then stared at the house again. We could hear sounds inside now quite plain, men's voices, and women's too. Ugly sounds besides, that I couldn't understand; such howling and shrieking as though all Bedlam were let loose inside—wailing like some creature in pain, and roars of mocking laughter. I turned deadly cold, and shivered as if it were midwinter.

"'For mercy's sake, let's get away from this madhouse—if it's not something worse!' said I. 'All's not right here; and I'd go afoot all night before I'd rest in that place.'

"'Nonsense!' returned Vermudyn in his impetuous way. 'I'm going in, anyhow; and you'll stop to see fair-play, I know.'

"The upshot of it was he seized my arm and led me into the house; while a gipsy-looking fellow came out for our horses, after we'd unloaded our knapsacks and blankets. My gold was sewed in a belt round my body, and I determined to fight hard for dear life, if need be; whilst I was equally determined to see Vermudyn through the night's adventure, as far as it lay in my power.

"If the outside of the house was strange to us, the inside was still stranger. The furniture appeared to be hundreds of years old. The presses, chairs, and tables were all of polished black oak, which reflected the light of many candles; while a big fire roared in the open fireplace, near which a table was laid for supper, and everything on it matched all we'd already seen. There were drinking-horns mounted in silver; cups of the same; such a load of plate as I'd never seen in my life, and such as, I was pretty certain, belonged to no country inn in a wild district where the only travellers were miners, and the only natives Injuns. On the top of a carved press in one corner there was a fine show of bottles—long-necked, slender flasks, crusted over with age and cobwebs; and short squat bottles, that held hollands and Kirschwasser, Vermudyn told me.

"Well, while we took stock of the room and its contents, there wasn't a soul to be seen, yet the noise and hubbub continued still all around us; the clatter of a hundred voices rising and falling far and near like the wind. Laughter, screams, and low moans all together, or following each other quickly. The longer I listened, the less I liked it; yet, as I sat in a corner of the big chimney, I seemed to grow drowsy and stupid-like, as if I had no power of my limbs or my voice. I think I couldn't have walked a dozen steps for a thousand pounds; yet I could still hear and see all, through a light mist that fell betwixt me and everything I looked at.

"Vermudyn didn't appear afraid or surprised in the least; and the spell—I can call it nothing else—that was over me had no effect on him. He stood in front of the fire, warming his hands, and looking round him quite gaily, and pleased with all he saw.

"'Wake up, mate!' he called to me; 'we've fallen in luck's way this time, surely. You've no cause to fear. It seems to me that I must have been here a score of times before, I know the place so well; and yet'—he stopped for a minute and put his hand over his eyes—'and yet—it can't be!—I know it. That press,' he went on, 'should hold the green suit.' And stepping across the room, he opened a worm-eaten cupboard in the far corner, and took out a suit of faded green velvet, the cut of which reminded me of old pictures I'd seen at home; and when Vermudyn took them out and looked them over carefully, the whole thing struck me so absurdly, that I began to laugh like a maniac, though still I had no power to speak. I wanted to tell him he would look like a tumbling mountebank at a fair, if he rigged himself out in the velvet suit; but I only laughed and nodded at him silently from the chimney corner, like some drivelling old dotard.

"However, he didn't put it on, but, as if struck suddenly by another thought, threw it aside, and opened a cupboard near the fireplace. He smiled again. 'I knew it was here,' he said softly, as he returned to the fire, and stooping down, held something to the light. It was a little box of carved ivory, yellow with age, and strangely shaped; but Vermudyn seemed as familiar with it as he was with the rest of the wonders in that house, for he pressed a spring, and the lid flew up, disclosing a sparkling chain made like a snake, with shining scales of beaten gold that glittered in the flickering firelight.

"While Vermudyn was still looking at its twisted coils and muttering to himself, the door opened, and a troop of figures crowded into the room."

II

"Of the troop of figures who came flocking into that strange and mysterious house, I observed that some of those behind held more lights, though the room was bright enough already, while the foremost carried dishes. But I had no eyes for the meat and drink they brought, or for anything but a girl in their midst; and it was just the same with Vermudyn, I saw in an instant; only, whilst I was full of horror and a dread I couldn't shake off or overcome, Vermudyn felt no fear, no surprise; only an intense delight flushed his face with joy, and his eyes glittered, as he came forward eagerly to meet the girl, who, it seemed to me, was pale as death, with eyes that glowed like flame.

"I think I never saw so colourless a creature to live and move—if indeed she did live. And her hair—redder, and yet more golden than the chain Vermudyn held—was coiled round her beautiful head in the same snaky folds. She never looked at me for an instant, but went straight to Vermudyn, and putting both her hands in his, said some words in a strange language that sounded like spoken music. It was the sweetest voice I ever heard, and the softest. He answered in the same tongue, laughing and clasping the hands she put in his. From that minute, he fell under her spell, and had no eyes or ears for anything save that strange white woman.

"She poured out wine for him, and he drank it with feverish haste, still looking at her and holding her hand. I noticed, though, that he shuddered when she first touched him, as if her hands were icy-cold; but he felt that no longer; he was just mad-like and stupid, as a bird is with a snake. He could only watch her with wild eyes that never left her face.

"The men and women who came in with this awful, beautiful creature were dark, mostly, and reminded me of the gipsies I used to see when I was a boy at home in England. One of the girls, dressed in outlandish clothes, embroidered in scarlet and gold, came up and offered me some wine—even held it to my lips—and the scent of it made me mad to taste. The girl's arm was close round my neck, and her wicked eyes, dry and bright as a toad's, were looking into mine with a mocking smile, as she sang a soft, strange song, like laughing and crying all in one. But I shut my teeth hard, and turning away my head, closed my eyes, determined to resist her with all the strength of my will so long as I was conscious. Even in that dreamy, bewildered state, I felt afraid of entirely losing my senses, and something seemed to tell me I was lost if I yielded for an instant. My tempter laughed then, a loud hideous laugh, and flung down the silver cup she had offered me. The wine was spilt, and I fancied it turned to liquid flame as it touched the floor.

"Still I had no power to speak or move from my place, but I watched Vermudyn more eagerly than ever. The supper-table was pushed on one side; and the room was now filled with dancers, dancing fiercely and madly to a wild tune, like the song of the gipsy when she leant over me with the poisoned wine. The tune rose louder and higher, and the dancers moved faster to keep time with the unearthly music—unearthly and wild, but so beautiful that I could have listened for ever, I thought. At times it sounded like the wind sighing through the aspens at night; then it rose to a roar like waves breaking on the beach in a storm. Yet, with all the changing sound, the roar of a storm, and the wailing of the wind—tears and laughter and pain—the music still kept time and tune, and the mad dance went on without a pause.

"Foremost amongst them all was Vermudyn, and the woman in white with the glittering eyes and hair. He was holding her fast in his arms as they flew round; her head lay on his shoulder, and his face was bent down over hers. But I could see, as I watched him, that he had grown almost as white as the girl he held; and now her great eyes blazed with such awful light, I shuddered to look at them; while, as she danced and clasped Vermudyn, I fancied a tinge of colour came into her white lips, and her cheeks were a shade less deathly.

"Still they danced, and still she grew brighter and warmer, but not like a living woman yet. And Vermudyn, like a mere straw drifting round and round in a whirlpool, became weaker and fainter every minute, and his face now was something ghastly to see; but his eyes were still fixed on the girl, and he could see nothing and feel nothing beside. Her shining hair had got loosened in the dance, and seemed to be flying round them like thin golden flames as they moved.

"It was she, now, who held Vermudyn up and forced him still to dance. His arms were round her yet; but her strength alone sustained the fainting man. She flew round as easily as ever; her feet scarcely touching the ground. The noise grew furious and deafening—music and laughter, shouts and screams that made my blood run cold, with snatches of old songs between, were all mingled together in one hideous mighty roar.

"The faces of the men, or the demons who took their shape, got more fiendish as they danced; when suddenly the dancers swept out of the room in a wild crowd, just as they had entered it, and in their midst Vermudyn, lying dead, or senseless, on the floor. I tried to move—to reach him somehow at that desperate pass; but I couldn't stir a finger. I struggled to shout aloud—to call his name. I might have been dead, for all the help I could give him. I had no power to speak or move.

"Directly that demoniacal crew left the room, the lights seemed to fade and the fire grow dim. Thick darkness fell over everything, and I could not see a ray of light from where I now lay like a helpless log.

"I remembered nothing more until I opened my eyes in broad daylight, stiff, and shivering with cold. I was lying at the entrance of a little cave among the rocks, wrapped in my blanket, and close to the embers of a dying fire. My horse, I saw, was picketed not far from me.

"I was still in the Devil's Panniken, sure enough. I saw the road by which we had come last night; but the place was strange to me; these were not the rocks I had seen before, which surrounded the place where we had spent the night.

"*We?* I was quite alone now, and broad awake! The house and all else had vanished. As the recollections of the past night came crowding back, I sprang up and looked around in wonder. The house—the very room—in which I'd been was so distinctly before my mind's eye, that I stood staring in amazement to find myself alone. No vestige of the house I've described to you, and no Vermudyn either! I told myself that I was clean mad. I searched for him in a sort of frantic hurry, and shouted his name, but heard only the echoes answer me.

"I tried to get farther into the cave at the mouth of which I'd been lying; but I soon found the way closed by a big chunk of rock. There was no other outlet to the cave, and there was nothing to explain the mystery. There was no sign of Vermudyn or his horse; *that*, no doubt, had strayed during the night. But where was *he*, and where, above all, had we two spent the night? I was fairly stunned. I felt for my knife, my revolver. These, with my belt, were safe enough. I had lost nothing. I was simply cold, hungry, and quite alone—save for my nag; and how glad I was of that companion, I can't tell you! He would be the means of getting me away from that awful place faster than my legs could carry me.

"I found a hunch of bread and some meat in my wallet; but I was too excited and wretched over Vermudyn's disappearance, to light a fire and boil some tea. As soon as I'd swallowed down my breakfast, I mounted my horse, and rode backwards and forwards for a good two hours, searching for the body, for I was clear in my own mind that my poor old mate was dead.

"Dead or alive, I hated to think of riding away and leaving him there in the Devil's Panniken. But it was no good. I hunted every hole and corner within a mile of the place—as near as I could judge—where we had spent the night. At last I gave up the hopeless search—no signs of Vermudyn anywhere; and before noon, I had turned my horse's head away from the wretched place, and for the first mile or so I rode so hard and fast that I began to blame my own folly in running away in broad daylight. From what, too?

"Ay, there was the rub! What was I riding away from? and how had I escaped, while Vermudyn was lost? I was almost mad when I went over the past twenty-four hours. I couldn't believe my senses. All I'd seen and heard too; and the only other witness was gone, vanished as completely as if he had been a spectre or part of some nightmare dream!

"I felt my brain reel as I passed mile after mile along the lonely road, till at last I began to wonder if the Vermudyn I thought I knew was ever a living man, or if he made part of a long hideous dream, which I thought I should never forget or get over.

"But I couldn't cheat myself so; the man had written his name inside my pocket-book, 'C. Vermudyn,' and had given me a ring he told me he once bought in an eastern bazaar. I've worn the ring ever since, in memory of him and that awful Halloween night.

"Sure enough, Vermudyn was no dream; but from that day to this his name has never crossed my lips; and nothing would induce me ever again to ride through the Devil's Panniken either by day or night.

"In my own mind, boys, it's as clear as daylight that the body found in that cave Gentleman Jack was telling you of a while since was neither more nor less than the skeleton of my poor old mate Vermudyn. I never thought to hear of his bones being found after all these years, poor old chap; or of telling you tonight what happened to us that Halloween in the Devil's Panniken. I only hope he wasn't alive in that awful place!—alive, and shouting for help, shut up there alone, and hopeless in the dark, whilst I was riding away in sunshine and clear air!—Phaw!" muttered the old man; "it's no good to think of that now; and talking's dry work.—Another go of whisky, Pat!"

The murmurs of admiration, astonishment, and feeble doubt over this wondrous story of Old Grizzly's were arrested almost ere they began, and each man stopped short, as a low, long laugh sounded through the room, and they then perceived what, being absorbed in the "tale of mystery," they had been too preoccupied to notice before—namely, that a stranger had entered the room some time during the progress of the narrative, and it was he who had dared to laugh! All eyes were turned significantly and inquiringly upon this presumptuous stranger; and one gentleman had gone so far as to deliver himself of the original remark, that "he calculated to call that mighty cool," when the newcomer advanced into the light of the flaring kerosene lamp, and Old Grizzly sprang to his feet, speechless and aghast.

"Well, old boy, don't you know me now?" asked the stranger. "Am I so little like the Vermudyn you chummed with in Cherokee Dick's claim?"

"It's Halloween *again*," muttered the other hoarsely, still delaying to take the proffered hand.

"And an unlucky night for me to turn up, after the scurvy trick I played you," laughed the stranger. "But look here, mate—if you kept my ring, I've kept yours; and I'm flesh and blood safe enough—no spirit or demon, as you seem to fancy."

Old Grizzly grasped both his hands, looking long and earnestly in his face meanwhile. "It is Vermudyn!" he at last exclaimed. "Though how they found your bones yonder in the Devil's Panniken, and yet you're alive and hearty here tonight, is more than Pat Murphy or any other Irishman could explain!"

"I had better say at once that there's no mystery about this—this—gentleman's arrival tonight, at least," interposed Gentleman Jack. "He is a chance companion and fellow-traveller of mine, and like myself, he hails from 'Frisco last."

"As you seem to be in the humour for telling stories tonight, mates," observed the newcomer, "perhaps it wouldn't be amiss if I explained to my friend here, in your presence, the truth of his strange Halloween experiences on the night he parted company with me—or I with him—whichever you prefer.

"I told you once," said he, addressing himself to Old Grizzly, "I had travelled a good deal and spent some years in the East; but I never told how much I had learned of the manner and customs of the people I lived with; or that, amongst other diverting knowledge, I acquired the art of smoking and eating that extract of hemp known in eastern countries as 'hashish'; and no one save those who have been under its marvellous influence can ever understand the wonderful reality of the illusions it produces—stronger and more powerful than any opium in its effect, and less harmful to use. Years ago, the drug was almost unknown; today, there are 'hashish' eaters and smokers in most of the big cities of the States.

"At the time I'm speaking of, it was little known, and its effects scarcely understood. I had taken it often enough myself; but some idle whim prompted me to try the result of a dose on my friend here, that special and memorable night of which he has just told you something. Well, I administered a biggish dose in a pill I gave him for an aguish turn he'd had; and after that, as we rode along I let him have some tobacco, as his own was smoked out, and this tobacco of mine consisted almost entirely of the dried hemp, the true 'hashish'. We had not ridden a great way into the Devil's Panniken, talking, as we rode, of the bad reputation of the place and the various legends concerning it, when the drug began to take effect on my old friend here, and he would have fallen from his horse, if I had not kept close beside him and supported him with my arm. As matters were then, I decided to dismount and camp for the night. For myself, I'd never been afraid of man or demon, and I knew my companion could go no farther; so I easily persuaded him to stop, though several times he muttered something about riding on.

"Well, I wrapped him in his blanket like a babby, lighted him another pipe, just to compose him, and set to work to make a rousing fire, for the night was cold, and a keen frosty wind came sweeping down the ravine. He behaved strangely enough for some time, muttering and talking, while I watched by him; then by turns singing and laughing, while he stared at me or the fire. Once or twice he struggled hard to get up; but by-and-by the hashish overpowered him, and he slept soundly. I remained by him the whole night, and then tried in the early dawn to awaken him, as we wanted to push on. But he slept so heavily, that the idea occurred to me to ride off and leave him to wake alone, thoroughly mystified between his hashish visions and the loss of me!

"It was a bad, mad sort of practical joke, but I was full of such follies in those early days. After I'd left him, I made tracks for the town we'd determined on visiting together, and waited for him some days; but he never turned up; and then an uneasy fear that some harm had befallen my friend through my own folly, got hold of me; and taking a sudden distaste for a digger's life, I made my way to the nearest port, and went on board a ship just starting for Europe, and which, luckily for me, stood in need of an extra hand.

"Since then, I've led a roving life on sea and shore, till fate landed me here tonight in time to listen to the account of my mysterious end, as it appeared to my worthy friend. I am sorry to spoil a good story, mates;

but the pleasure two old chums experience in finding each other alive and hearty after so strange a parting—twenty years ago—will, I hope, in some degree compensate for your disappointment in discovering that the White Witch of the Devil's Panniken had no hand in my fate after all!"

"But," interrupted Gentleman Jack, "a skeleton with a ring on its finger was found recently in the cave."

"Quite possible," returned the newcomer; "but I am happy to say it is not that of Cornelius Vermudyn."

OUT OF THE NIGHT

Elizabeth Phipps Train

Published in Peterson's Magazine, *vol. 96, issue 5, 1889*

Elizabeth Phipps Train (1856–1940) was an American author, touted as a literary sensation by the press of the day. Before her first novel, *Doctor Lamar* (Thomas Y. Crowell & Co., 1891) was published, she honed her craft writing for *Peterson's Magazine* (where this story was originally published in 1889), *10 Story Book* and *The Saturday Evening Post*. She was interviewed by *The Boston Globe* in 1894 on the serialization of *The Autobiography of a Professional Beauty* (this would go on to be published in book format by J. B. Lippincott Co., 1896) in *The Boston Globe* in May 1894. She was deeply interested in hypnosis, saying that "everything of a psychic nature interests me greatly". Her only other genre credit appears to be the short story "The Evil Eye" published in *Frank Leslie's Popular Monthly* (May 1887), although in *Doctor Lamar*, the protagonist does appear to administer a "death-producing drug" which warrants further research. She died at eighty-two, following a long illness.

MIRIAM Jerrold was called a peculiar girl, and, in fact, there was enough of the unconventional and unusual about her to justify the adjective. By many, her foreign birth and rearing were offered as a reason for her unlikeliness to American girls, while others urged that these traits had not characterized her when, at the age of sixteen, she had, upon the death of her father, come to make her home in his native land, having been consigned by the will which had made her a great heiress to the care of his only sister, Mrs. Maturin Bullock, of Fifth Avenue and Newport.

Even then her individuality had, of course, been sufficiently pronounced, but the latter class of commentators held that this was due to her marked accent and the somewhat Bohemian laxity of thought and conduct which had been acquired in the free artistic circles where her father had chosen to set up his Lares.

Those who best remembered the exquisitely lovely child whose wavy masses of golden hair had fallen in unconfined wealth over her shoulders, shading with a curling fringe the low sweet brow and seeming to frame the rarely beautiful face in a burst of sunshine, were earnest in their asseverations that in those days no touch or promise of gravity clouded the perfect features, no hint of sadness underlaid the smiling innocence of the frank blue eyes, and that every indication of the child's nature gave evidence of a temperament attuned to laughter and merriment.

Among those who argued thus was her aunt, who, having grown in her six years' guardianship of the girl to love and admire though never to comprehend her, found the unfulfilled predictions of those early days a sorely perplexing puzzle which she was extremely fond of discussing with her husband.

"Maturin," she would say, "what do you suppose makes Miriam so odd? I can't get her to join the Patriarchs; she turns the cold shoulder upon afternoon teas—says that a man sipping tea and talking gossip is the ignoblest work of God—and spends all her time and money on dirty creatures with horrible diseases; though, I daresay, many of them are as well as you or I, and only pretend sickness to wheedle money out of her."

"Well, they certainly succeed in that," replied her husband, on one of these occasions, about the time of the beginning of this story, "for she has as little left of her income at the year's end as if she were a society girl of the most extravagant tastes and habits."

"Think of that! And yet she dresses like a nun, and her only self-indulgence is in the matter of music. That taste, I suppose, she inherits from her mother."

The late Mrs. Jerrold would have been a famous prima-donna, had not love, in the shape of a rich American, stepped in and broken her contract with destiny.

"I suppose so; and it's a sufficiently ruinous one, if she keeps on as she has begun. Fancy paying the prices those conscienceless foreigners ask, for the purpose of educating the souls of a dirty lot of beggars, who would all find more melody in the Fisher's Hornpipe than in the finest aria that ever was composed! What she needs is a good, sensible husband to bring her to reason."

Mrs. Bullock sighed heavily.

"Yes, my dear; but I fear she is incorrigible there also. There is Frank, poor fellow—he worships the very ground she walks on; and yet, much as I desire the match, I cannot persuade myself that it will ever be accomplished."

"I thought you said, a little while ago, there was some sort of understanding between them," Mr. Bullock remarked, blowing a cloud of pearly smoke from the fragrant Havana between his lips—for it was in the library, during the hour consecrated to the enjoyment of his post-prandial cigar, that Mrs. Bullock had sought sympathy from her husband regarding Miriam's erratic conduct.

"Well, yes, and so there is; but I fear it promises little satisfaction to Frank. It is to the effect that, if nothing occurs before the first of November to make her change her mind, she will marry him."

"Well, I call that very satisfactory. Here it is the middle of October, and she is still at least tolerating his attentions. But why should she have set that particular day? It seems as though she must be anticipating some unusual occurrence about this time."

"Oh, no! I have put it rather peculiarly, that is all. Somewhere about the first of August he asked her—for the fourth time, I think—to marry him, and, instead of refusing again, as she had formerly done, she told him that, if he would give her three months, she would consent, unless she had good occasion to change her mind."

"Why, that's excellent!" Mr. Bullock exclaimed, cheerily; for this same Frank was his own and well-beloved nephew, his junior partner, and a charming fellow of irreproachable character and position. "In the name of all that's reasonable, Naomi, what more could you want?"

"Better assurance that Frank's desire may be fulfilled than Miriam's conduct affords. I feel sure that she cares no more—not, indeed, as much—for the dear boy than she does for you, and I cannot believe she is a woman to marry without love. But hush! here she comes."

The warning was uttered none too soon, for scarcely had the last word fallen from Mrs. Bullock's lips than the girl stood before them. Whatever exceptions frivolous-minded folk might have taken to Miriam Jerrold's strange indifference to their amusements and distractions, surely not even the most captious critic among them could deny her claim to a most exquisite and uncommon style of beauty.

She was a trifle above the medium height, but so justly and symmetrically proportioned that she seemed less tall than was really the case. Her wealth of lustrous hair was as rich and radiant as in those days when it had rioted in unconstrained luxury about the joyous childish face; but alas! how the features that its decorously-confined glory enshrouded had lost their charm of gayety and careless mirth. A strange expression of sadness had fallen like a shadowy mask over them, and into the great golden-lashed eyes had crept a look of wistful yearning that made their gaze at times hard for those who loved her to meet. This expression was especially dominant tonight, and, observing it, Mr. Bullock held out his hand to the girl, and, clasping hers, drew her to his side.

"Well, puss," he said, affectionately, as she sank upon her knees by his chair and dropped her head upon his broad shoulder with a gesture of abandon so rare in her as to be doubly precious when she gave way to it, "been working yourself to death among the hospitals today?"

Miriam drew a long sigh.

"No; that work never tires me."

"You imply that some other work does; if so, give it up, little one. We cannot have our child overworked, can we, mother?"

Before Mrs. Bullock could respond, a servant appeared in the doorway announcing visitors, and the lady hurried away to fulfil her social duties, leaving Miriam and her uncle to prolong their conversation *en tête-à-tête*.

"Little one," he said, "we were talking about you, mother and I, when you came in. What do you think she was telling me?"

"Uncle dear, you know I never could guess a riddle."

"Well, then, it was that perhaps you were going to make the old folks very happy—you and Frank."

A sudden shiver passed over the girl's kneeling figure; but the habit of self-control was a strong one, and she hid her emotion at once, while scarcely a quiver disturbed the music of the sweet, earnest voice that replied:

"And it would really please you to have me marry Frank?"

"If you love him, little one. But, Miriam—no, do not turn your eyes away: I want to see what they, as well as your lips, say—you must not marry the boy unless you want to do so. No consideration for us, no pity for him, must weigh with you in this matter. I won't have my little girl worried into marrying any man she doesn't love—and I thought that might be what was ailing her this evening."

The girl shook her head and murmured a few reassuring words, evidently afraid to say more, for fear of losing her self-control; for tonight her heart was very heavy, and the tender loving words of her uncle touched and well-nigh overcame her. Seeing that she could bear no further allusion to the matter at present, and desiring to give an entirely new turn to the conversation, Mr. Bullock took up one of the slender white hands that lay clasped upon the arm of his chair, and, touching a curiously-wrought ring of silver and platinum that bound the third finger—the only ornament, if so it might be called, that her hand wore—said playfully:

"Come, puss, tell me where this ring came from. It's a cumbrous affair for such a slight finger. Come, let me take it off, and—Hey! What's this! Why, bless my soul—Miriam—child—what is the matter?"

For some word, or look, or memory—some cause utterly unknown to Maturin Bullock—had overset the fine balance of self-repression, and Miriam had drawn herself down into a crouching, sobbing heap upon the floor at his feet.

It is two weeks later, and in a very different scene, that we next see our heroine. The occasion is a somewhat novel one to her, being that of the celebration of Hallowe'en, which is being held in a large private ballroom belonging to one of New York's most potent magnates.

The girl seems scarcely herself tonight. Her usually pale face is flushed; her eyes burn brilliantly with a fire that gives unwonted animation to her face; her laughter rings out clear and frequent, but seems pitched in a different key—a higher and less musical one—than that of its ordinary soft minor cadence. People look at her in amazement, and, failing to detect the unwholesome nature of her excitement, wonder if it is possible that this is the same sad-eyed, reserved and ungenial girl whom they have always seen shrinking and retiring from like scenes of festivity.

Tonight she is the centre of attraction, entering into the evening's amusements with such apparent enjoyment that Frank Haviland's spirits rise buoyantly, as it is their nature to do—the more so as they have long suffered repression.

"Surely," he tells himself, "if she meant to refuse me tomorrow, she could not be so heartlessly gay tonight." Then a bold thought occurs to him, and he immediately seeks to put it in practice; but so hemmed-in is the girl he loves by admirers, that not until supper is announced does he find it possible to speak with her alone.

With this one purpose in view, he enters the brilliant banquet-hall, where tables, gleaming with gold and silver plate and groaning beneath wondrous marvels of the confectioner's art, bar, for a few moments, his way to the figure which stands out from all other women in the world for him, and which, he rejoices to see, is withdrawn a little into a recess—alone, temporarily, during the absence of her cavalier in search of refreshments.

Quiet as Miriam Jerrold's dress usually is, tonight it is sufficiently conspicuous even in that magnificently-apparelled throng. It is all of the richest, rarest, filmiest white lace, over shimmering satin, while diamonds thickly besprinkle the *décolleté* corsage and gleam from arms, ears, and hair.

As Frank approached her now, he noticed that the mask had fallen from her features, and that a terrible weariness and wistfulness had settled on them. For a moment he felt horribly disconcerted. Surely, not to this sad-eyed suffering woman could he broach the request he had come to make; but, in another moment, Miriam's face had changed and resumed its former brilliancy.

"Well, well!" she cried, accosting him in a light, somewhat artificial tone, which, while it aided his purpose, yet was hateful to him, as being foreign to her. "A pretty way, this, to treat me during the whole evening! Not once have you come near me, sir, but left me wholly to the mercy of any compassionate cavalier."

"Your vanity has been sufficiently fed tonight, Miriam," he said, "and I shall refrain from ministering further to its egregious appetite." Then, dropping his tone of badinage, he added, gravely, in a voice that showed that the young fellow was terribly in earnest in his request: "Miriam, darling, you have promised to give me my answer tomorrow; it will be tomorrow in half an hour. Say that, after you have had some supper, I may come for you and take you a little away from all this mummery, and that you will have mercy upon me before we leave this place, and tell me at twelve o'clock whether, hereafter, Hallowe'en shall indeed be regarded by me as a hallowed evening, or whether I must forever associate it with the destruction of all my dearest hopes."

Miriam looked at the handsome lad—for he seemed only that to her—and the kindest light that had ever shone in her eyes for him warmed his heart, as, laying her hand gently, almost tenderly, on his arm, she said, in the tone he loved so well: "Yes, come for me in twenty minutes, and I will go with you where you will."

The words seemed almost to prophesy the fulfilment of his desires, and on this evening, when every simplest word and action is supposed to teem with omen and significance, it was not strange that Haviland laid these words to his heart as symbolical of the unity of his and Miriam's future.

The spot which Frank Haviland designated as being "away from all this mummery" was an alcove of a small withdrawing-room leading off the noisy ballroom; and here, at a little before twelve, he brought Miriam.

The little room was comparatively deserted. Here and there a couple—who, like themselves, had sought retirement—stood and chatted together in lowered tones, but these were so occupied with themselves—so intent upon their own affairs—that they accorded scant heed to the entrance of another pair of lovers.

The feverish glow of excitement had faded from Miriam's eyes and cheeks, and as she sank upon the bench beside a long French window to which Haviland led her, she looked so pale and exhausted that the man's heart smote him with direful forebodings. He drew out his watch and glanced at it.

"Miriam," he said, gently, "it lacks ten minutes of the hour. Shall I use them in telling you again how passionately I love you, how tenderly I will guard you, how wholly I am yours to command through time and eternity? Or will my words make no difference? Is your heart already decided as to its answer, and shall I leave you these few minutes for rest and silence?"

She looked at him gratefully, and, leaning impulsively forward, laid her small, gloved hand on his large one.

"Oh, Frank," she said, "how good you are to me; how considerate after all my hard-heartedness! Yes, grant me one more favor: Give me these few minutes to rest in, but keep your watch out, and, when the hands reach twelve, speak to me, for I will not tax your forbearance a single moment."

It was certainly a strange situation for these two, sitting there in utter silence, side by side, with hearts agitated by the strongest emotions which come to mankind, while, from the near ballroom, came the melodious rise and fall of viol and violin, the echo of merry maidens' voices mingled with deeper masculine tones. As the watch ticked softly on, a change came over the man and woman, a change which formed a strong contrast between them. As the momentous hour drew near which was to fix their destinies forever, to unite them into one or separate them as widely as two parallel but never-meeting currents, Haviland's manner lost its nervous restlessness, a marble pallor stole over his face, and his features settled into a tense fixity of expression, while his eyes never for an instant quitted their guard upon the small watch-dial. Miriam, on the contrary, began to show signs of intense excitement. The working of her lips, the fluttering motions of her hands, her great dilated pupils and quivering nostrils—all gave evidence of the mighty struggle and conflict going on within her breast. Her customary self-control had as utterly vanished as if she had never acquired it. Her heart seemed to contract and beat in dull heavy thumps against her white satin corsage.

The music suddenly ceased in the adjoining room. The spell of midnight—of the witching hour of Hallowe'en—had taken possession of the gay assemblage. Mystic time-honored spells were about to be indulged in, to prove to the men and maids gathered there the constancy and faith—the fidelity or fickleness—of their sweethearts.

"Ah, what a bitter reality was this love they made a jest of! Dear God! that they should make a sport and game of life's most tragic element! God grant that they, these merry revelers, may never know the suffering and anguish, the weight of misery and hopeless despair which love might mean! Oh, Godfrey, Godfrey!"

Miriam started with a sharp cry as Haviland's touch fell upon her, and wondered if she had been talking aloud. The young fellow's face was almost rigid in its intensity, and it was easy to see that he had staked his all on this throw. Refused now meant rejected forever. He had touched her gently to attract her attention, and, as her eyes followed the direction of his, she saw that his hand was held out toward her, that an object lay within it, an object as relentless and inexorable as fate—a gleaming golden thing, with a white glaring face staring mockingly at her and pointing with its gloomy hands to three Roman numerals.

A mighty shudder convulsed the girl; she shrank back a moment; then, pushing the baleful thing harshly away, she sprang to her feet, passed Haviland, and threw wide the huge French windows as if panting, suffocating for fresh air. Standing thus, with the full glare of the gas-jets flaming brilliantly upon her, her gems scintillating gleams and flashes of rainbow tints about her, her wonderful beauty framed in the open casement, she made a marvelously effective tableau for any chance passer-by. Regardless of notice from without or within, with a sort of exaltation beaming from her face, she stretched out her arm and pointed to a church-spire which rose needle-like against the midnight sky.

"Hark!" she cried; "your watch is fast. The church-clock has not yet struck. Even yet something may separate us."

"But if—if, Miriam, before the clock strikes, nothing intervenes, you mean that you will marry me? Remember, I swear to cherish you."

His words seemed to recall the girl to herself: the strange excitement slowly died from her.

"Yes," she said, grasping the swinging sashes firmly, as if for moral support; "yes, if nothing intervenes—" She paused and looked once more far into the night, yearningly, beseechingly, imploringly, as if from out of its cold shadows a deliverer might appear; then, turning to Haviland, "No," she said, "I will wait no longer. If you will have me as I am, I who love you merely as a brother, I promise—"

A dull heavy boom interrupted her, then another and another. She stopped, and again looked out into the midnight—the Hallowe'en midnight, when witches and fays and elves disport themselves abroad, and play mad pranks with the affairs of men—and, as she stood thus, waiting for the bell to cease, a small tiny object, projected from without, came flying in at the open casement, struck her sharply upon the breast, and fell at her feet.

With a smothered cry, she stooped and snatched it from its lowly resting-place; then, as her dazed senses recognized what the tiny messenger was, she cried: "At last, at last, it has come! Oh, my God, I thank Thee for Thy Goodness!" And, in her abandonment of relief and selfish joy, she raised it to her lips, pressed them upon it again and again with the tenderness that a mother bestows upon a relic of her long-lost child, and then, coming to a sudden consciousness of her surroundings, she turned to Haviland, and a shade of sadness stole over her radiant features—sadness for the pain she must inflict.

"Frank," she said, gently, extending her hand, in which lay a small object, "there is the obstacle which must separate us forever."

Haviland bent forward and looked at the tiny foe which had vanquished him. So small it was, and yet so potent! Nothing but a thin-worn hoop of gold—a wedding-ring.

*

64

The next morning, Frank Haviland was toying with a scarce-tasted breakfast, when a letter was handed to him. He had parted from the woman he loved the night before, without any explanation of the mysterious obstacle which had intervened to thwart his passionate hopes. All night had he pondered on the meaning of that ring, only to reject as impossible the only solution which presented itself. Never would he believe that the girl whose pure true nature had won first his respect and then his love had stooped to the duplicity of a clandestine marriage! And yet, what other meaning could that small golden circlet enclose? He eagerly seized the envelope, on which he recognized Miriam's characteristic handwriting, and, impatiently tearing aside the cover, plunged at once into the contents, which ran as follows:

FIFTH AVENUE, Nov. 1, 1887.

DEAR FRANK:

I have just left you with the promise of an explanation of the mystery attached to the little ring which came, a strange Hallowe'en messenger, from out of the darkness to me last night. A little ring? And yet no mighty hoop of forged and ponderous metal could have so bound and fettered my happiness as this tiny trifle of gold. I told you a few minutes ago it must separate us forever; but, if it stands between you and your love, it is not the first time it has served such a purpose—as, for four weary terrible years, it has been an insurmountable barrier between me and the only man I have ever loved.

People call me odd, queer, eccentric; and yet, Frank, you know that when I first came from abroad I was none of these. No, my heart was naturally a light one, loving brightness, gayety, and pleasure, until the heavy cloud of sadness and suffering shadowed it.

For two years after I came to Uncle Maturin's, I was a careless happy child; then, one summer, at Newport, sorrow overtook me. Heavens! how I remember it all! I was, as you know, passionately fond of bathing and a good swimmer, but loved best to bathe alone, and, hating the publicity of the more frequented places, generally chose a spot just back of

65

our cottage. Here I was permitted to go alone, with only a maid to stand by and see that no harm befell me; and here it was that, bathing one day, I was seized with cramp, and, being some distance from shore, could do nothing but turn myself upon my back and call Jenny to run for help. Ah! shall I ever forget the sensation of those few moments? It seemed to me that the tide was carrying me further from shore, and the cramp, which affected all my limbs, rendered me utterly helpless. A terrible fear came over me. I thought that Jenny would never come back. I lost my presence of mind, and felt myself sinking beneath the surface. The very agony of death swept over me, and I raised my voice and screamed aloud. Again I called "Help! Help!" and again I sank beneath the pitiless waves; then, as once more I rose to the surface, I felt that further struggling was useless. "Goodbye", I called, softly; "goodbye, dear aunt and uncle; goodbye—". Before I could sigh forth another word, I heard a shout—a cheery inspiring promise of help in a voice that I have hungered, thirsted, yearned to hear again through every day and night of my life since.

Frank, they talk of love at first sight, but it was even before I saw him that I loved Godfrey Bogart. I loved him as his clear strong voice smote my ear, as his firm protecting clasp touched my spent and exhausted body; then and there, a passionate abandonment of myself to him swept over me, and never for a single moment has any other man caused me to waver in my allegiance. He is the man whom God has created for me, and if, in the mysterious working of His Will, He has sought to bar our union, yet I knew, even before that little messenger of hope came to me last night, that, some time, here or in heaven, we should be united.

We kept my accident a secret, for I feared that I should be forbidden my favorite recreation were it to reach Uncle Maturin's ears, and Jenny was easily bribed to say nothing of it. She had met Godfrey as she was speeding homeward for help, and brought him to my rescue. Many, many times we met in that summer. Godfrey was a universal favorite and was asked everywhere, and, in the giddy whirl of Newport life, it escaped notice that he singled me out whenever opportunity offered. Perhaps, as he was of limited wealth and no *parti*, the object of his attentions was not a person of much consequence to the world. Ah, that summer! Whatever happens, I shall always have had that.

The days flew by and the season drew to a close. Newport was becoming deserted, and at last the night came when Godfrey told me that he, too, was leaving the next day. I was a mere child, unused to hiding my feelings, and I gave a little gasp and laid my hand on my heart as he said it. He bent down and looked full into my eyes.

"Miriam, child," he said, "it is hard to leave you."

"But it will not be for long," I faltered. "You will come to see me in New York?"

He kept his eyes fixed intently on my face for a full minute without replying, then raised my hand very gently to his lips and dropped his clasp of it.

"No," he said, drawing himself erect. "No; I swear I will not. Miriam, do you know I am a married man?"

Ah, Frank, if he had, instead, plunged a knife into my heart, what suffering I had been spared! I don't think I said a word; I simply could not grasp the truth, but sat staring blankly at him with a wide uncomprehending gaze which he could not bear to meet, for in another moment he had turned away, buried his face in his hands, and I heard the most awful sound that ever strikes upon a woman's ear—the deep bitter sobs of the man she loves. I cannot write more of that scene, which is a sacred one to me.

The woman whom Godfrey had married was notoriously unworthy of him. They had separated, and he offered to get a divorce which would be easily procurable. I would then marry him. He did not urge it, for his ideas of my girlish purity and innocence were so exalted that he could not bear to smirch them with the stain of a union with a divorced man.

"No," I said, "I never will marry you while she lives. She is your wife still, and the Bible forbids your taking another. Should she die, come to me or send me her wedding-ring, and I will marry you."

He did not seek to alter my decision, but drew a ring, the singular one you have often remarked on my hand, from his finger and placed it on mine, bidding me wear it for his sake. Then we parted.

Now you know my story, Frank, and can guess the joy that the little ill-treated and disgraced ring brought to my heart. He is free; where, I know not; but I shall soon see him, I feel. Forgive me for the pain I have brought you, and pardon me that sudden relief from my long probation caused me, last night, to be unmindful of your grief.

Always affectionately and sincerely yours,

MIRIAM JERROLD

A week later, Miriam Jerrold was seated in the convalescent-ward of one of the New York hospitals—reading, as was her wont, to a number of the patients who were able to listen to her. She wore the simple soft-hued gown which her uncle called her hospital-uniform, as it was kept for such occasions; and on her breast lay a great bunch of violets, which breathed their sweet fragrance through the room. Her pale face wore already a more hopeful, brighter expression than had been its wont, and her voice had a more buoyant, elastic ring than hitherto. Yet a week had passed and no further tidings had reached her of Godfrey Bogart.

The entrance of a nurse brought her reading to a sudden period.

"Miss Jerrold," the young woman said, approaching her, "have you a plain gold ring on?" Miriam looked surprised, and the nurse added explanatorily: "We have a patient who has been here nearly a week and has been growing steadily worse, dying of typhoid fever. Of course, he has been delirious most of the time, and his one idea seems to be in some way connected with a gold ring. He is very violent now, and we can hardly keep him in bed. He keeps trying to get up, flings his arms about as if he were trying to throw something into the air, and mutters constantly about a wedding-ring. Sometimes, if we humor them, they grow more quiet; and, I thought, if I could borrow a ring from you—why, Miss Jerrold—what is it?" For the girl had risen with white startled face and terror-stricken eyes and had grasped the nurse by the arm.

"Where is he? Take me to him at once! Dying, you say? Godfrey Bogart dying? Where? Quick, I say—quick!"

Utterly perplexed and bewildered, yet feeling that Miss Jerrold, whom she dearly loved, had some good reason for the privilege she demanded—that of being taken to the private room where the sufferer lay—the nurse led the way, and stood back a little as Miriam entered and approached the bed.

A man of about thirty lay there, with a dreadful fever-flushed face, from which the great gray eyes gazed gloomily forth with a haggard hungry expression, which altered not as they fell upon Miriam.

"Godfrey! Godfrey!" she cried, "do you not know me? It is I—Miriam. Oh, God! after all these years, to meet you like this!"

The nurses, compassionate but filled with a sense of duty to their patient, came forward, and the sound of their steps roused Miriam to forestall their protest.

"Yes, yes," she said, hurriedly drying her eyes. "I know I must control myself, and I will do so—only, I beseech of you, do not send me away: let me try my power over him. You say sleep may save him: let me try to induce it. I have had much experience with sick persons."

They were touched by her pleading, besides appreciating the efficacy in some cases of certain influences, and offered her a chair; but, preferring to retain her position on the floor, she took the two restless hands in hers, smoothed them between her palms with a gentle regular movement, murmuring the while soft tender love-words, as a mother croons to her sleeping child.

Gradually, the spell took effect—the strained weary eyelids drooped over the burning balls, the twitching, muttering lips fell into peaceful silence, and the spasmodic movements of the muscles yielded to the caressing touch upon them: the sufferer slept.

*

It was not till many days later that Miriam learned how Godfrey Bogart had but recently returned from a long, long absence abroad, to receive a message from his wife to the effect that she was dying, and begged him to come to her. He went, and devoted himself to her comfort until she died; then, weary and worn, with fever already beginning to burn in his veins, he determined to seek Miriam. On All-Hallowe'en, he went to her home, only to find her absent. He inquired and learned where she was, and hurried with eager excited footsteps thither, prowling restlessly, hungrily about the brilliant house with a strange purposelessness which craved only to be near her.

Suddenly he saw what seemed, to his feverish fancy, a vision: A beautiful figure—that of the woman he loved, only tenfold more lovely than he had ever seen her—came and flung wide a window, and stood, like an exquisite apparition, gloriously illuminated by the glare of myriads of gas-jets, in the aperture. His heart throbbed and his brain seemed on fire. There she was—the woman whom he had loved, whom he had longed for so yearningly for four weary years. She stood in a flood of brilliant light, and he was without, in the shadow. How could he make his presence known?

Like a flash of lightning, a thought swept across his brain—the ring. He took it from its safe hiding-place in his pocket, measured the distance carefully with his eye, and then, with a sudden swift motion of his arm, threw the little object to its rightful destination. What followed was a blank.

It is a year later, and Hallowe'en again. The Bullock mansion on Fifth Avenue is ablaze with lights. A high festival is in progress here, for which that of last year was but a preparation. The chief celebrators stand beneath a huge wedding-bell, and a rich odor of orange-blossoms proclaim the fact that Hymen has been receiving sacrifices tonight; and the voluntary offerings are a goodly pair to look at—a man, charming of face and proud of bearing, and a woman, whose birthright of beauty has of late been increased by a rich dowry of happiness.

THE FACE IN THE GLASS

Letitia Virginia Douglas

Published in Godey's Lady's Book, *October 1891*

Letitia Virginia Douglas was a poet and author who lived in Philadelphia. Her poetry appeared in syndicated papers and *Good Housekeeping*. Her fiction was mainly written for *Godey's Magazine* (also known as *Godey's Lady's Book*), edited by Sarah Hale. She wrote the short story "The Spirit of the Desert: A Mesmeric Mystery" in 1886, an interesting, if slight genre tale about a gentleman being saved from dying in the desert by someone who has been "dead many years". Two years later two Gothic prose poems, "The Wizard's Spell" and "The Keepers of the Light" were published in *The Speaker's Garland and Literary Bouquet*. Her last poem, the slightly spooky "Farewell to the Roses" ("But soon the vampire will depart, though it all be too late") was published in *The Presbyterian* in August 1939. She died nine months later on 30 May 1940.

BLYTHE Hurst's busy tongues wagged an excited buzz of comments when it became known for a fact that the old Manor House in Witches' Walk was taken.

The place had an eerie look, and a reputation for being haunted; but the "new folks" had evinced no curiosity as to its history, else a score of old inhabitants had stood ready to pour the same into their ears, with variations.

The *fact* is, the old Manor House had been the scene of a tragedy, in itself rather pathetic than horrifying. A fair girl had been stricken by lightning on her wedding eve. The stone had gathered so much moss as it rolled that the Manor House in Witches' Walk now boasted a ghost in the likeness of the dead maiden, with magnified horrors of a kindred nature. But the new tenants were not disturbed by the faint, far-off, dark whispers that reached their ears unasked. They brought their own servants with them, and these, too, were of a nature so stolid that they did not appear to be at all in awe of "the ghost." The "new family" consisted of Mr. Arthur Whitting, a humorous writer and something of a recluse—bachelor—and his spinster sister, Miss Florimel, who kept house for her dreamy and unpractical brother.

Mr. Whitting was in the habit of forgetting, so lost was he to all interests not literary, and in all probability he would have meal-time, forgotten so absent-minded was he in regard to such trifles, but Florimel was firm on the subject. So it happened that Mr. Whitting had his sister to thank for his excellent health and goodly avoirdupois. That same determined lady was also in the habit of thrusting her brother out for a "constitutional" regularly after breakfast each morning, deaf to his meek entreaties that he might be allowed to "finish that chapter first." And it was during one of these strolls that he was first awakened to the startling fact that his Manor House was "ha'nted," by the following little occurrence: He passed afield, and stumbled upon worthy Farmer Mayhew.

"You're fr'm the old Manor House, hain't you?" observed Mayhew, with a curious glance of his shrewd grey eyes, from under the big brim of his sun hat.

Mr. Whitting replied that he was.

"Never see anything queer yet o' nights?"

"Any—I beg your pardon?" faltered Mr. Whitting, with a puzzled stare.

"Why, land alive man! didn't you know the place is ha'nted? Has been ever sence a young gal—twin, she was, too, the rector's twin darter, and *powerful* pretty!—was struck dead by lightnin' in the little back room with the vines runnin' all over the winder and the porch under it? No? Well, I'll tell ye—"

And he proceeded to edify the new tenant of the Manor House with a hair-raising chapter of horrors.

Mr. Whitting was disturbed, even though he had forced his loquacious informant to a reluctant acknowledgment that "he hadn't seen nothin' himself, and couldn't lay his hand on any one as could *swear they'd* seed it with their *own* eyes, but *everybody* 'lowed—"

"Whew! The sun's getting hot. I must be going," interrupted Mr. Whitting, impatiently. Why couldn't people have let him and his delicious old woodland rat trap alone? He had left the busy whirl of Philadelphia and come here, thinking to bury himself in the seclusion of a sylvan paradise, where he might pursue his literary labours undisturbed by any whisper from the outside world. And, lo! his beautiful dream was straightway dispelled by the harsh voice of the multitude buzzing its everlasting tattle. "They say," his pet aversion, had even pursued him into these woodland depths!

Mr. Arthur Whitting, the humorist, forgot his pet jokes now. This was no joking matter. If the servants should get tainted with this silly superstition (he recollected, with a start, having seen Stephens cast a nervous glance behind him in the library at dusk last evening), they would be giving notice next, and if there was anything he hated it was having new servants about. They mussed his MSS., mislaid his books, put him out of temper, and drove his plots out of his head. They *shouldn't* take fright. They should be coerced into sense if not coaxed, the first sign of shying they showed.

Half an hour later, Mr. Whitting, hot with his energetic homeward tramp, although a crisp October breeze was blowing, burst into the kitchen and confronted Stephens.

"Here, you! listen to what I tell you, now, and see you heed it, or *I'll make you;* do you hear? No matter what silly babble you may hear from these country gawks, don't you believe it—it's nonsense.

"About the—the—ghost, sir?" faltered Stephens, in a whisper, with a sheepish look behind at the yawning cellar-way.

Mr. Whitting laid a forcible hand on the fellow's coat-collar by way of a gentle reminder.

"You blockhead! If I ever see you looking like that again I'll—I'll *shake you!* You're old enough to know better. No giving notice, mind! If you threaten to leave this I'll lock you up. You can tell your wife the same thing *from me!* I'm not going to have my household demoralized by a lot of idle talk."

"All—all—right, sir!" sputtered Stephens, when he had at last succeeded in extricating his coat-collar from his employer's energetic grip, and had placed a safe distance between himself and that irate gentleman.

While Mr. Whitting was talking, Miss Florimel entered the room.

"Why Arthur!" she cried, "what has disturbed you?"

Arthur deigned not to enlighten her then, but plunged at once into a vigorous plan of his own for setting his household an example.

"Florimel, my dear," he said, "I am thinking of changing my sleeping apartment. I shall take the little chamber in the wing—the back one on the ground floor, with the porch outside and the vines running all over the window. I observe that my ceiling leaks, and I certainly discover a draught. Be good enough to have the room thrown open and aired today. I shall occupy it tomorrow night."

Mr. Whitting had rented the Manor House as the last occupants left it furnished. The rector, its owner, had placed it in the hands of an agent immediately after the sad accident that befell his daughter, and had taken his family abroad.

Miss Whitting looked at her brother, under the impression that he had gone suddenly out of his senses. Stephens, too, was staring, but with the glare of horror added to the amazement in his eyes.

It had not occurred to Mr. Whitting that the next night was that deliciously-horrible gala night of the spooks, Hallowe'en.

Stephens quaked in his shoes as he lighted his master to the ground floor chamber at nine o'clock, and the latter turned a disapproving eye on his trembling hands as the sputtering candle they held quivered nervously, and the fellow stared superstitiously into the black gulf beyond the rays of light.

"You may go," said Mr. Whitting, coldly. When he was alone he speedily lost himself in his book. The effect he had worked for was produced; or, rather, would be produced when he stepped forth whole and from the "ha'nted" room the next morning, and the news should have gone abroad on Maria's loquacious tongue that the master hadn't "seen anything queer there," nor even been disturbed by an unquiet dream. Then people would begin to feel ashamed of themselves, and maybe they would let him live out the remainder of his lease in quiet. Mr. Whitting's interest in the chamber, or the subject of which it was the keystone, did not extend beyond the impression he wished to make on his servants in thus sacrificing his comfort to destroy a popular bugaboo. He turned to his work with a sigh of relief, and speedily forgot his surroundings.

So absorbed was he that he did not hear Miss Whitting's low tap at the door until it was repeated more emphatically, and her voice said through the keyhole: "Arthur, if you have not yet retired, open the door; I have something for you."

When he had obeyed, he was confronted by his sister and a dainty tray of smoking pippins, their plump cheeks shriveled to darkest tan, with the white foam of the roasted meat just showing here and there on their shining skins. A plate of baked chestnuts and a jar of home-brewed ale completed the contents of that festive tray.

The *littérateur* opened his eyes in astonishment. There was but one night in all the year when he was wont to indulge in a midnight feast, and that particular night was observed as religiously by the brother and sister as though it had been the festival of some saint. For they had been born on a New England farm, and had been trained to love that "night in the lonesome October" when nuts, apples, games, and ghost-stories hold the tapis by common consent.

"Have you clean forgotten that this is Hallowe'en?" prattled Miss Florimel, cheerily. "Why, Art! what a sleepy-head you are growing to be, with your everlasting books and ink-pots in your old age, I was going to say; but forty-eight is young. I'm fifty-five myself, and see how I have to exert my faculties for us both. You ought to be ashamed—we haven't missed keeping Hallowe'en in at least forty-five years-you haven't, that is. I've kept it ever since I could remember, and there, now, close that book, and sit down and toast your feet by the fire, and drink your drink while it's warm. Good-night, dear."

Mr. Whitting blew out his candle and pulled the curtain aside, to let in the bright moonlight.

But the thick vine-tendrils outside, still loaded down with their luxurious leafage of crimson and freckled gold, barred the way, so that only a gleam of silvery light struggled through into the inner darkness. They had probably forgotten to air the room as he had ordered, and so the vines had been overlooked. There was a suspicious dimness in the glass as seen by the uncertain light, too, which suggested dust the bachelor's pet abhorrence. He drew a long track down the obscured pane with his forefinger. Yes, the glass was thick with it. Ugh! No matter. Tomorrow he would order Maria here with buckets and brooms; and in the meantime he would soon rid himself of those superabundant vines, so as to get a little more light on the subject. No sooner thought of than done. He threw up the sash, and, penknife in hand, began the work of destruction. In ten minutes not a tendril remained clinging to the window, through which a flood of fairest moonlight poured, subdued a little by the thick veil of dust.

Suddenly, as he lingered there looking out upon the pleasant landscape, he was conscious of a faint, dim profile between himself and the outer world.

He rubbed his eyes, and looked again intently. It was gone no, the faintest shadow of a shape still remained, like a thought undefined. He snatched his flannel pen-wiper off the desk, and hastily rubbed it over the dusty glass, so that he might see more clearly. Then he quickly threw up the sash, and stepped out onto the little porch beneath. He could have sworn that some one—a woman had stood there, with her profile turned toward him, stiff and immovable as a creature turned to stone. Where had she gone? He stepped off the low porch, and moved softly round to the rear of the house. But only the cool night wind sighing a lonely lullaby to the crisped leaves was there. Not a moving thing in sight.

"Pshaw!" he muttered to himself, with an impatient laugh at "his folly," "has the silly tattle of the country turned *my* brain, too, I wonder?" And he turned sharply about, stepped into the room again, and shut the glass down; resolutely undressed, and sprang into bed.

But soon that unpleasant consciousness of a mysterious presence intruded on the would-be sleeper again, this time strongly.

With a low exclamation of disgust at himself and everything in general, he raised himself upon his elbow and looked toward the window, with difficulty restraining a positive start as he did so, for, clearer than before, it appeared again—a distinct face and figure, apparently standing just outside the window-pane, in a position sidewise to him. The face, beautiful in profile, yet sphinx-like in its calm solemnity, almost to expressionlessness, shone clear out as a face done in cameo, amongst a surrounding halo of hair, the whole-woman, hair, and gown—colourless with a kind of lambent whiteness that was only semi-opaque. Soft and indistinct shone through the shape: the bright outer world; the hills; the forest shadows.

Mr. Whitting could not have told, so unreal was the whole experience, even while its spell was on. He leaned a little forward to see the eyes. *Were they open?* Only on the faces of sleeping children was that expression of utter oblivion to be seen. This was not the face of a child, but that of a young maiden, just budding into womanhood. There was not the faintest change of attitude. There it stood, stock-still, with hands clasped before it; not like a maiden indulging in pensive thoughts, as she stands in idle mood; not in an attitude of assumed stiffness, like one posing for effect; but with an air of solemn indescribableness, like a creature turned to stone by some sudden bolt hurled from the hand of a swift Fate.

A feeling that he could not have put in words swept over Mr. Whitting. We have demonstrated that he was not a superstitious man; yet he actually shuddered, to his own immediate disgust. For the next moment he had thrown the feeling off and bounded to the window, with his dressing gown thrown about his shoulders, confident that, in his own words, "some one of those fool idiots was playing a confounded Hallowe'en joke on him, because he had shown his contempt of their foolish ghost-rubbish."

The fact that the figure had mysteriously disappeared by the time he had reached the sash and thrown it up, only strengthened this conviction and stirred up Mr. Whitting's latent ire, as he closed the window again and crept shiveringly back to bed; but not to lie down and slumber. One backward glance at the window showed him the still figure in its place again, distinct as ever.

"I'll see how long this thing will last," quoth Mr. Whitting, grimly, to himself. "If she can stand it mooning out there in the cold, with a thin frock on, surely so can I stand it in here. We'll see who gives up first."

And fixing himself comfortably, Mr. Whitting glued his wide-awake eyes upon the serene profile, and waited. Yet, through the slow hours of

the night, that sphinx never moved. Goodness would this last all night—
or rather, all morning? For the clock was striking again now—one—
two—three! The creature's fondness for a joke must certainly be extreme
to carry her this length, or she was mad!

He threw on his dressing gown and sprang to the window again; and
again she, or *it*, was gone.

Perplexed and angry at having lost his night's sleep, Whitting sat
down, with the calmness of despair, to "see it out."

The cheerful voice of a distant chanticleer ushered in the pale grey
light of dawn. The moon's sickly pallor mingled with it; dissolved into
it; yielded itself to annihilation, and it was day. For a brief half-hour Mr.
Whitting yielded to tired nature's demands, and dozed off into forgetful-
ness. When he awoke, the bright first rays of the rising sun were streaming
in upon him. The mysterious profile at the window was gone.

Dressing himself, hurriedly, he stepped out into the fresh air, and carefully looked about for the lightest trace of footsteps; but there were none.

Miss Florimel laughed cheerfully when he related his experience, and
declared "it was the nuts and ale, and things." They had disturbed her
own digestion a little, she admitted, but had not carried her the length of
seeing ghosts.

Mr. Whitting was not convinced. He was vehement and angry; not at
Miss Florimel, but "at that confounded agent for misrepresenting his old
spook-hole," and at those vague individuals who had dared to "put up a
joke on him."

It was the agent's business to protect his tenants against annoyance of
this species. He decided, against Florimel's discreet counsel, to complain
to the agent, to protest, and otherwise vent his indignation.

So his morning walk was directed toward Blythe Hurst, with a purpose. The agent heard his story in silence.

"Last week," he said, briefly, "the owner of the Manor, the rector,
returned from abroad. He is on his way to visit friends in Boston, and has
stopped with us for a few days in order that his daughter, who is not very

strong, may get completely rested before continuing the journey. I had best let him hear your complaint and he will explain. Ah, there is Miss Benton now. Miss Frances, will you tell your papa there is a gentleman here to speak to him, please."

A young woman had come languidly out upon the porch from an adjoining room. She had not noticed, probably, that there was a stranger in the parlour, which also opened on the wide porch with long French windows. So she had carelessly taken up her station in front of the latter, standing with profile turned toward them, her hands loosely clasped in front of her, looking away toward the distant hills.

The face was fine and fair; but pale, either from ill health or one of those immobile, placid temperaments which never betray a thought through the medium of the features by so much as a tinge of colour. A mass of loose blonde hair framed the profile. Still as a statue the girl stood until the agent's voice roused her from her apparent lethargy. The likeness was complete! Whitting was startled—so startled that he felt himself actually grow pale. For *this*, with a ghostly difference, was the very picture that had kept him awake all night.

There *must* be some lucid explanation of it all; though how explain what he had seen? The dull semi-opaque shadow—the clear profile; the colourlessness—were absent here; this was a girl of flesh and blood. He would probe to the bottom of the mystery. Now or never. He was determined on that. His own perplexity and helplessness had one effect only, it made him angry with himself and everybody. He was in no mood to be trifled with now; and if this pale faced automaton with the white hair and expressionless face thought to play upon his superstition, by prowling about her old home masquerading as a ghost to frighten the tenants off, she should pay for her prank—he would tell her father! He would—he would sue the agent! He would move! He would—would—

"Please, will you step into the other room? Papa is not feeling very well this morning, and is lying down," said a soft, timid voice at his elbow. The agent had vanished. Whitting stood there alone, looking foolish enough, no doubt, with the flush and frown of anger adding their unbecoming emphasis to the deep sunburn he had lately acquired, owing to Florimel's foolish whim of making him tramp for miles in the open air every morning after breakfast.

"Ah!" he murmured sarcastically on the impulse of the moment, "this is the young lady, I presume, who had such a vast amount of fun at my expense by haunting my window on Hallowe'en. I trust you didn't catch cold, *and that you enjoyed it more than I did!*"

A deep wave of crimson surged over the girl's pale face; a look of incredulous amazement, of haughty anger, followed in its train.

"I—!" she faltered, making a little gesture with her hand—a gesture of scorn and hurt dignity.

"*I haunt your window, man? I!*" The scorn expressed in that soft, contemptuous tone of slow disdain would have cut a less sensitive man to the quick; especially her way of saying "*man*"—"as though she had been speaking to her coachman," quoth Mr. Whitting to himself, crestfallen.

Ere he had time to rally to the attack a deep voice called from the other room: "Frances, my love!"

"Coming, papa!"

Miss Benton deigned to turn her flashing eyes—Heaven knows there was no lack now of expression in the angry face she turned upon him in his direction, while her straight mouth writhed in indescribable curves of contempt as she imperiously waved him into her father's presence.

"Papa," she began at once, leaving no loophole for attack to poor Mr. Whitting, "this *man*—your Manor tenant—comes here with a strange complaint. He says—he dares to say—that I masqueraded before his window last night *as a ghost*, or something!"

"My daughter, my daughter, do not be hasty. You forget the—" and the white-haired old rector drew his daughter to his side and murmured something.

To Whitting's amazement the expression of haughty anger and insulted pride instantly faded from the girl's face, giving place to one of pensive sadness, as when one recalls some tender memory inseparable from sorrow.

She gave him one glance as she passed him swiftly in leaving the room, and he fancied that there were tears shining in the soft blue eyes.

"Sir," said the old rector, courteously, "you sleep in the little ground-floor bedroom in the back wing, do you not? But I know you do, else you would not have been annoyed."

Whitting explained his reason for the transfer.

"Then let me solve the problem for you in a few words," resumed the old rector, in tones of gentle emotion.

"A few years ago I lived in the old manor-house with my wife and my twin daughters. My children were born there, and they had never known any other. I brought my wife there as a bride—I buried her there.

"One of our daughters gave her heart to a worthy man, and they were shortly to be married, when, quite unexpectedly, he was summoned to Europe to attend the dying-bed of a relative. He cabled home, however, that he would surely be back in time for the 30th, which had been the original date set for the wedding, so that no change need be made on the cards. The night before the 30th he wired from New York: 'Will be with you early in the morning.' And my child's happiness was complete. As she was in somewhat delicate health, being at all times constitutionally fragile, she retired early to her chamber that night, the small back one on the ground floor—in order that she might gather fresh strength for the morrow. There came up that night one of those sudden, violent thunderstorms so common here in the summertime. As she stood dreamily beside her little window, looking out through the pane at the grandeur of the storm the crashing branches and bending trees—a fearful flash of vivid, blue sheet lightning suddenly enveloped the whole world in blinding brightness, flaring full upon her face and figure, and, by some curious freak, photographing both indelibly on the glass!... But my child uttered one piercing shriek and fell to the floor—*dead*."

The speaker's voice died away in a tremulous whisper, and for one moment there was deepest silence in the room. All of Whitting's indignation had vanished. At length he said, respectfully: "But why was the pane of glass never removed? *That* would be a very easy mode of getting rid of this annoyance to your future tenants who may *not* know the story, but may object may even be frightened off by *it* if they are of a superstitious turn."

"Because my poor wife pleaded that the wonderful picture of our child painted upon the glass by the hand of God, as it were, might never be destroyed or removed. 'It would be almost sacrilege to touch it,' she said. 'Let it always stay. Promise! Never a mortal artist could have given us as true a picture of our beloved. It is as though her spirit came back to visit us.'

"The strangest part of it is, the face of my daughter cannot be seen from the outside of the window by broad daylight, or at close quarters, except vaguely. I would never," he concluded, "have consented to leave the old place even temporarily had my own health not failed as well as that of my surviving child. And I hesitated to put it at the disposal of strangers, but could not well afford to go abroad leaving it lying idle. However, I hope soon to re-enter my old home to leave it no more."

A month later the Manor House received another family into its capacious recess—the old rector and his child came home to live. But Mr. Whitting did not move; for shortly thereafter the two families became one. And the beautiful face in the glass still looks out at twilight upon the pleasant hills, while its counterpart in the flesh smiles at Whitting across the cosy tea-table in another room.

'STRUTHER KANNOCK'S HALLOWEEN

Edgar L. Wakeman

Published as part of Tales of Ten Travelers, a newspaper
serial that was syndicated throughout America, 1893

Edgar L. Wakeman (1863–c.1910) was a California-born author, trav-
eller and journalist who took a keen interest in Britain and Ireland and
wrote about life there for American newspapers in the 1880s and 90s.
Visiting both countries, he wrote "Afoot In Ireland: A Poet's Wandering
in the Emerald Isle" for the *Topeka Capital Commonwealth* in 1888 and
"Marriage Superstitions in Scotland" for the *Boston Transcript*, in 1891.
Writing in *Old Scottish and English Border Towns* (also 1891) he remarked:

> American travelers hastening between the English and Scottish capitals
> miss what I have often felt is the most interesting portion of the two
> countries. That is the Border country with its ancient border towns, in
> and around which have been fought more ferocious contests than else-
> where in all.

In 1910 he was forced into an asylum and "preservation of a very considerable estate" ($70,000—$2.2 million in today's money) by some of his
children. The reason was said to be Wakeman's hard drinking that had
begun twenty years before, on the death of his wife. His daughter and her
mother-in-law said his drinking became so bad he had to be moved out of
the family house and into a barn to keep him away from a dying daughter. The jury, at Queen's County Court, where he was on trial for three
days, found him competent ("he proved more than an ordinarily bright
witness") and able to look after his own affairs and ordered him released
from the State Hospital for the Insane in Central Islip. In late 1910 he

walked out of *The Current*, the magazine he co-owned with its business manager Mr. Nesbitt. In 1911 his son George was jailed for deserting the Navy and an article on the story remarked that he was the son of "the late Edgar L. Wakeman".

A selection of his works appear to have been serialized in newspapers then issued as privately printed books; the titles can be found in the *Catalog of Title Entries of Books Jan 1–June 30 1894*. Genre titles appear to be: *The Bogle of the Wishing Gate, Baba Sy'ra's Quest, A Manx Phynnodderee* and *The Casket of Manaca Isnaga*.

OLD Anstruther Kannock sat at his desk in his dingy library, in ancient Kannock Manse, and listened moodily to the moaning night wind of autumn as it swept wildly through the almost bare branches of the elms and sycamores which shut in the gray old place darkly from the highway that led to the near and pleasant New England village below.

Old Stone 'Struther, he was called by the villagers who had most cause to dread the cruel power his heartless nature and considerable wealth enabled him to exercise. Miser Kannock was his commonest title among the many who knew only his niggardliness and greed.

Brother Anstruther, he was always called by his dead brother's wife, who, as his sole housekeeper and servant, tremblingly slaved on through the years to thus protect her two children from want. Ogre Anstruther these children, Edith and Herbert Kannock, whisperingly spoke of him to each other, to their mother and to one loyal friend, the village schoolmaster, Charles Penruth, between whom and old 'Struther Kannock there existed something akin to mortal hate.

"Here's another cursed Halloween!" muttered 'Struther Kannock at his ramshackle old desk.

He struck outward and backward with his fist. It broke a piece of leather out of his frayed and time worn armchair.

"Everything's going to rack and ruin," he continued as he noticed the rent his fist had made.

He sat back in his chair and crabbedly closed his eyes. A slight sputtering of the candle started him into an upright position.

"Of course! That's got to waste, too. The wick actually turns over and burns the side all down into the socket!"

He snuffed the light with a savage snap of his fingers. It burned up brighter for a moment, and some sort of relevancy took his attention to the antiquated fireplace near.

"See there! Look at that waste. That woman'll ruin me!"

He stepped to the chimney side and with his foot kicked ashes over the edges of the blazing logs.

"Wood costs money. But, Lord! Little they care. That's what comes of feeding a dead brother's wife and brats!"

He turned back to his chair and, just as he was about to reseat himself; he caught sight of his own shadow upon the wainscotted wall. It was high as the cracked ceiling and was swinging its giant arms wildly.

He wheeled about to look at it. It seemed to confront him threateningly.

"Shadows, shadows, shadows!" he growled. "More waste! Why shadows? Just the same everywhere. Shadows under trees, shadows behind buildings, shadows alongside gravestones. Unnecessary. All folderol. All waste!"

He advanced to his own shadow on the wall and it gradually shrunk to his own stature. Then he put his hard fist against the paneling with a grinding motion.

"That's it, now. Go right at anything that threatens and it'll wilt. Beat it out. Grind it out. Wipe it out. If you don't, it'll wipe you out. That's Anstruther Kannock's way; and it's a mighty good way, too!"

Despite his blustering bravery, the man seemed to be environed with shadows. They worried him. The tapping of some little branch against the pane brought him with a start to the window.

"Why ain't them blinds shut?" he querulously muttered. "Just like their pesky carelessness. I don't want anybody looking in here, and they know it. Confound them all! They'd be even glad to have pranks played on me here tonight—the brats and that devilish schoolmaster would, anyhow!"

He stood at the window a moment and seemed to relapse into his former miserable reflections. It was one of those eerie nights when it is dark and clear by turns, and the wind leaps across the face of nature in cutting, withering pulsations filling all the outer world with invisible forces and presences.

"Yes," continued the man at the window in an ugly tone, "waste, waste, waste! Look at that cloud of leaves. Every one's got to go. That's waste. Grass is all bent and matted. That's waste. Birds fussed and fumed all summer building their nests. Dead now; and that's waste, too. If I'd made the earth and the things in it, there'd been no such dodrotted folderol!"

He turned his great eyes peeringly into the night. The roof of a gray old church loomed darkly above the writhing branches of surrounding trees, and 'Struther Kannock's face darkened.

"That cost ten thousand," he muttered. "What all-fired nonsense and waste that is!"

At that moment the scant moonlight revealed a little huddle of white tombstones like crouching ghosts against the hills beyond the church front, and one, taller than the rest, seemed to fill the man at the window with hateful resentment and bitterness.

He shook his fist menacingly toward it, railing horribly at it for a time while walking back and forth in the old library with a hard, impatient tread.

"I'll level you yet, too!" he went on with passionate vehemence, "What's your miserable white face got to be everlastingly looking this way for? You'd a-starved but for me. Your wife and brats would a starved but for me. You wouldn't even have had a head stone but for me. Anson Kannock, you're dead and dust ten year! Stay there, you fool. Keep away from me. Lie quiet now! or I'll—I'll—Who says I ain't done right by you? Who says I ain't done right by them? Who says—"

The door to the library opened. Its inmate screamed out as though his brother's ghost had stalked from the graveyard to answer his self-justifying questions.

But the one at the door was only dead Anson Kannock's widow, stooped, apologetic, humble, patiently ready for complaint or curse, and timidly bearing a few letters in her hand to the master of Kannock Manse.

The pale, bent little woman looked at 'Struther Kannock in fear and trepidation.

He took the letters, glared at their bearer as if to fathom her thoughts and said, with a pretence of rough jocularity:

"Susan, I was just practicing my part, in case any of those young scalawags come around here with their Halloween doings tonight. I've made up my mind to have no more of 'em; not any, mind!"

"Yes, brother Anstruther."

"I'll lame some of 'em for life; for life, mind. No pranks tonight, now. And if that boy and young woman of yours are up to anything, you better get 'em to bed early. Are they up to anything, now, Susan?"

He turned on her with the question so suddenly and savagely that the woman retreated in fright, faltering only:

"Yes, brother Anstruther."

"And yes, brother Anstruther, what?" he returned, glaring and snapping like an animal at the helpless woman before him.

"Only—only some little innocent amusement, I'm sure, brother Anstruther. But, I'll stop it, sir. Oh, I will stop it, sir, if it annoys you; indeed I will!"

She pleaded so, in her tones, her manner, her very cowardly and worn-out helplessness, for some responsive manhood and compassion in the remorseless image of man before her, that her very pleading angered him.

He railed at her, at her children, at her dead husband who lay in the windswept graveyard beyond the manse walls, at countless things he had railed at over her cowering body and spirit without ceasing before, until livid with passion and rage; and then, instantly changing his manner, snapped at her like some vicious animal:

"Get out!"

Scarcely before the door had quickly and softly closed, he snapped out again:

"Come back here!"

The door now only partially opened and the voice behind it, in which was mingled the tremulousness of tears, submissively asked:

"Well, brother Anstruther?"

"Who brought these letters?"

"Mr. Penruth, sir."

"Oh, of course, Mr. Penruth! That fellow haunts this house like a specter! Sparking Edith, I s'pose? Now, what's up tonight? Out with it, or you'll regret it, Susan Kannock!"

"Yes, yes, yes, brother Anstruther;" she faltered, half beside herself with fear. "The young folks thought you wouldn't mind if they used the kitchen—it's the largest room in Millvale—and they'll surely bring all the apples and nuts and such things themselves; and we'll be very sparing of the wood and lights!"

"Who's—who's doings is this, woman?"

"Oh, sir, it's mine and Edith's and Herbert's and—and Mr. Penruth's—"

"That scoundrel! And you beggars dare do this in Kannock Manse, without my permission?"

Here, 'Struther Kannock's voice merged into something like a howl of rage, rose into a gurgling shriek and died away into a gasp of impotent condemnation and detestation.

"I'll see about this. I'll see about this!" he growled. "See here, now. You keep that cur of a schoolmaster in the house half an hour or so. I may want to look him over a minute. Understand?"

"Oh, yes sir."

"Then get out!"

'Struther Kannock tossed the letters upon his desk and paced his room, consumed with passion and anger.

But there was a certain cowardice and impotence in his rage which rendered its expression puerile as it was brutal and inhuman. Something restrained it, held it just within the bounds of actual objective outbreak, curbed it from its own natural tragedies and their punishment; and so these storms were driven more wildly and mercilessly through his own unpitying heart.

When this storm had died away he plunged into the armchair and betook himself to the letters before him. He cunningly examined each superscription postmark and envelope and balanced each letter in his hands, as though they were scales, before he opened it.

"Umph! Check for this fellow's last quarter's rent. Month behind. He'd better look lively. Umph! This one can't meet his mortgage. Oh, no, of course he can't. Prays for a little time. Oh, yes, he'll get a little time. 'Struther Kannock gets that place. Umph!—Bah! Can't 'Struther Kannock help the Millvale charity fund? Hard winter coming on—many mouths to feed. Not much!"

And thus, on and on he told his own miserable story to his own miserable self; joyous in ruin, unmoved by piteous appeals, scorning all human suffering and hating all humankind.

He gathered up the littered mass to place it in a pigeonhole of his desk. To do this he had partly raised himself to a standing posture and was leaning forward. Suddenly he sank back into his chair with wildly staring eyes.

There before him, where it had previously escaped notice, lay a letter plainly addressed to him in his dead brother's familiar hand.

He rubbed his eyes fiercely, as if he could not believe them longer. He loosened the collar at his throat, as though the drafty room were suffocating him. He mopped his forehead with one hand and another and beat away the cold drops which had instantly gathered there. He bounded from his chair and backed into his shadow against the wall, and, seeming to remember its presence there, sprang from that subtle darkness as though it held revengeful life; when, finally like a beast at bay, he wriggled to the middle of the room, peering and panting in quick succession towards its every side.

"Anson Kannock here again!—and on Halloween night? He said he'd curse me in his grave, if—if—who dare say I haven't done right by 'em? Well, well! Ghosts eh? Bah! Didn't I bury him? Didn't I put the stone over him? Only fools like Susan would be frightened of ghosts or letters from a ghost!"

He edged up to his desk craftily. With a quick lunge of his arm he brought his fist down with a crash upon the letter.

"There, Mister Anson Kannock! That's what I'd do if you were in its place. Bah! Who's afraid of a letter?"

He still held his fist upon it. Glancing covertly about the room, he clutched the missive and tremblingly tore it open. Then he read these words:

ANSTRUTHER:

You have been false to your trust. My poor wife and her children are without mercy at your hands. You will meet me beside my grave, between it and our father's tomb, alongside the old footpath from the village, an hour before midnight. If you fail to do this, every vestige of your wealth and your power to harm others shall pass before morning from your hands.

ANSON KANNOCK

Never had 'Struther Kannock in all his worthless life been so still and hushed as now.

There is no such bravery as the unconscious valor of integrity; no such cowardice as that skulking behind human injustice. 'Struther Kannock, pale and trembling before the accusative and threatening words penned by a dead and harmless hand, was now infinitely a more abject creature than the weakest human he had ever ground to nothingness and despair.

The blow had shrunk and withered him. It had swept his passion and rage from him. It had silenced his brawling tongue. As water vanishes in a deadly flame, so had his very vitalities been consumed within him. The wretch who but a moment before had found his keenest delight in scourging helplessness, in planning ruin for the upright and the good, now with a sickening quiver of human dependency found himself reaching out appealingly to the feeble strand of hope and pity binding him to the outraged ones about him.

He burned the letter and its envelope and rubbed the black and crinkly particles to powder between his hands. He staggered to the window and, peering into the dark toward the silent graves hoarsely whispered:

"Anson?—Anson? Don't—don't come here. Don't! I got the letter. I'll—I'll be there at the time you say."

Then he made his way haltingly to the library door, opened it and listened long and anxiously as if for approaching footsteps.

"Susan? Susan Kannock?" he called faintly and apologetically.

The woman was beside him in a moment, leading him timorously back to his old armchair.

"Mercy! Brother Anstruther, are you ill? Has anything happened?" she begged in frightened tones.

"Eh? Happened? Oh no, no, no. Nothing happened; nothing happened, Susan. Sister Susan, nothing's happened. I just wanted to say I've—I've changed my mind about Halloween; about the kitchen; about the young folk; about the wood and the lights and any—any little things that'll make 'em all welcome!"

The poor woman looked at him as though doubtful of her own senses.

"And Susan, I would somehow like to feel as though we've got along since Anson—since Anson left you all here, fairly friendly and comfortable, Susan?"

The man was actually pleading to the tortured human before him.

Perhaps a faint flush mantled her face; a flush kindled by her endless indignities which had been borne in silence for the sake of the dead and the living; but she only answered amazedly,

"Yes, brother Anstruther."

He had now fumbled about until he had grasped her hand. She remembered ever after that it was icy cold, that it fluttered as if palsied, but that it still clung to hers as though it held fast to 'Struther Kannock's only hope.

"Sister Susan," he began slowly and huskily and as though it were difficult for him to speak. "Sister Susan? I've been thinking for a—a time you were doing too much around here; too much. I've been thinking, and I just now thought of it again, that Bert might have a few more—a few more advantages; a few more, Susan. There's Edith too. Now Edith ought to spruce up a bit; like other girls, you know. You see I've been thinking about—about all these things, when, maybe, you thought I wasn't thinking about 'em, Susan?"

He said it all so deprecatingly, so justifyingly and with the tone of a sufferer begging for sympathy and encouragement, that the broken life before him, in a maze of wonder, anxiety, dread and hope, faltered feebly,

"It's good of you—it's like you—brother Anstruther!"

"So it is; so it is! I wish somehow Anson could know it, Susan."

Tears now flowed silently down her care-worn face.

"That is—if he could know it." This with a stealthy glance toward the desk and the window. "Dry your tears before you go back among—among 'em, Susan. Everything will go right here now, sister. Won't you ask Mr. Penruth if he can come and sit with me here for a few minutes?"

She started immediately to do his bidding as was her wont. But he still held her hand, loath to let it go.

"Sister, is—is everything all right now at Kannock Manse; buried—" this word compelled another swift glance at the desk and the window—"forgotten; started right again, now?"

"Oh, yes, yes, yes!" she moaned with a sudden outburst of feeling. "Everything; everything. God bless you for all the kindness you mean, brother Anstruther!"

She disappeared quickly into the dark hallway, while 'Struther Kannock, dazed by the first reverential blessing of his life, sat there in the cheerless old room doubtful whether it was a benediction or a curse,

With a fine, strong tread, Charles Penruth soon entered the library.

He seemed to wholly ignore 'Struther Kannock's gestured invitation to a seat beside him, and, walking straight to the fireplace, set his arm solidly upon its tall mantle of time-stained oak, his head resting lightly within the palm of his hand.

In this posture, and with a silence and impassiveness which almost suggested some figure of unpitying Justice, he looked calmly down upon the abject man before him as, a moment before punishment, he might have sternly regarded some incorrigible culprit of the Millvale village school.

Not a handsome man was Charles Penruth. But there was a certain power revealed in his strong, huge and loosely-jointed frame, in his angular features, his quiet gray eyes and his almost massive head.

Two or three men the world has known with frame and face like his, stand on monuments for their humane and heroic deeds; and this man in his strange and placid face, told a story, to those who could see, of illimitable patience, compassion and determination; above all, of some purpose and quest and mission whose working out had so stormed his soul with pity, regret and with unbending resolve and implacable detestation, that lines of sadness were already furrowed in his face of stone.

The two men, each looked a long time into the face of the other before either broke the silence. 'Struther Kannock was the first to speak:

"Penruth, we haven't been friends since you first came to Millvale?"

"We have not."

"I have tried to oust you from your place and you have made me out infamous among my neighbors."

The man at the chimney merely nodded his head.

"Isn't there some way, Penruth—some way we can be friends?"

"Just men are never less than friends!"

Old 'Struther Kannock seemed dejected by this reply. Impassable barriers, then, had been raised between them. "I am powerless to defeat and subdue this man," he reflected bitterly. "What is there left for me to do? I must make peace here, with him, before I can meet that—my brother, tonight!"

He answered his own perturbed self-questionings with instant diplomacy.

"Penruth, you and your brother, Judge Penruth, hold my last agreement with Anson, in trust?"

"With other papers, Mr. Kannock, bearing on your robbery from your brother of this great Kannock Manse estate; your second robbery of his inventions, from which millions in profit have already been realized by yourself and others; your false representations to him of their failure, and your final robbery of your brother, on his deathbed, through inconceivable duplicity, of all right and title to the result of his splendid genius and life of sacrifice, on the pretext that you would fittingly provide for his wife and children so long as they might live!"

"Penruth!"

"Do you wish further reasons why we cannot be friends? Shall we speak of the shameless manner in which you have carried out your doubly sacred trust?"

'Struther Kannock attempted to rise, but could not. With one hand clutching the frayed arm of his chair and the other working uneasily among the papers upon his desk, he leaned far forward, his miserly face grimacing hideously, as though impotent murder lurked in the black heart behind. At last he gasped:

"And that's what you've been at, like a hungry ferret, through all these years?"

"Precisely."

"Penruth, you're—you're a poor man; and the judge ain't over well-to-do?"

A slight pallor came into the face of the man of stone against the chimney.

"I ain't rich, mind. Far from it, Penruth. But I've been thinking. I've been thinking this very evening, that I'd like to sort of, well, do something handsome for—for somebody. I wouldn't mind starting with you and the judge, Penruth; and making you both independent for life! Understand?"

"No!" came quickly, tremulously, but with an inflection of unutterable loathing, from the schoolmaster's scarcely parted lips.

"Damnation!" blurted 'Struther Kannock with a burst of his former brutal energy. "I mean, Penruth, if you'll bring me those papers, every one of them, and put them in my hands within the next hour, mind!—you may name your own price for them! Will you do that, Charles Penruth?"

"Do you know what that price would be?"

"Eh? Maybe five or ten thousand. Maybe not so much—considering I'm not rich; considering what I've done for them!" This with groveling wheedling and a shamefaced gesture of his head in the direction of the old manse kitchen.

"Do you wish to know it?"

"Yes, yes, yes!"

"Well, then, it is one-half of everything you now possess, transferred to those to whom it rightly belongs; and the absolute conveyance of your entire interest in Anson Kannock's inventions to his maltreated wife and children!"

"Penruth! Penruth! This is madness!" almost shrieked 'Struther Kannock, sinking back helplessly in his chair.

"For years the madness has been yours alone;" was the schoolmaster's quiet response, as he started to leave the room.

"Don't go! Don't go! Oh, let me think; let me think!" cringingly pleaded the wretched master of Kannock Manse.

"It is good to think;" said Penruth, pitilessly resuming his place against the chimney-piece.

The old man turned his head from the light of the candle and ground it crushingly into the upholstering of the chair. He held it there for a long, long time, motionless as the gray eyes which he now rested with almost fiery intentness upon him. At last he spoke in a muffled way, without turning his face to the one he questioned.

"Penruth, you are a scholar; a man who digs and burrows and thinks. Do—you—believe—there—are—ghosts?"

"Implicitly."

The schoolmaster's face lighted splendidly as this was said. The word came firmly, convincingly, almost solemnly, from his lips. He moved a step or two forward toward the huddled form in the old arm chair. His head was even now partly turned toward him, with a listening, eager movement, almost as to a scholar whom he was impressively leading to irresistible conclusions and facts.

"Real ghosts—ghosts that can help or harm?" half whispered the muffled voice in the chair.

"Actual, tangible, palpable ghosts!" The schoolmaster almost stood over him as he spoke. "'Struther Kannock, an awful, avenging, pitiless ghost springs from the grave of every wrong we place among the shadows of the past, deeming it hidden and still! It lurks beside us, taunting us in happiness, flouting our power, maddening us into more desperate expedients. It is never voiceless, never hidden, never still! It is ever present; and at last—like that face of Anson Kannock there, now!—at your window, 'Struther Kannock!—"

"My God!—You lie!" shrieked the frenzied wretch, plunging out of the chair past the schoolmaster to the chimney corner, where he cowered, whimpering and muttering in almost imbecile and mortal terror.

"Oh, I didn't mean that! Don't go!—don't go!" he pleaded as his inquisitor again turned away.

Penruth hesitated, immediately wheeled the arm chair close to the flickering fire and gently forced the ghost-haunted master of Kannock Manse within it.

"I must go now. I promised to help the young folk with their games for a little—it's Halloween, you know; and I must meet my brother later at his office. We are to meet about those papers, 'Struther Kannock!"

"Yes, yes, yes!—the papers! Oh, yes, yes, yes!"

He clutched the skirt of the schoolmaster's coat almost fiercely.

"I've been thinking—I told Susan that! I am thinking. I'll keep thinking. Don't let Judge Penruth go to bed this night! Bring him here, here to Kannock Manse, along toward midnight. Yes, yes, yes!—along toward midnight!"

Penruth disengaged himself, not without effort, and moved slowly toward the door.

"Penruth! Penruth! Tell Susan—tell Bert and Edith!—tell 'em all out there! 'Struther Kannock ain't against 'em. Tell 'em all, all now, Penruth, to dance and sing and play games and cut up, Penruth; cut up. Tell 'em 'Struther Kannock says that. Tell 'em—"

But the schoolmaster had left him with his incoherent pleadings; left him with the recriminations of his cruel life, while their remorseless wraiths goaded on his despair.

The door closed but halted an instant as it closed. If in that instant the darkness of the ancient hallway could have been penetrated, in Charles Penruth's face might have been seen a wondrous look of triumph, subdued by traces of compassionate sadness and unalterable sternness and resolve.

Back in the library of Kannock Manse the candle sputtered and flickered upon the desk where countless wrongs had been done. The paling embers in the ashes of the fireplace now and then shot feeble tongues of flame within the cavernous chimney, in faint response to the echoing challenges of the blast. Like ghostly knuckles against the panes, shuffled and pattered dead leaves and bits of branches which the giant trees tossed furiously as they lashed and cried in wild abrasion. Ghostly voices moaning whimpered from cracks and crannies, or whispered querulously from doorways, niches and dark corners of the shadowy room.

But what is that? The old man shrinks from it as if the sound carried it with some strange and deadly hurt. There it is again; clearer, louder, more penetrating than before! No wonder it beats and pounds the miserable frame into a writhing mass within the age-eaten chair. It is the sound of innocent mirth, ever a fearsome trumpeting to bigotry, envy and greed! ringing for the first time in half a century now a merry peal of gladness through and through the whitened skeleton of olden hate haunted Kannock Manse!

But listen! There is another and more ominous sound to 'Struther Kannock's heart. Its solemn and vibrant peal is not half through, when the old man lunges from his chair, grasps the chimney-piece as if for support, nods piteously toward the ghostly window panes and staggers through the library door into the dark hallway beyond.

A moment more and a wild soughing of the blast, as the outer door is closed, tells that the man of coward heart and dark purpose is beating tremulously against the wind and the innumerable phantoms of the night, drawn by illimitable fear, rather than by a single strand of human love or reverence, toward the gray old church beyond the moss grown wall.

The light streams out upon him as he passes the vast old kitchen, half-filled with the merry-makers of genial Halloween. It cuts him like flame. The melodious murmurs of the place fill his ears and he turns his head quickly as if from a stinging blow. What impetuous, sacred, saving youth-tide memory hands reach out to him through light and life and sound and song from that blessed old kitchen of other days, no human soul save his may know; but he plunges and staggers on.

The wall is gained. The ancient oaken gate is turned upon its rustic hinges. The wind plays mad antics among the tall grasses and the waving weeds. He even feels he hears a saddened sobbing and sighing from the throats of the tremulous bells in the ponderous tower above his head. He stumbles and staggers on. The gravestones dance into his eyes and away, and huddle about him gruesomely. With mighty effort and a despairing groan he leaps fiercely to the side of the tall marble shaft standing at the head of Anson Kannock's grave. He can go no further. He cannot scream out. He can neither bound madly away nor even fall among the crowded graves. For there before him, rising slowly from the crumbling slab above his father's tomb, is a majestic spectral form. Its long white arm is slowly lifted. Its ghastly face begins to move; and its stern and mournful voice smites the wretched being's soul with the measured and solemn words:

"Anstruther Kannock, I knew you dare not refuse to come!"

Whatever the dread mystery enacted, whatever the measureless misery to such a nature as this in the inexorable accounting which was surely had, and whatever the blighting judgment passed by the dead or supposititious dead upon the groveling living, among these lone and windswept graves, the folk of Millvale ever after knew only that some mighty and wondrous change had come upon the master of Kannock Manse this night of Halloween—a change that had made him an old man; a man of blanched locks and face; a man of trembling and halting step and hesitant, thoughtful speech; and yet a man more in the sunlight than the shadows of remaining peaceful days, into which had come a blessed quickening of ministration to the humble, weak and poor.

Two only knew of his absence from the manse; and but one of these ever possessed the secret of what had left him prone and unconscious upon his father's crumbling tomb.

On their way to the manse, as bidden by the distracted miser, Charles Penruth and his brother, Judge Penruth, bearing some legal papers in their hands, had taken the shorter but unfrequented path which led from the village through the churchyard on the hill.

Here they had stumbled over 'Struther Kannock as he lay witless and almost lifeless on his father's grave. They took him between them and without disturbing the merry-makers at the manse, at last got him safely in his own bed. Here, as they were vigorously chafing his hands and limbs, he suddenly sat bolt upright and calmly said:

"Please bring the papers and a pen!" This, with the first inflection of gentleness the two at his side had ever heard escape his lips. The documents were brought and the old man read them aloud, still in clear and kindly tones. Then, as one brother held a light and the other a book upon which the papers rested, he signed them decisively without the slightest tremor of hand or pen.

"Shall we burn these others now?" the schoolmaster quietly asked.

"No. You may leave them with me."

He took them, crunched them in his hand a little and then placing them carelessly beneath his pillow, added:

"They hold no more harm or hurt now than the vanishing shadows of Kannock Manse!"

"Amen!" came heartily and solemnly from the other voices in the room; and in a moment more, as Charles Penruth and his brother stole softly out of the doorway, old 'Struther Kannock's head lay close upon his pillow and his sleep was dreamless and peaceful as a babe's.

Was there joy this Halloween night in the ample olden room of cheer, to which the two now hurried? No need to ask the lips and eyes and hearts of mother, daughter, son; of pupil Edith, blushing, demure and sweet, and of master Penruth, grave and grand and tall; nor of all the assembled "company," athrill with this ecstasy-bringing change and glow, until the thrilling and the glowing of it all broke into such peals of gladness as Millvale hamlet had never before known.

And, think you, was there a dance here this Halloween night, where the shadows had so long gathered and lowered like a close and stifling pall? Ask the rafters of oak above them that shivered a century's splinters and mold upon the vaulting heads and heels of these glad-hearted Millvale villagers. And ask the stars that looked softly down upon this scene of peace and joy until their shining eyes went out in the brighter All Hallow-dawn which lifted flaming cones upon the peaks of fair and far New England hills!

THE PHANTOM RIDE
A HALLOWE'EN GHOST STORY
Lyllian Huntley

Published in The Sunny South, 26 October 1901

Lyllian Huntley Harris (1883–1939) was the grandniece of Georgia State Treasurer Robert Emory Park and a past president of the Georgia Division United Daughters of the Confederacy. She spent her life working for a State music club and had a trophy named after her. Harris had been ill for more than a year with heart problems when she died at home at 1:30am on January 12, 1939, and was buried the next day in Sandersville Cemetery.

Harris appears to have only written two stories during her lifetime, and unusually, both are Hallowe'en-themed. The first was published in *The Sunny South* entitled "The Phantom Ride: A Hallowe'en Ghost Story" (27 October 1901) and is attributed to "Lyllian Huntley". I'm publishing it here for the very first time since its original appearance alongside "The Vow on Halloween" which was published in *Weird Tales* (May 1924). I'm certain that the authorship of both tales is by the same woman. The facts are that she was born in Fulton County, near Atlanta. "The Phantom Ride" was written for *The Sunny South*, an Atlanta newspaper, and Lyllian married John Joseph Harris in 1905.

This lack of contemporary information about Harris meant that for whatever reason, and only known to anthologist Peter Haining himself, he "passed off" Harris's *Weird Tales* story as being by the Irish author and founding member of Fianna Fáil, Dorothy Macardle, in his themed anthology *Hallowe'en Hauntings* (William Kimber, 1984). Sadly, this may not have been a simple mistake on Haining's part. From information discovered in the years since his death (2007), it appears that he fraudulently and blatantly invented or misattributed numerous citations, as well as facts about stories and their authorship in several other anthologies and works. Haining's involvement with the Harris tale wasn't reported until 2011 by Douglas A. Anderson.

I T was on the 31st of October, that fascinating night popularly known as All-Hallowe'en, when bogies abound and nature gives way to marvelous revelations and wonders, that my friend, Viola Lyndchurst. and I spent the night with my aunt, who lived in a rambling old house on the outskirts of the village. Being extremely imaginative and of an inquisitive turn of mind, I was fond of exploring the nooks and secret recesses of the old mansion and hunting up old traditions to fit. On this memorable occasion, however, my ardor was checked, and forever afterwards I never cared to inquire or deal in the weird or supernatural.

A few of our friends had collected to assist us in the usual festivities and games that characterize the evening. Chestnuts had been roasted, apples pared, and we girls had entered a dark room with our hair unbound and peered into a mirror, hoping to see the features of our fate, with the usual results.

Viola suggested that all should go down to the well and look in to see what mysteries would be unveiled. "Horrors!" cried my cousin, Edward, "let's not try any such grewsome tricks. Do you all not remember last Hallowe'en here when poor Joe Forrester looked in the well and saw his own coffin?"

"Ah, yes, and three weeks later he was murdered by his own brother," chimed in Viola. "How could we forget that terrible tragedy?"

"Do you all recall how quiet he was, and how he looked as if someone had injured him, or he had something on his mind?" continued Edward.

I felt a pained dark flush cross my face and quietly recede, leaving me deathly pale and faint. This had been the one sad experience of my happy young life. It was I who had offended him, having refused to accompany him to my aunt's entertainment, whereupon he had vowed vengeance.

One of my peculiarities was an abhorrence of drink, and it was a source of deep and sincere regret to me to learn that my old-time friend had but recently formed this habit, especially as prayers and entreaties on my part proved unavailing.

Just then refreshments were served, greatly to my relief, and merrier topics being discussed, our gloomy conversation was not resumed and was apparently forgotten by all, but myself. As for me, I could not shake off the melancholy which had thus surreptitiously taken possession of me, an indescribable something which caused me to start and tremble at every sound.

After refreshments the company dispersed, each going alone and in a different direction, to sow hemp seeds, the grinning "countenances" of the lighted pumpkins affording sufficient light for this uncanny employment.

Being left alone, who can tell what subtle power directed my steps toward the well—the same that had betrayed to Joe Forrester his untimely end?

Trembling at every sound, and starting at every rustling leaf, I had sowed my allotted handful of seeds, while repeating over and over the well-known couplet:

"Hemp seed I sow, hemp seed I sow,
My true love come behind me and mow."

By so doing I had hoped to regain my lost gayety, but the monotony of the hollow tones, which barely escaped my frozen lips, sounded to my nervous fancy like a dirge.

The sardonic smile on the face of the pumpkin, which had hitherto been horrible to look at, seemed suddenly to change! In place of the grinning features, at which I had been staring, I saw in its flickering light the face of Joe Forrester! The light wavered for a moment, then went out, leaving me in total darkness, except for the pale rays of the crescent moon, half hidden behind a cloud!

Inexpressibly terrified, I turned to flee, but spellbound, I could move neither hand nor foot!

Calling all my energies and will power to bear, by a supreme effort, I turned to retrace my steps when looming up before me, with noiseless tread and horrible visage, was a frightful skeleton, his bones rattling as he moved the hemp seeds I had sown.

Just then a distant clock tolled out the mystic hour of twelve!

Horror stricken and frenzied, almost to madness, I tried to scream, but my lips gave forth no sound. In place of my own voice, which I expected to hear, a hollow laugh grated on my already jaded nerves. My limbs gave way beneath me, and I was falling—!

But no—a bony arm caught me, at which I recoiled to hear, uttered in sepulchral tones, these words:

"Come with me!"

Surprised at my own temerity, I ventured to say tremblingly:

"Who are you, and where are you taking me?"

"My name you ought to know," he replied, in meaning tones, "but I come from the city of the dead! Perhaps you imagine that you dream?"

"Oh, no: I'm fully awake," I said, trying to put on a bold face, which I was far from feeling.

"Then come, you are to take a drive with me. No refusal, mind! I say come!"

I started forward, fearing to disobey my strange companion. Almost paralyzed from fear, I moved slowly, but nothing could exceed his impatience.

"Come!" he said again, "my carriage awaits, and I am anxious to tell you the story of my life and death. There is no more fitting time than now."

I looked despairingly around for some of my friends, but in vain. The grounds seemed suddenly to have become deserted.

"Come faster," continued my relentless midnight guide, and I obeyed. Suddenly I gave a start.

"What is the matter," he asked.

"Why—why, your carriage is all white and made of bones!" I gasped. "Surely I see human skulls! You won't compel me to ride in that?" entreatingly.

"Certainly they are, and, indeed, I will," he replied decidedly.

He at once assisted me into the horrible hearse of bones, and seeing his determination I made no opposition. He seated himself beside me, and soon we were going at full speed.

Leaning back. half fainting with terror. I tried to close my ears to the sound of his rattling bones, but to no avail.

"Well," he condescended to say, after a pause, during which the phantom horse had raced madly on, "now you shall hear my story," he continued, as we drove rapidly on. I made no reply, being utterly incapable of speech.

My weird escort heaved a sigh, then—

"Mine is a sad story," he said, slowly and sorrowfully. "I once lived at the turnpike road cottage. I started, with my brother. We had been friends in the true sense of the word as well as brothers, and 'what's mine is yours' had been the motto that guided our lives. We worked together and kept our savings in common. My brother and I had never quarreled"—here a lump seemed to rise in his throat. "As I said, we never quarreled until one day I saw him stealthily slip a bottle from his coat pocket and take a long drink, and another, and another, until he was terribly intoxicated. 'Give me a drink,' I said, 'I helped to earn it. you know.'

"'Get out with you.' he answered gruffly. 'I haven't enough for myself, much less to waste on you.'

"I grew angry at his injustice and sprang at him, for the whisky was as much mine as his.

"'Don't come too near,' he cried warningly, an ominous ring in his voice.

"'Why not?' I demanded.

"'I will kill you if you do!'

"'Nonsense!' I exclaimed loudly, 'nonsense!' With this he quickly approached me. I saw the flash of glittering steel, and realizing my life was actually in danger. I sprang at him with the fury of a tiger. My brother was never a fighting man, but that night he seemed possessed by a devil. We were fighting desperately—"

I shuddered.

—"and I thought I would have conquered," turning his empty eye sockets on me as he spoke, "but with a quick movement he gave me a stab in the heart which proved to be my death blow. My brother disappeared and I was buried—"

I felt the quick thumping of my heart.

—"the next day." He paused. The phantom horse raced on, everything had a weird look, the marrow in my bones was chilled, while shudder after shudder shook my whole frame. Presently—

"Here we are," he said, offering to assist me to alight, as we neared the gates of the cemetery, and again I felt that icy touch on my hand which made my blood run cold, and which I tried so hard to evade.

Ignorant as to my fate, fearing I knew not what, together we walked for a few moments, which seemed so many hours.

Presently, stopping before an open vault—

"Come in," he said, and fearing that icy touch, I entered the tomb:

It was dark, damp, cold and horrible!

"Why—why," as I glanced about aghast, "this is where Mr. Forrester is buried, isn't it?"

"Did you know Forrester?" he returned, ignoring my question.

"Quite well. We were once friends, but he became offended with me. I never saw him again, and I finally heard—"

"What caused his death?" he interrupted.

"I had heard he had become addicted to drinking and on that account—"

—"refused to drive with him to your aunt's Hallowe'en party last year."

"Yes, and he vowed I should yet accept his invitation—"

"Whether you were willing or not—"

"How do you—"

"He has kept his word!"

"No—"

"Yes," he hissed.

Aghast I looked at him, and fearing I was going to faint, leaned against the cold marble for support.

The truth suddenly burst upon me: Could it be possible that—

For some unaccountable reason and sorely against my will I felt impelled to look at him again, and fancied I saw a sinister smile play over his hideous visage.

"Surely you are not—you can't be—"

"Forrester!"

With a great effort I opened my eyes and looked about me.

I was surprised to find myself in my own bed.

A woman with a sweet face and dressed in gray was sitting by my side. The old family physician was bending over me, feeling my pulse, with a look of eager anxiety on his kind face.

"At last she is conscious." I heard him murmur, as in a dream.

"How did I get back?" I asked, struggling to sit up.

"You have been nowhere, dear, only very ill with brain fever for three weeks, but you will recover now," as a soft hand folded mine in her own.

"But the skeleton—"

"She is beginning to rave again, nurse, so give her another sleeping portion."

"Indeed, I am not! Doctor, I must tell you—"

"There, go to sleep and tell me all tomorrow."

The "tomorrow" when he will listen and believe me will never come, for I have a strong conviction that I will never convince him that my story was other than the fancy of a fevered brain; but we, dear reader, you and I, knew better. We know all that really happened during that terrible adventure, which to this day has left its silvery marks on my head.

THE VOW ON HALLOWE'EN

Lyllian Huntley Harris

Published in Weird Tales, May 1924

I T was Hallowe'en, the time of revelry, when mysticism holds full sway and hearts are supposed to be united beneath the magic glow of dim lanterns. It was the time of apple bobbing, fortune telling, and masking in motley raiment, the whole glamoured over by the light of wishing candles.

Amid such scenes one never thinks of tragedy, but it treads apace, sometimes among the gay revelers, and many a domino or cowl covers that which would make the staunchest heart quake and is as different from the gay exterior as darkness is from light.

The lanterns glimmered, the varicolored lights shading and darkening with the winds that soughed through the beautiful old garden where the fete was held.

The pergolas, standing whitely aloof from surrounding density, made wonderful trysting places for the age-old stories of love to be whispered.

"You have made me very happy tonight, Audrey," a deep voice was whispering. "I think that all my after life will be a paean of gratitude for this moment of bliss. When you would vouchsafe no word of hope, not even one of pity, I felt hopeless, broken. Life seemed as senseless as a stupid rhyme! But now, dearest, life's cup is filled to overflowing!"

His lips met hers in a lingering caress.

For a moment the lanterns seemed to flicker and dim. A slight shudder ran over her slender frame. She freed herself gently.

"I cannot expect you to understand, Arthur," Audrey replied, "why you were kept waiting. The silence encompassed the whole of the earth and sky to me. It has been a frightful reality, which my tongue refused to explain until today, and my mental anguish has well nigh swayed my reason. A year ago tonight I experienced a terrible ordeal, more uncanny because it has seemed impossible for me to shake off the pall of it. It has changed the course of my life. For a year I have lived the life of a senseless thing, a piece of clay, merely breathing, eating, sleeping, but with no soul left me—"

Her voice trailed off into nothingness, and for a while both were silent. He was awed by her utterances. His arm tightened about her.

"Poor Audrey," he whispered, "you must have worried yourself needlessly. Is not illusion a sort of night to the mind which we people with dreams?"

"It was no illusion, Arthur, but grim reality. But last night a dream came to me which seemed to awaken my dead sensibilities, cut loose the spell under which I was living. In it I was commanded to tell you all."

Gently he caressed her.

"Tell me what you wish, dear, and nothing more. Remember, hope is better than memory. I am listening."

"I shall tell you all. You suffered, so nothing shall be withheld. My troubles began when my father had financial reverses. I gave music lessons to eke out a meagre income. About this time Rothschild Manny came into my life. He loved me at sight, as intensely as I loathed him. One glance from his slanting, shifty eyes was sufficient to set me cowering in my chair, and if his hand by chance touched mine, cold chills chased over my body. He was like some demon, waiting his chance to spring upon his prey.

"Imagine my dismay, when my parents immediately began insisting on my marriage with this monster! His fortune would retrieve ours and

would regain the position we had lost by financial reverses. The horror
of it! After one lengthy argument I felt my brain reel, and I fell upon my
knees crying and imploring my father to spare me this ordeal. He was
obdurate and insisted upon my consent. Finally he sent for Manny, placed
my hand in his, and gave me to him formally But not once did I encourage
him, and he seemed to change into a veritable demon. His eyes would
become crafty as he looked at me and his face assume an expression of
sardonic intensity.

"One day, the day that is seared upon my memory, one year ago
tonight, he sought me out. I was alone in the house, my father having
gone to the lodge. Manny was trembling under some terrible emotion.

"'Your welcome does not shine forth from your eyes, my dear,' he said
as he seated himself and took my hand.

"With a gesture of horror I jerked it away. The motion seemed to infu-
riate him, and deepened the intensity of his eyes.

"'I came to take you driving,' he said, with a quick intake of his breath.
'The night is lovely and my new car is without. It will be yours when you
are mine.'

"There was a steely intensity in his gaze directed upon me. 'I don't care
to go,' I said quietly.

"'Pray reconsider. I may be able to persuade you to feel differently if
you give me a chance.'

"Here I interrupted.

"'I will do nothing of the sort,' I cried, 'I will go nowhere with you.
I want nothing to do with you, and, God willing, I will never be your
wife!'

"My words infuriated him. He was under some powerful influence
of evil. He seized my wrist and, jerking me out of my chair, shook me
violently.

"My senses reeled, and I must have lost consciousness. All I remember
was being held up by main force, those horrible evil eyes boring malevo-
lently into mine while he shouted in my ear:

"'Remember—young lady, you will drive with me—yet! Maybe not now, but some day! This is not a threat, it is a declaration, and neither stars, moon nor even heaven itself, shall deliver you from it.'

"I was thrown violently upon the floor. Merciful oblivion came to me.

"For days I was ill—not knowing, not caring what happened, craving death to relieve me from the sinister influence and deliver me from the effect of that horrible vow on Halloween. When I recovered I learned that Manny, driving his car that day madly, had lost control and had come to a horrible end. His evil influence seemed to hold me drugged in its power. I longed to die. But death does not come when one craves it. I lived, a piece of senseless clay, until you came to me; and when I looked into your eyes I felt that heaven had been kind in denying me my desire. My heart, my soul, went out to you, but I couldn't let you know. I could never become your wife with that terrible vow sounding in my ears, that terrible power controlling me.

"Then yesterday, in the dim watches of the night a dream came to me. A voice spoke and said: 'Love beyond price is yours. Take and cherish it, lest this priceless gift be withdrawn!'

"I awoke, happy, myself once more, grateful that life could come to me again."

She nestled close and his hand caressed her hair.

"My darling, how you have suffered. My whole life shall be spent in keeping you free of the mirage of this terrible experience—"

"Beg pardon," a suave voice interrupted, and a cowled figure drew near, "this is my dance, I believe. Is it not too warm to repair to the ballroom? I have my car here. A spin will refresh us both."

The cowled figure bowed low. Audrey glanced at her card, and arose with a little laugh.

"You will excuse me, Arthur, won't you? It seems that this august domino person has prior claim."

With a light hand on the newcomer's arm she was lost in the crowd. The music from the palm-shaded orchestra stirred forth, hummed, throbbed, and sobbed into a soft requiem.

Two days later, some belated wayfarers came upon a young woman, who seemed unable to move from her seat in an automobile. Upright beside her was a skeleton, whose sightless eye-sockets even then bored into the soul from which the light of reason had fled forever more!

Manny had kept his threat.

And in an old moonlit garden, under the white pergola where he had lived his one moment of bliss, a figure fell, turned into sudden clay, as the smoking weapon in his hand could testify.

THE BANSHEE'S HALLOWEEN

Herminie Templeton Kavanagh

Published in McClure's Magazine, *May 1903*

Herminie Templeton Kavanagh (1861–1933) was a British-born Irish short story writer, best-known for the fairy adventure *Darby O'Gill and the Good People* which was first published in *McClure's Magazine*, before being published in book form in 1903. The Darby O'Gill character proved popular, and would eventually led to a Disney film, *Darby O'Gill and the Little People*, being released in 1959.

She met her second husband Judge Marcus A. Kavanagh whilst he was touring Europe; they married in Des Moines in 1905. Herminie died on 30 October 1933, from heart troubles, following a week's stay in St. Luke's, Chicago and was buried in New York. A year after her death, her widower, then 75 years old and dean of the Superior court judges, married his 27-year-old secretary.

I

HALLOWEEN night, to all unhappy ghosts, is about the same as St. Patrick's Day is to you or to me—'tis a great holiday in every churchyard. An' no one knew this betther or felt it keener than did Darby O'Gill, that same Halloween night, as he stood on his own doorstep with the paper of black tay for Eileen McCarthy safely stowed away in the crown of his top-hat.

No one in that barony was quicker than he at an act of neighbourly kindness, but now, as he huddled himself together in the shelter of his own eaves, and thought of the dangers before, an' of the cheerful fire an' comfortable bed he was leaving behint, black raybellion rushed shouting across his heart.

"Oh, my, oh, my, what a perishin' night to turn a man out into!" he says. "It'd be half a comfort to know I was goin' to be kilt before I got back, just as a warnin' to Bridget," says he.

The misthrayted lad turned a sour eye on the chumultuous weather, an' groaned deep as he pulled closer about his chowldhers the cape of his greatcoat an' plunged into the daysarted an' flooded roadway.

Howsumever, 'twas not the pelting rain, nor the lashing wind, nor yet the pitchy darkness that bothered the heart out of him as he wint splashin' an' stumbling along the road. A thought of something more raylentless than the storm, more mystarious than the night's blackness put pounds of lead into the lad's unwilling brogues; for somewhere in the shrouding darkness that covered McCarthy's house the banshee was waiting this minute, purhaps, ready to jump out at him as soon as he came near her.

And, oh, if the banshee nabbed him there, what in the worruld would the poor lad do to save himself?

At the raylisation of this sitiwation, the goose-flesh crept up his back an' settled on his neck an' chowldhers. He began to cast about in his mind for a bit of cheer or a scrap of comfort, as a man in such sarcumstances will do. So, grumblin' an' sore-hearted, he turned over Bridget's parting words. "If one goes on an errant of marcy," Bridget had said, "a score of God's white angels with swoords in their hands march before an' beside an' afther him, keeping his path free from danger."

He felt anxious in his hat for the bit of charitable tay he was bringin', and was glad to find it there safe an' dhry enough, though the rest of him was drenched through an' through.

"Isn't this an act of charity I'm doin', to be bringin' a cooling drink to a dyin' woman?" he axed himself aloud. "To be sure it is. Well, then, what rayson have I to be afeared?" says he, pokin' his two hands into his pockets. "Arrah, it's aisy enough to bolsther up one's heart with wise sayin' an' hayroic praycepts when sitting comodious by one's own fire; but talkin' wise words to one's self is mighty poor comfort when you're on the lonely high-road of a Halloween night, with a churchyard waitin' for ye on the top of the hill not two hundred yards away. If there was only one star to break through the thick sky an' shine for him, if there was but one friendly cow to low or a distant cock to break the teeming silence, 'twould put some heart into the man. But not a sound was there only the swish and wailing of the wind through the inwisible hedges.

"What's the matther with the whole worruld? Where is it wanished to?" says Darby. "If a ghost were to jump at me from the churchyard wall, where would I look for help? To run is no use," he says, "an' to face it is—"

Just then the current of his misdoubtings ran whack up against a sayin' of ould Peggy O'Callaghan. Mrs. O'Callaghan's repitation for truth and voracity, whin it come to fairy tales or ghost stories, be it known, was ayquil if not shuparior to the best in Tipperary. Now, Peggy had towld

Ned Mullin, an' Ned Mullin had towld Bill Donahue, the tinker, an' the tinker had adwised Darby that no one need ever be afeared of ghosts if he only had the courage to face them.

Peggy said, "The poor crachures ain't roamin' about shakin' chains an' moanin' an' groanin', just for the sport of scarin' people, nor yet out of maneness. 'Tis always a throuble that's on their minds—a message they want sint, a saycret they're endayvouring to unload. So instead of flyin' from the onhappy things, as most people generally do," she said, "one should walk up bowld to the apparraytion, be it gentle or common, male or faymale, an' say, 'What throubles ye, sir?' or 'What's amiss with ye, ma'am?' An' take my worrud for it," says she, "ye'll find yourself a boney-factor to them when you laste expect it," she says.

'Twas a quare idee, but not so onraysonable afther all whin one comes to think of it; an' the knowledgeable man fell to dayliberatin' whether he'd have the hardness to folly it out if the chanst came. Sometimes he thought he would, then agin he was sure he wouldn't. For Darby O'Gill was one who bint quick undher trouble like a young three before a hur-rycane, but he only bint—the throuble never broke him. So, at times his courage wint down to a spark like the light of a candle in a gust of wind, but before you could turn on your heel 'twas blazing up sthrong and fiercer than before.

Whilst thus contimplatin' an' meditaytin', his foot sthruck the bridge in the hollow just below the berrin'-ground, an' there as the boy paused a minute, churning up bravery enough to carry him up the hill an' past the mystarious gravestones, there came a short quiver of lightning, an' in its sudden flare he was sure he saw not tin yards away, an' comin' down the hill toward him, a dim shape that took the breath out of his body.

"Oh, be the powers!" he gasped, his courage emptying out like wather from a spilt pail.

It moved, a slow, grey, formless thing without a head, an' so far as he was able to judge it might be about the size of an ulephant. The parsecuted lad swung himself sideways in the road, one arrum over his eyes an' the other stretched out at full length, as if to ward off the tumble wisitor.

The first thing that began to take any shape in his bewildhered brain was Peggy O'Callaghan's adwice. He thried to folly it out, but a chatterin' of teeth was the only sound he made. An' all this time a thraymendous splashin', like the floppin' of whales, was coming nearer an' nearer.

The splashin' stopped not three feet away, an' the ha'nted man felt in the spine of his back an' in the calves of his legs that a powerful, unhowly monsther towered over him.

Why he didn't swoonge in his tracks is the wondher. He says he would have dhropped at last if it weren't for the distant bark of his own good dog, Sayser, that put a throb of courage intil his bones. At that friendly sound he opened his two dhry lips an' stutthered this sayin':

"Whoever you are, an' whatever shape ye come in, take heed that I'm not afeared," he says. "I command ye to tell me your throubles an' I'll be your boneyfactor. Then go back dacint an' rayspectable where you're buried. Spake an' I'll listen," says he.

He waited for a reply, an' getting none, a hot splinther of shame at bein' so badly frightened turned his sowl into wexation. "Spake up," he says, "but come no furder, for if you do, be the hokey I'll take one thry at ye, ghost or no ghost!" he says. Once more he waited, an' as he was lowering the arrum from his eyes for a peek, the ghost spoke up, an' its answer came in two pitiful, disthressed roars. A damp breath puffed acrost his face, an' openin' his eyes, what should the lad see but the two dhroopin' ears of Solomon, Mrs. Kilcannon's grey donkey. Foive different kinds of disgust biled up into Darby's throat an' almost sthrangled him. "Ye murdherin', big-headed imposture!" he gasped.

Half a minute afther a brown hoot-owl, which was sheltehred in a nearby black-thorn three, called out to his brother's fambly which inhabited the belfry of the chapel above on the hill that some black-minded spalpeen had hoult of Solomon Kilcannon be the two ears an' was kickin' the ribs out of him, an' that the langwidge the man was usin' to the poor baste was worse than scan'lous.

Although Darby couldn't undherstand what the owl was sayin', he was startled be the blood-curdlin' hoot, an' that same hoot saved Solomon from any further exthrayornery throuncin', bekase as the angry man sthopped to hearken there flashed on him the rayilisation that he was bating an' crool maulthraytin' a blessing in dishguise. For this same Solomon had the repitation of being the knowingest, sensiblist thing which walked on four legs in that parish. He was a fayvourite with young an' old, especially with childher, an' Mrs. Kilcannon said she could talk to him as if he were a human, an' she was sure he understhood. In the face of thim facts the knowledgeable man changed his chune, an' puttin' his arrum friendly around the disthressed animal's neck, he said:

"Aren't ye ashamed of yerself, Solomon, to be payradin' an' mayand-herin' around the churchyard Halloween night, dishguisin' yerself this away as an outlandish ghost, an' you havin' the foine repitation for daciency an' good manners?" he says, excusin' himself. "I'm ashamed of you, so I am, Solomon," says he, hauling the baste about in the road, an' turning him till his head faced once more the hillside. "Come back with me now to Cormac McCarthy's, avourneen. We've aich been in worse company, I'm thinkin'; at laste you have, Solomon," says he.

At that, kind an' friendly enough, the forgivin' baste turned with him, an' the two keeping aich other slitherin' company, went stumblin' an' scramblin' up the hill toward the chapel. On the way Darby kept up a one-sided conwersation about all manner of things, just so that the ring of a human woice, even if 'twas only his own, would take a bit of the crool lonesomeness out of the dark hedges.

"Did you notice McDonald's sthrame as you came along the night, Solomon? It must be a roarin' torrent be this, with the pourin' rains, an' we'll have to cross it," says he. "We could go over McDonald's stone bridge that stands ferninst McCarthy's house, with only Nolan's meadow betwixt the two, but," says Darby, laying a hand, confaydential on the ass's wet back, "'tis only a fortnit since long Faylix, the blind beggarman, fell from the same bridge and broke his neck, an' what more natural," he axed, "than that the ghost of Faylix would be celebraytin' its first Halloween, *as a ghost*, at the spot where he was kilt?"

You may believe me or believe me not, but at thim worruds Solomon sthopped dead still in his thracks an' rayfused to go another step till Darby coaxed him on be sayin':

"Oh, thin, we won't cross it if you're afeared, little man," says he, "but we'll take the path through the fields on this side of it, and we'll cross the sthrame by McCarthy's own wooden foot-bridge. 'Tis within tunty feet of the house. Oh, ye needn't be afeared," he says agin; "I've seen the cows cross it, so it'll surely hould the both of us."

A sudden raymembrance whipped into his mind of how tall the stile was, ladin' into Nolan's meadow, an' the boy was puzzling deep in his mind to know how was Solomon to climb acrost that stile, whin all at once the gloomy western gate of the graveyard rose quick be their side.

The two shied to the opposite hedge, an' no wondher they did.

Fufty ghosts, all in their shrouds, sat cheek be jowl along the church-yard wall, never caring a ha'porth for the wind or the rain.

There was little Ted Rogers, the humpback, who was dhrownded in Mullin's well four years come Michaelmas; there was black Mulligan, the gamekeeper, who shot Ryan, the poacher, sittin' with a gun on his lap, an' he glowerin'; beside the gamekeeper sat the poacher, with a jagged black hole in his forehead; there was Thady Finnegan, the scholar, who was dis-appointed in love an' died of a daycline; furder on sat Mrs. Houlihan, who dayparted this life from ating of pizen musherooms; next to *her* sat—oh, a hundhred others!

Not that Darby *saw* thim, do ye mind. He had too good sinse to look that way at all. He walked with his head turned out to the open fields, an' his eyes squeeged shut. But something in his mind toult him they were there, an' he felt in the marrow of his bones that if he gave them the encouragement of one glance two or three'd slip off the wall an' come moanin' over to tell him their throubles.

What Solomon saw an' what Solomon heard, as the two wint shrinkin' along'll never be known to living man, but once he gave a jump, an' twice Darby felt him thrimblin', an' whin they raiched at last the chapel wall the baste broke into a swift throt. Purty soon he galloped, an' Darby wint gallopin' with him, till two yallow blurs of light across in a field to the left marked the windys of the stone-cutter's cottage.

'Twas a few steps only, thin, to the stile over into Nolan's meadow, an' there the two stopped, lookin' helpless at aich other. Solomon had to be lifted, and there was the throuble. Three times Darby thried be main strength to hist his compagnen up the steps, but in vain, an' Solomon was clane dishgusted.

Only for the tendher corn on our hayro's left little toe, I think maybe that at length an' at last the pair would have got safe over. The kind-hearted lad had the donkey's two little hoofs planted on the top step, an' whilst he himself was liftin' the rest of the baste in his arrums, Solomon got onaisy that he was goin' to be trun, an' so began to twisht an' squirm; of course, as he did, Darby slipped an' wint thump on his back agin the stile, with Solomon sittin' comfortable on top of the lad's chist. But that wasn't the worst of it, for as the baste scrambled up he planted one hard little hoof on Darby's left foot, an' the knowledgeable man let a yowl out of him that must have frightened all the ghosts within miles.

Seein' he'd done wrong, Solomon boulted for the middle of the road an' stood there wiry an' attentive, listening to the names flung at him from where his late comerade sat on the lowest step of the stile nursin' the hurted foot.

'Twas an excited owl in the belfry that this time spoke up an' shouted to his brother down in the black-thorn:

"Come up, come up quick!" it says. "Darby O'Gill is just afther calling Solomon Kilcannon a malayfactor."

Darby rose at last, an' as he climbed over the stile he turned to shake his fist toward the middle of the road.

"Bad luck to ye for a thick-headed, on-grateful informer!" he says; "you go your way an' I'll go mine—we're sundhers," says he. So sayin', the crippled man wint limpin' an' grumplin' down the boreen, through the meadow, whilst his desarted friend sint rayproachful brays afther him that would go to your heart.

The throbbin' of our hayro's toe banished all pity for the baste, an' even all thoughts of the banshee, till a long, gurgling, swooping sound in front toult him that his fears about the rise in McDonald's sthrame were undher rather than over the actwil conditions.

Fearin' that the wooden foot-bridge might be swept away, as it had been the year purvious, he hurried on.

Most times this sthrame was only a quiet little brook that ran betwixt purty green banks, with hardly enough wather in it to turn the broken wheel in Chartres' runed mill; but tonight it swept along an angry, snarlin', growlin' river that overlept its banks an' dhragged wildly at the swaying willows.

Be a narrow throw of light from McCarthy's side windy our thraveller could see the maddened wather sthrivin' an' tearing to pull with it the props of the little foot-bridge; an' the boards shook an' the centre swayed undher his feet as he passed over. "Bedad, I'll not cross this way goin' home, at any rate," he says, looking back at it.

The worruds were no sooner out of his mouth than there was a crack, an' the middle of the foot-bridge lifted in the air, twishted round for a second, an then hurled itself into the sthrame, laving the two inds still standing in their place on the banks.

"Tunder an turf!" he cried, "I mustn't forget to tell the people within of this, for if ever there was a thrap set by evil spirits to drownd a poor, unwary mortial, there it stands. Oh, ain't the ghosts tumble wicious on Halloween!"

He stood dhrippin' a minute on the threshold, listening; thin, without knockin', lifted the latch an' stepped softly into the house.

II

Two candles burned above the blue and white chiney dishes on the table, a bright fire blazed on the hearth, an' over in the corner where the low bed was set the stone-cutter was on his knees beside it.

Eileen lay on her side, her shining hair sthrealed out on the pillow. Her purty, flushed face was turned to Cormac, who knelt with his forehead hid on the bed-covers. The colleen's two little hands were clasped about the great fist of her husband, an' she was talking low, but so airnest that her whole life was in every worrud.

"God save all here!" said Darby, takin' off his hat, but there was no answer. So deep were Cormac an' Eileen in some conwersation they were having together that they didn't hear his coming. The knowledgeable man didn't know what to do. He raylised that a husband and wife about to part for ever were lookin' into aich other's hearts, for maybe the last time. So he just sthood shifting from one foot to the other, watching thim, unable to daypart, an' not wishin' to obtrude.

"Oh, it isn't death at all that I fear," Eileen was saying. "No, no, Cormac asthore, 'tis not that I'm misdoubtful of; but, ochone mavrone, 'tis you I fear!"

The kneelin' man gave one swift upward glance, and dhrew his face nearer to the sick wife. She wint on, thin, spakin' tindher an' half smiling an' sthrokin' his hand:

"I know, darlint, I know well, so you needn't tell me, that if I were to live with you a thousand years you'd never sthray in mind or thought to any other woman, but it's when I'm gone—when the lonesome avenings folly aich other through days an' months, an' maybe years, an' you sitting here at this fireside without one to speak to, an' you so handsome an' gran', an' with the penny or two we've put away—"

"Oh, asthore machree, why can't ye banish thim black thoughts!" says the stone-cutter. "Maybe," he says, "the banshee will not come again. Ain't all the counthry-side prayin' for ye this night, an' didn't Father Cassidy himself bid you to hope? The saints in Heaven couldn't be so crool!" says he.

But the colleen wint on as though she hadn't heard him, or as if he hadn't intherrupted her:

"An' listen," says she; "they'll come urging ye, the neighbours, an' raysonin' with you. You're own flesh an' blood'll come, an', no doubt, me own with them, an' they all sthriving to push me out of your heart, an' to put another woman there in my place. I'll know it all, but I won't be able to call to you, Cormac machree, for I'll be lying silent undher the grass, or undher the snow up behind the church."

While she was sayin' thim last worruds, although Darby's heart was meltin' for Eileen, his mind began running over the colleens of that town-land to pick out the one who'd be most likely to marry Cormac in the ind. You know how far-seeing an' quick-minded was the knowledgeable man. He settled sudden on the Hanlon girl, an' daycided at once that she'd have Cormac before the year was out. The ondaycency of such a thing made him furious at her.

He says to himself, half crying, "Why, then, bad cess to you for a shameless, red-haired, forward baggage, Bridget Hanlon, to be runnin' afther the man, an' throwing yourself in his way, an' Eileen not yet cowld in her grave!" he says.

While he was saying them things to himself, McCarthy had been whuspering fierce to his wife, but what it was the stone-cutter said the friend of the fairies couldn't hear. Eileen herself spoke clean enough in answer, for the faver gave her onnatural strength.

"Don't think," she says, "that it's the first time this thought has come to me. Two months ago, whin I was sthrong an' well an' sittin' happy as a meadow-lark at your side, the same black shadow dhrifted over me heart. The worst of it an' the hardest to bear of all is that they'll be in the right, for what good can I do for you when I'm undher the clay," says she.

"It's different with a woman. If you were taken an' I left I'd wear your face in my heart through all me life, an' ax for no sweeter company."

"Eileen," says Cormac, liftin' his hand, an' his woice was hoarse as the roar of the say, "I swear to you on me bendid knees—"

With her hand on his lips, she sthopped him. "There'll come on ye by daygrees a great cravin' for sympathy, a hunger an' a longing for affection, an' you'll have only the shadow of my poor, wanished face to comfort you, an' a recollection of a woice that is gone for ever. A new, warm face'll keep pushin' itself betwixt us—"

"Bad luck to that red-headed hussy!" mutthered Darby, looking around disthressed. "I'll warn father Cassidy of her an' of her intintions the day afther the funeral."

There was silence for a minute; Cormac, the poor lad, was sobbing like a child. By-and-by Eileen wint on again, but her woice was failing an' Darby could see that her cheeks were wet.

"The day'll come when you'll give over," she says. "Ah, I see how it'll all ind. Afther that you'll visit the churchyard be stealth, so as not to make the other woman sore-hearted."

"My, oh, my, isn't she the far-seein' woman?" thought Darby.

"Little childher'll come," she says, "an' their soft, warm arrums will hould you away. By-and-by you'll not go where I'm laid at all, an' all thoughts of these few happy months we've spent together—Oh! Mother in Heaven, how happy they were—"

The girl started to her elbow, for, sharp an' sudden, a wild, wailing cry just outside the windy startled the shuddering darkness. 'Twas a long cry of terror and of grief, not shrill, but piercing as a knife-thrust. Every hair on Darby's head stood up an' pricked him like a needle. 'Twas the banshee!

"Whist, listen!" says Eileen. "Oh, Cormac asthore, it's come for me again!" With that, stiff with terror, she buried herself undher the pillows.

A second cry follyed the first, only this time it was longer, and rose an' swelled into a kind of a song that broke at last into the heart-breakingest moan that ever fell on mortial ears. "Ochone!" it sobbed.

The knowledgeable man, his blood turned to ice, his legs thremblin' like a hare's, stood looking in spite of himself at the black windy-panes, expecting some frightful wision.

Afther that second cry the woice balanced itself up an' down into the awful death keen. One word made the whole song, and that was the turruble worrud, "Forever!"

"Forever an' forever, oh, forever!" swung the wild keen, until all the deep meaning of the worrud burned itself into Darby's sowl, thin the heart-breakin' sob, "Ochone!" inded always the varse.

Darby was just wondherin' whether he himself wouldn't go mad with fright, whin he gave a sudden jump at a hard, sthrained woice which spoke up at his very elbow.

"Darby O'Gill," it said, and it was the stone-cutter who spoke, "do you hear the death keen? It came last night; it'll come tomorrow night at this same hour, and thin—oh, my God!"

Darby tried to answer, but he could only stare at the white, set face an' the sunken eyes of the man before him.

There was, too, a kind of fierce quiet in the way McCarthy spoke that made Darby shiver.

The stone-cutter wint on talkin' the same as though he was goin' to dhrive a bargain. "They say you're a knowledgeable man, Darby O'Gill," he says, "an' that on a time you spint six months with the fairies. Now I make you this fair, square offer," he says, laying a forefinger in the palm of the other hand. "I have fifty-three pounds that Father Cassidy's keeping for me. Fifty-three pounds," he says agin. "An' I have this good bit of a farm that me father was born on, an' his father was born on, too, and the grandfather of him. An' I have the grass of seven cows. You know that. Well, I'll give it all to you, all, every stiver of it, if you'll only go outside an' dhrive away that cursed singer." He trew his head to one side an' looked anxious up at Darby.

The knowledgeable man racked his brains for something to speak, but all he could say was, "I've brought you a bit of tay from the wife, Cormac."

McCarthy took the tay with unfeeling hands, an' wint on talking in the same dull way. Only this time there came a hard lump in his throat now and then that he stopped to swally.

"The three cows I have go, of course, with the farm," says he. "So does the pony an' the five pigs. I have a good plough an' a foine harrow; but you must lave my stone-cutting tools, so little Eileen an' I can earn our way wherever we go, an' it's little the crachure ates the best of times."

The man's eyes were dhry an' blazin'; no doubt his mind was cracked with grief. There was a lump in Darby's throat, too, but for all that he spoke up scolding-like.

"Arrah, talk rayson, man," he says, putting two hands on Cormac's chowlders; "if I had the wit or the art to banish the banshee, wouldn't I be happy to do it an' not a fardin' to pay?"

"Well, then," says Cormac, scowling, an' pushin' Darby to one side, "I'll face her myself—I'll face her an' choke that song in her throat if Sattin himself stood at her side."

With those words, an' before Darby could sthop him, the stone-cutter flung open the door an' plunged out into the night. As he did so the song outside sthopped. Suddenly a quick splashing of feet, hoarse cries, and shouts gave tidings of a chase. The half-crazed gossoon had stharted the banshee—of that there could be no manner of doubt. A raymembrance of the awful things that she might do to his friend paythrefied the heart of Darby.

Even afther these cries died away he stood listenling a full minute, the sowls of his two brogues glued to the floor. The only sounds he heard now were the deep ticking of a clock and a cricket that chirped slow an' solemn on the hearth, an' from somewhere outside came the sorrowful cry of a whipperwill. All at once a thought of the broken bridge an' of the black, treacherous waters caught him like the blow of a whip, an' for a second drove from his mind even the fear of the banshee.

In that one second, an' before he rayalised it, the lad was out undher the dhripping trees, and running for his life toward the broken foot-bridge. The night was whirling an' beating above him like the flapping of thraymendous wings, but as he ran Darby thought he heard above the rush of the water and through, the swish of the wind Cormac's woice calling him.

The friend of the fairies stopped at the edge of the foot-bridge to listen. Although the storm had almost passed, a spiteful flare of lightning lept up now an' agin out of the western hills, an' afther it came the dull rumble of distant thunder; the water splashed spiteful against the bank, and Darby saw that seven good feet of the bridge had been torn out of its centre, laving uncovered that much of the black, deep flood.

He stood sthraining his eyes an' ears in wondheration, for now the woice of Cormac sounded from the other side of the sthrame, and seemed to be floating toward him through the field over the path Darby himself had just thravelled. At first he was mightily bewildhered at what might bring Cormac on the other side of the brook, till all at once the murdhering scheme of the banshee burst in his mind like a gunpowdher explosion.

Her plan was as plain as day—she meant to dhrown the stone-cutter. She had led the poor, daysthracted man straight from his own door down to and over the new stone bridge, an' was now dayludherin' him on the other side of the sthrame, back agin up the path that led to the broken foot-bridge.

In the glare of a sudden blinding flash from the middle of the sky Darby saw a sight he'll never forget till the day he dies. Cormac, the stone-cutter, was running toward the death-trap, his bare head trun back, an' his two arrums stretched out in front of him. A little above an' just out of raich of them, plain an' clear as Darby ever saw his wife Bridget, was the misty white figure of a woman. Her long, waving hair sthrealed back from her face, an' her face was the face of the dead.

At the sight of her Darby thried to call out a warning, but the words fell back into his throat. Thin again came the stifling darkness. He thried to run away, but his knees failed him, so he turned around to face the danger.

As he did so he could hear the splash of the man's feet in the soft mud. In less than a minute Cormac would be sthruggling in the wather. At the thought Darby, bracing himself body and sowl, let a warning howl out of him.

"Hould where you are!" he shouted; "she wants to drownd ye—the bridge is broke in the middle!" but he could tell, from the rushing footsteps an' from the hoarse swelling curses which came nearer an' nearer every second, that the dayludhered man, crazed with grief, was deaf an' blind to everything but the figure that floated before his eyes.

At that hopeless instant Bridget's parting words popped into Darby's head.

"When one goes on an errant of marcy a score of God's white angels, with swoords in their hands, march before an' beside an' afther him, keeping his path free from danger."

How it all come to pass he could never rightly tell, for he was like a man in a dhrame, but he recollects well standing on the broken ind of the bridge, Bridget's words ringing in his ears, the glistening black gulf benathe his feet, an' he swinging his arrums for a jump. Just one thought of herself and the childher, as he gathered himself for a spring, an' then he cleared the gap like a bird.

As his two feet touched the other side of the gap a turrific screech— not a screech, ayther, but an angry, frightened shriek—almost split his ears. He felt a rush of cowld, dead air agin his face, and caught a whiff of newly turned clay in his nosthrils; something white stopped quick before him, an' then, with a second shriek, it shot high in the darkness an' disappeared. Darby had frightened the wits out of the banshee.

The instant afther the two men were clinched an' rowling over an' over aich other down the muddy bank, their legs splashing as far as the knees in the dangerous wather, an' McCarthy raining wake blows on the knowledgeable man's head an' breast.

Darby felt himself goin' into the river. Bits of the bank caved undher him, splashing into the current, an' the lad's heart began clunking up an' down like a churn-dash.

"Lave off, lave off!" he cried, as soon as he could ketch his breath. "Do you take me for the banshee?" says he, giving a dusperate lurch an' rowling himself on top of the other.

"Who are you, then? If you're not a ghost you're the divil, at any rate," gasped the stone-cutter.

"Bad luck to ye!" cried Darby, clasping both arrums of the haunted man. "I'm no ghost, let lone the divil—I'm only your friend, Darby O'Gill."

Lying there, breathing hard, they stared into the faces of aich other a little space till the poor stone-cutter began to cry.

"Oh, is that you, Darby O'Gill? Where is the banshee? Oh, haven't I the bad fortune," he says, sthriving to raise himself.

"Rise up," says Darby, lifting the man to his feet an' steadying him there. The stone-cutter stared about like one stunned be a blow.

"I don't know where the banshee flew, but do you go back to Eileen as soon as you can," says the friend of the fairies. "Not that way, man alive," he says, as Cormac started to climb the foot-bridge, "it's broke in the middle; go down an' cross the stone bridge. I'll be afther you in a minute," he says.

Without a word, meek now and biddable as a child, Cormac turned, an' Darby saw him hurry away into the blackness.

The raysons Darby raymained behind were two: first an' foremost, he was a bit vexed at the way his clothes were muddied an' dhraggled, an' himself had been pounded an' hammered; an' second, he wanted to think. He had a quare cowld feeling in his mind that something was wrong—a kind of a foreboding, as one might say.

As he stood thinking a rayalisation of the caylamity sthruck him all at once like a rap on the jaw—he had lost his fine brier pipe. The lad groaned as he began the anxious sarch. He slapped furiously at his chist an' side pockets, he dived into his throwsers and greatcoat, and at last, sprawlin' on his hands an' feet like a monkey, he groped savagely through the wet, sticky clay.

"This comes," says the poor lad, grumblin' an' gropin', "of pokin' your nose into other people's business. Hallo, what's this?" says he, straightening himself. "'Tis a comb. Be the powers of pewther, 'tis the banshee's comb."

An' so indade it was. He had picked up a goold comb the length of your hand an' almost the width of your two fingers. About an inch of one ind was broken off, an' dhropped into Darby's palm. Without thinkin', he put the broken bit into his weskit pocket, an' raised the biggest half close to his eyes, the betther to view it.

"May I never see sorrow," he says, "if the banshee mustn't have dhropped her comb. Look at that, now. Folks do be sayin' that 'tis this gives her the foine singing voice, bekase the comb is enchanted," he says. "If that sayin' be thrue, it's the faymous lad I am from this night. I'll thravel from fair to fair, an' maybe at the ind they'll send me to parliament."

With these worruds he lifted his caubeen an' stuck the comb in the top tuft of his hair.

Begor, he'd no sooner guv it a pull than a sour, singing feelin' begun at the bottom of his stomick, an' it rose higher an' higher. When it raiched his chist he was just going to let a bawl out of himself only that he caught sight of a thing ferninst him that froze the marrow in his bones.

He gasped short an' jerked the comb out of his hair, for there, not tin feet away, stood a dark, shadowy woman, tall, thin, an' motionless, laning on a crutch.

During a breath or two the parsecuted hayro lost his head completely, for he never doubted that the banshee had changed her shuit of clothes to chase back afther him.

The first clear aymotion that rayturned to him was to fling the comb on the ground an' make a boult of it. On second thought he knew that 'twould be aisier to bate the wind in a race than to run away from the banshee.

139

"Well, there's a good Tipperary man done for this time," groaned the knowledgeable man, "unless in some way I can beguile her." He was fishing in his mind for its civilist worrud when the woman spoke up, an' Darby's heart jumped with gladness as he raycognised the cracked voice of Sheelah Maguire, the spy for the fairies.

"The top of the avenin' to you, Darby O'Gill," says Sheelah, peering at him from undher her hood, the two eyes of her glowing like tallow candles; "amn't I kilt with a-stonishment to see you here alone this time of the night," says the ould witch.

Now, the clever man knew as well as though he had been tould, when Sheelah said thim worruds, that the banshee had sent her to look for the comb, an' his heart grew bould; but he answered her polite enough, "Why, thin, luck to ye, Misthress Maguire, ma'am," he says, bowing grand, "sure, if you're kilt with a-stonishment, amn't I sphlit with inkerdoolity to find yourself mayandherin' in this lonesome place on Halloween night."

Sheelah hobbled a step or two nearer, an' whuspered confaydential.

"I was wandherin' hereabouts only this morning," she says, "an' I lost from me hair a goold comb—one that I've had this forty years. Did ye see such a thing as that, agra?" An' her two eyes blazed.

"Faix, I dunno," says Darby, putting his two arrums behind him. "Was it about the length of ye're hand an' the width of ye're two fingers?" he axed.

"It was," says she, thrusting out a withered paw.

"Thin I didn't find it," says the tantalizing man. "But maybe I did find something summillar, only 'twasn't yours at all, but the banshee's," he says, chuckling.

Whether the hag was intentioned to welt Darby with her staff, or whether she was only liftin' it for to make a sign of enchantment in the air, will never be known, but whatsomever she meant the hayro doubled his fists an' squared off; at that she lowered the stick, an' broke into a shrill, cackling laugh.

"Ho, ho!" she laughed, houldin' her sides, "but aren't ye the bould, distinguishable man. Becourse 'tis the banshee's comb; how well ye knew it! Be the same token I'm sint to bring it away; so make haste to give it up, for she's hiding an' waiting for me down at Chartres' mill. Aren't you the courageous blaggard, to grabble at her, an' thry to ketch her. Sure, such a thing never happened before, since the worruld began," says Sheelah.

The idee that the banshee was hiding an' afeared to face him was great news to the hayro. But he only tossed his head an' smiled shuparior as he made answer.

"'Tis yourself that knows well, Sheelah Maguire, ma'am," answers back the proud man, slow an' dayliberate, "that whin one does a favour for an unearthly spirit he may daymand for pay the favours of three such wishes as the spirit has power to give. The worruld knows that. Now I'll take three good wishes, such as the banshee can bestow, or else I'll carry the goolden comb straight to Father Cassidy. The banshee hasn't goold nor wor'ly goods, as the sayin' is, but she has what suits me betther."

This cleverness angered the fairy-woman so she set in to abuse and to frighten Darby. She ballyragged, she browbate, she trajooced, she threatened, but 'twas no use. The bould man hildt firm, till at last she promised him the favours of the three wishes.

"First an' foremost," says he, "I'll want her never to put her spell on me or any of my kith an' kin."

"That wish she gives you, that wish she grants you, though it'll go sore agin the grain," snarled Sheelah.

"Then," says Darby, "my second wish is that the black spell be taken from Eileen McCarthy."

Sheelah flusthered about like an angry hin. "Wouldn't something else do as well?" she says.

"I'm not here to argify," says Darby, swingin' back an' forrud on his toes.

"Bad scran to you," says Sheelah. "I'll have to go an' ask the banshee herself about that. Don't stir from that spot till I come back."

You may believe it or not, but with that sayin' she bent the head of her crutch well forward, an' before Darby's very face she trew—savin' your presence—one leg over the stick as though it had been a horse, an' while one might say Jack Robinson the crutch riz into the air an' lifted her, an' she went sailing out of sight.

Darby was still gaping an' gawpin' at the darkness where she disappeared whin—whisk! she was back agin an' dismountin' at his side.

"The luck is with you," says she, spiteful. "That wish I give, that wish I grant you. You'll find seven crossed rushes undher McCarthy's doorstep; uncross them, put them in fire or in wather, an' the spell is lifted. Be quick with the third wish—out with it!"

"I'm in a more particular hurry about that than you are," says Darby. "You must find me my brier pipe," says he.

"You omadhaun," sneered the fairy-woman, "'tis sthuck in the band of your hat, where you put it when you left your own house the night. No, no, not in front," she says, as Darby put up his hand to feel. "It's stuck in the back. Your caubeen's twishted," she says.

Whilst Darby was standing with the comb in one hand an' the pipe in the other, smiling daylighted, the comb was snatched from his fingers and he got a welt in the side of the head from the crutch. Looking up, he saw Sheelah tunty feet in the air, headed for Chartres' mill, an' she cacklin' an' screechin' with laughter. Rubbing his sore head an' mutthering unpious words to himself, Darby started for the new bridge.

In less than no time afther, he had found the seven crossed rushes undher McCarthy's doorstep, an' had flung them into the stream. Thin, without knocking, he pushed open McCarthy's door an' tiptoed quietly in.

Cormac was kneelin' beside the bed with his face buried in the pillows, as he was when Darby first saw him that night. But Eileen was sleeping as sound as a child, with a sweet smile on her lips. Heavy purspuration beaded her forehead, showing that the faver was broke.

Without disturbing aither of them our hayro picked up the package of tay from the floor, put it on the dhresser, an' with a glad heart sthole out of the house an' closed the door softly behind him.

Turning toward Chartres' mill he lifted his hat an' bowed low. "Thank you kindly, Misthress Banshee," he says. "'Tis well for us all I found your comb this night. Public or private, I'll always say this for you—you're a woman of your worrud," he says.

THE GRAVEYARD

Alphonse Courlander

Published in The Sketch, *6 March 1907*

Alphonse Courlander (1881–1914) was a well-known journalist and novelist whose most popular book was *Mightier than the Sword* (1913), an intriguing insight into the machinations of Fleet Street. For eight years he was one of the lead reporters for the *Daily Chronicle* before becoming the Paris correspondent for the *Daily Mail*, the Montenegro correspondent for *The Express* and then one of the reporters who tracked down the serial fraudster Violet Chatsworth after she faked her death in 1909. In 1911 *The Daily Mirror* reported that Courlander was an "undesirable alien" when *The Daily Express* sued the newspaper he was working for, the *Penny Illustrated Paper*, due to an article they printed entitled "Is *The Daily Express* a German Spy?"

Courlander's suicide at thirty-three was recorded by the newspapers as "succumbed to an illness which came as a culmination of strain during the early days of the war." "The Graveyard" is a delightful story and gives clear warning: if you are going to go round there at the dead of night, please take a friend. You don't know what's amongst the leaning headstones...

THERE were three girls and two men sitting round the fire in the library. The married men of the house-party were in the morning-room playing bridge, and the married women were gathered in the drawing-room, reading or engaged in the matronly occupation of sewing. Someone was playing on the piano Grieg's *Peer Gynt*, and the echoes of it came to the library, where the three girls and the two men were sitting with the lights turned down, because Christina had said that it was such fun to see the firelight making distorted shadows of the chairs and tables on the wall. One of the men, Harlesden, stretched his arms above his head (they became giant arms of Shadowland, reaching to the ceiling) and yawned.

"Afraid we're borin' you, Dickie," said Christina. They were cousins, and, taking advantage of the relationship, she censored his manners at every opportunity. "Don't you know, Dickie, it's very rude to yawn in the company of ladies?" She shook her finger in admonition—the firelight transferred it to the wall and magnified it into a Cleopatra's needle.

"Oh, don't tease him, Tina," said Beatrix. "Let him yawn. It's simply heavenly sitting like this in front of the fire and saying nothing, and listening to the creepy-crawly music. Doesn't 'Peer Gynt' suggest graveyards and family vaults to you?"

"B-rr-rr!" said the other man. "I wish to goodness she'd change the tune and give us something lively from *The Belle of New York*."

The conversation drifted on, until the subject of Harlesden's yawning was forgotten, and then came silence again, while everyone in the room looked dreamily at the logs putting out their gleaming red and blue tongues and crackling in laughter, as though they were inhabited by mischievous sprites. Suddenly Peggy, the third girl, spoke from out of the shadows of the big armchair in which she had almost buried herself.

"Do you believe it was true?" she said absently.

"What was true?" they asked in return.

"Why, that about churchyards—you remember Tina said it. That if you crossed the graveyard at night and picked flowers from a grave a hand would spring out of the grave over which you walked and seize you. Do you believe it was true?"

"I know that in most West Country villages," said Christina. "there's a superstition to that effect. You wouldn't get any villager to walk through the churchyard and pluck flowers from a grave after sunset."

"I think I have heard of the same superstition in Germany," said the man next to Harlesden. "There the peasants believe that ghouls sit on the tombstones when dark sets in."

"I wouldn't go through a churchyard in darkness," said Beatrix positively. "Ghouls or no ghouls, I shouldn't like the idea."

"No more would I," said Christina.

Peggy raised her face so that it was lit up by the fire-glow. It was a dark, oval face—the nose short and pugnacious, the lips masculine in firmness and feminine in their red colour and outline, the chin smooth and strong.

"Would you go, Dickie?" she asked.

"Would if I had to," he replied promptly. "Otherwise—er—I wouldn't."

"Would you?" she asked, turning to the other man.

He laughed, and moved uneasily. "I've been a sailor, you know," he said, "and when you've been under the stars and moon at sea you get all sorts of silly superstitions into your head. Frankly, I wouldn't go."

There was an awkward silence for a moment, as Peggy gave a short laugh, which the others thought was unkindly done. Christina, with her gentleness, came to the rescue.

"Didn't you save three men from drowning once, Mr. Vallance?" she asked quietly. "You got the Royal Humane Society's medal, didn't you, for it."

"Oh, that happened a long time ago," he answered.

"I see," replied Christina.

Peggy began again. "I'm not afraid of graves or ghosts," she announced. "I'll just show you, you people are all cowards."

"What are you going to do, Peggy?" asked Beatrix nervously.

Peggy rose to her feet, and laughed. "I'm going to bring you back a flower from the churchyard—I'll bring you back a bouquet of flowers Peggy, don't be foolish," said Christina.

"Tell her to be quiet, Tina," said Beatrix.

"Oh, nonsense!" laughed Peggy, and looking at Mr. Vallance with eyes that had challenge in them. "Come, choose your graves. Would you like the rose from Peter the Miser's last resting-place? His granddaughter placed some new ones there yesterday."

"I shouldn't go if I were you," said Vallance quietly and gently.

"You said that once before," retorted Peggy. Why was she cruel to him, thought Vallance, when she must have remembered that evening when they had talked of each other's lives?

"Oh," said Peggy, "think of me in half-an-hour's time, stalking through the churchyard," she walked mincingly across the room, "like this—and bending over the graves, and plucking roses and periwinkles and geraniums. Well, you'll see me back in less than an hour." She waved her hand airily and left the room.

"Peggy is too bad. I'll go and stop her," said Beatrix.

"She'll catch her death of cold. Will you fetch her back, Mr. Vallance?" said Christina.

"No," said Vallance savagely, and then—"I beg your pardon, no."

"Peggy's all right," said Dick, with a yawn. "Jolly plucky girl. I'd be too lazy to do the job, and I don't like graveyards."

On the piano in the drawing-room someone crashed out a mad tune from *The Belle of New York*.

*

Peggy had run half-way down the lonely village road, in the rain swept darkness, before she realized what a mad, unnecessary thing she was doing. She could feel her cheeks burning and tingling, refusing to be cooled even by the cold rain that beat upon her face, tingling because—well, Peggy would not have admitted this to herself: that she was angry with Vallance because he had shown himself to be such a coward.

The road was empty, and the silence was broken only by the sigh of the trees, as the branches bowed to the wind and the rain. She ran on, urged by the spirit of adventure and daring which she inherited from her forefathers. Even as a schoolgirl Peggy had scaled perilous walls in search of forbidden fruit on the other side, and had climbed trees, swinging from branch to branch as recklessly as any boy. And now, just over twenty, the same love of daring inspired her, though, thought she, there was nothing very daring in what she was about to do now, for the churchyard held no terrors for those who were not superstitious.

She came to the old lych-gate of the ancient churchyard and paused. Through the gate she could see, as in a frame, the picture of the square-towered church, rising gloomily out of the darkness, and looking grey and awesome in the chill light of the moon, which gleamed mistily through the gauzy rain-clouds. All around it, wrapped in sempiternal silence, were the graves of those who were dead, in crooked rows, as if the tombstones had grown out of the ground in the fashion it pleased them best. Some of them reflected the white glamour of the moon—they were the newly erected tombstones; others were dark and full of desolate shadows. The latch on the lych-gate answered her touch with a noisy click, and the next moment she was at the skirts of the graveyard. She smiled to herself, and told herself there was nothing to fear. Nobody could do her harm, for death was death, and the only people who were in the graveyard were locked fast under the earth by the heavy stones above them. The wind sped with a whimper along the alleys made by the tombstones, as if it were the voice of the souls of those who could not enter heaven, and were forced to ride the earth on the shoulders of the storming wind. She tried not to listen to it, but it screamed in her ears, and then rushed away to a lonely part of the graveyard, and yammered among the shivering poplars like an outcast beaten dog. Peggy walked along the slushy gravel, her feet crunching the ground. The noise she made in walking was the only sound in the graveyard that belonged to herself, and it comforted her. She stopped to read an inscription on a moonlit tombstone bordering the walk:

"HERE LIETH YE BODY OF THOMAS FRAZER, BORN FEBRUARY
9TH, 1789; DIED JUNE 11TH, 1856; AGED 67 YEARS.
AND HIS WIFE, ANGELA MARIA FRAZER, BORN MAY 21ST,
1786, DIED NOVEMBER 1ST, 1870.
AND IN DEATH THEY WERE NOT DIVIDED."

The winds and the rains of Time had eaten into the stone, and the letters were almost undecipherable, yet she spent some time figuring out the inscription. As for the motto, there was only:

"AND N   EA H   IVID D."

But it was easy to guess the thought that the graver had in his mind—a thought that he had carved, possibly, in his century, hundreds of times, just as his descendants are carving today, and may carve tomorrow, for us.

Peggy moved on. She was about to step on the grass, when something wet and clammy struck her face and whirred away again with a flapping of black wings and a croaking, raucous cry. It was only some night-bird, probably more startled than Peggy at the encounter; but for the first time her heart pumped quickly and drew the blood from her face, and left her tingling and trembling. Then she realized that she was being stupid and allowing her nerves the mastery. She reassured herself, saying it was a night-bird whose wings were wetted with the rain. However, she stepped back from the grass and followed the path until she came to the willows that bowed their dishevelled heads and wept over the mounds of earth that were in their shadows. In this part of the churchyard, were the sad graves of children—poor babes of the parish, sad graves, nameless in many cases, since the little people had no name of the earth and only flitted for a brief moment down from heaven and then flew back again; little mounds, over which the grass grew tidily, but over which no flowers were placed.

So Peggy moved on, and, gaining courage, strode across the grass, taking care to avoid stepping on the children's graves, and reached a splendid grave, from which the scent of flowers rose in the air. She smiled to herself, bent down, and picked a flower—a geranium, and then another. Her nerves were all right now, she told herself, and in half an hour she would be back again in the warm library, telling them all of the adventure. She sought for Peter the Miser's grave. She had promised to bring a flower back from Peter's grave. It meant passing through avenues of cold, grey stones, until she grew weary of the monotonous repetitions of texts and the stock mottoes of the stonemasons. She found Peter's grave at last. A low railing enclosed it, and kept people at a respectful distance from the flat slab that was sunk in the earth, telling them of Peter's virtues, chiefly and especially (according to his dying wish, for he was a pagan, and gold was his idol) that he died worth "one thousand pounds sterling". There were flowers at the foot of the railings, placed there by his granddaughter, and Peggy bent down and gathered a handful. She laughed to herself and turned to go. Her task was done.

And then—the hot blood within her seemed to turn to ice, and her heart, she thought, stopped beating for one swift moment, only to race away again until it thudded within her breast and set her temples throbbing like the beat of a thousand clocks. *For something clutched her skirt and jerked her back.* She looked about her doggedly, with eyes that saw only white tombstones. They seemed to change suddenly into pallid faces, the carving on them marking the eyes and nose and mouth—faces with a fixed, horrible grin upon them, mocking at her in her terror.

She tried to move away from the grave of Peter the Miser, and it seemed to her that she was being gently, persuasively pulled back again. She opened her lips wide. Her soul screamed within her, but no sound came from her lips—they were parched with fear. She saw gross, black spiders, bloated and loathsome, crawling lazily up and down a tombstone near at hand, and a bird with a wet wing went screeching and flapping by her head.

She tried once more to move, and in her imagination she could picture the clutch of fleshless fingers upon her skirt, and the skinny arm of Peter cleaving the earth, to hold her and to fulfil the superstition. The wind leapt about her and the rain swept about her face. All the fear and horror within her surged to her lips in a long, thrilling shriek, and she fell face forwards to the wet earth.

When they came with lanterns, an hour later, they found her crooning to herself, and rocking herself to and fro. The flowers she had gathered from the graves were clutched in her hand. Her skirt was found to be caught in the handle of a spade which the sexton had left by Peter's grave. She smiled wanly at them, and babbled to herself when they asked her questions. It was Vallance who lifted her in his arms as tenderly as a mother lifts her babe, and carried her back to the warmth, kissing her hands and making them wet with his tears.

ALL SOULS' NIGHT

Eleanor Fitzgerald

Published in New Ross Standard, *29 October 1909*

Eleanor Fitzgerald posed a slight problem. There was a Mary Eleanor Fitzgerald (1877–1955), an American editor, theatre professional and literary agent who edited the early anarchist magazines *Mother Earth* and *The Blast*. However, looking through her papers which are held at the University of Wisconsin-Milwaukee Library, there is no mention of short story manuscript holograms or anything pertaining to fiction writing, as in bills of sale, contributor copies, etc. As Mary Eleanor Fitzgerald's archival footprint is so large, I feared it may have inadvertently drowned out the author of "All Souls' Night".

Having said that, I believe that the author of this tale was from Loughguile in Northern Ireland. A short, "St. Brigid's Well: An Old True Story of the Castle of Cragane" appeared in the *Irish Weekly* in 1909, the same year as the following story was published. I believe that she was living in London by the early 1920s and was a member of the Irish Literary Society. She acted in Mr. Shan Bullock's *The Turf Cutters* and also wrote several plays, one called *The Sun Goes Down* (which she also acted in—a reviewer noted that: "some of the spoken words were a trifle 'flowery'") and another called *The Candle* that was performed in the Century Theatre, West London, in 1937. The play is based on the true story of Teresa Geoghegan who lost her "Christmas Candle" while waiting for a train for three hours at a small West of Ireland railway junction and accuses her sons of selling the candle "for drink." "All Souls' Night" is a neat little horror story. Martin is dead and buried six feet under, but why has he come back telling his wife he can't get to heaven until a debt is paid?

N o, your honour; I was a widow woman five long years afore I
knew the truth of it.

It was this ways. When my husband died—God rest his
soul—he told me not to fret; that there would be enough to keep me and
my little Maura away from the poorhouse; "and," says he, "God and His
Blessed Mother will look after ye."

But he got weaker and weaker, till he couldn't hold his tranheen (a
straw) in his hand; and one day his Reverence Father Fahey—the saint—
says to me, says he, "Mrs. Malone, prepare for the worst, for your husband
will soon be with his God."

I hurried to the bedside, but he was just dozing and wanderin' like; but
in a little while he called me and Maura to him and told us how happy he
felt. He knew God had forgiven him his sins, and though he would have
liked to have lived with us a while longer, still, "God's will be done," says
he; and at his asking I began the prayers for the dying, though my heart
was breakin'. I saw the death-sweat gathered on his brow; but I did not
cry—fearful I'd keep his spirit wandering on this cold earth, away from
God and his saints. I opened the window to let his pure soul go. Oh, my
poor darlin', he never injured anyone in his whole life—only trying to do
good and help everyone.

Next day I saw a white moth come flutterin' into the house—and then
I knew our lost one was with God and His blessed Mother.

I wouldn't let Maura see the body laid out nor let her kiss the cold,
unanswering lips, so I sent her to Mrs. Ryan, the Soggarth's housekeeper,
till after the funeral.

And oh, the day she came back! will I ever forget it? Only the two of us, in our little cabin—alone—alone. But we had the Holy Mother of Sorrows with us, and Martin's messenger; for the white moth never left us.

Maura, the pulse of my heart, loved her father well, and each night as she said her prayers she asked God to let her speak to him; and each word pierced my heart; for in her childish way, my jewel used to say aloud all she wished God to do for her father, and all she wanted to tell him. At night, when the candle was lighted, the white moth came, and we prayed as only a broken-hearted woman and an innocent child can pray.

Father Fahey advised me to start a little hucksterly on one side of the cabin, and he helped me with his purse as well. Ah, what would we poor people do without the soggarth, who teaches us, doctors us, advises us, and helps us? Well, I did as he told me, and the neighbours were very good and bought off me.

One day, when Martin was dead about six months, Murty Maguire said he wanted to speak to me in private like, when Maura wasn't there. Then he told me he was troubled with dreams of my Martin, and said he was certain my darlin' wasn't happy.

"Well," says I, "if Martin isn't happy, who is? Every year he made the Station and the rounds of the blessed well on his bare knees; and we never had anything that we didn't give part of to God's poor. For as Martin always said, nothing is ours: God lends it to us, and we must give some of it to them that is poorer still. But," says I, "I will have prayers said far and near for poor Martin–Heaven be his bed."

I was feelin' strong and well again, for, oh, the people are kind to the widow woman and the orphan, and while he was speakin' the white moth came and fluttered round about. Of a sudden Murty up with his hand and crushed it.

"Oh! Saints above," says I, "what have ye done? That was Martin's message of love to me and Maura, and never again will we see it now. Avoe! avoe!"

"Never mind," says he: "wait till All Souls' Night. Sure, he'll come to see ye himself then—he was that fond of ye."

I felt mighty queer, and Maura cried after the angel fly, as she called it.

All Souls' Night came, and I cleaned the hearth, lit a good fire, and put bread and water on the table for though the Soggarth is always angry with the people for doing this, sure don't we all do it, glory be to God! Didn't our mothers and grandmothers do it?—yes, and their grandmothers, too—for we believe the souls get power to come to us on that night.

Well, I lit the holy candle. It was late, and I was saying my Rosary by Maura's bed, when I heard a terrible noise in the back, near the haggard.

"May God have mercy on us," says I, "it must be a tremor (earthquake)," and I calls little Maura, and we peep through the window: but there was nothing to see.

"Maura," says I, "put the old shawl about ye, asthore, and we'll say the Rosary by the kitchen fire."

We went into the kitchen, and she cuddled herself up on the old settle. I was saying the prayers with my beads in my hands and my head bent low; when Maura's shriek made me jump to my feet, and there she was—screamin', screamin' and pointin' her finger. I looked round, and, Mother of God—there was Martin in his grave-clothes—and all the time Maura kept screamin'. She never knew me again—exceptin' a few minutes afore she died.

"Oh, Martin. Martin," says I, "what brings you back, at all, at all; and why—oh, why—did ye come when Maura was awake? It isn't like you to be forgetful;" and I crossed myself.

"Honor," says he, "I'm suffering. I owe a man fifty pound, and I can't get to Heaven till 'tis paid back. Will ye pay it, Honor? Ask Murty Maguire, for 'tis he is the man. Give it to him as soon as ye can," says he, "for I'm in great pain;" and then he walked out of the door, and I was left with sorrow—dark, dark sorrow—for my cushie was a natarel (an idiot).

At daylight I went to Father Fahey but he wouldn't listen to me. He said it was a dream—a bad dream—and blamed me for my superstition: but when he came and saw Maura macushla—"she's had a fright," says he; "I will get the doctor for her." Then he puts on his stole and reads and reads, and prays over her. When the doctor came he only shook his head. Five years she lived, gibbering away to herself, but never a word to me, barrin' afore she died. I was angered with his reverence misdoubting me seein' Martin, and so I went to Murty.

"Oh, then," says he, "himself oughtn't to have troubled. Sure I'd never have mentioned it to ye: faix, 'tis gospel truth."

I couldn't pay unless I sold out my home—small though it is—and then it was the poorhouse for us.

Well, your honour, I began, payin' Murty a pound now, and a pound then, whenever I could get it; but the amount always seemed to be the same—he said it was interest. Martin came to me again one night, and says he, "Marry Murty if he wants ye," says he.

"No, no, Martin allanah," says I; "do ye know our jewel is a natarel?" But he didn't seem to care. "Do as I tell you," says he. It didn't seem like Martin's talk at all—so loud and noisy it was.

I went again to the priest. "Honor Malone," says he, "ye are stark mad. Your husband was a good man, and I cannot think ye see anyone, only in your imagination; but if you do see a spirit, 'tis the devil himself. I will come to your house myself, and watch with ye."

He came and came, but the spirit never appeared when the Soggarth was present. Then I got very sick, and Father Fahey sent me to his sister's house in Mayo, so that I could get well; and he put one of the parish school-girls to mind my little shop. I got soon well enough, but Maura remained the same, though I took her to Knock, and to the Holy Well of St. Brigid.

I had only got back a week when Murty asked me to marry him, but I couldn't—I disliked him that much. Then he got cross, and told me he would let all the village know of my husband's trouble. I was near mad with sorrow, and Martin's ghost kept coming and telling me to do as he bid me. My dreams of my husband they were beautiful; but when he came, his spirit was, oh, so different. So I told him one night that he must be old Nick himself, and not my own good and holy man, and that

I would sell out and pay Murty up, and emigrate to America. Then he seemed satisfied, and went away,

I couldn't get anyone to buy the little place from me; and, in truth, the Soggarth wouldn't have let me give up my home.

Martin didn't trouble me now, and for six months I was quite free. Then one day Dr. Flynn come to me and asked me to go to Murty Maguire's. 'Twas the twelve-month day of Maura's death, and I was thinking o' what she'd said to me. She sat up in bed. Her eyes were changed to just what they were before that terrible night—and she spoke sensible.

"Mammy," says she, "kiss me, and listen to the angels singin'—'tis lovely. And there's Dad beckonin' to me—I must go to him. 'Tis my own Dad, and not that ugly man who frightened me last night." (Last night! Holy Virgin, 'twas nigh five years come Hallow Eve!) "Mammy, Mammy, come hurry," says she. "Dad is callin'," says she; and she crossed herself and died.

I was in no humour to go to Murty's with these thoughts in my mind, and I told the Doctor so.

"Well he asked for ye: but please yourself," says he. And just then Father Malone came rushin' in. "Hurry, Mrs. Malone," says he; "jump on the car, and don't wait—for the love of God!" says he. So I went with him, and he brought me to where Murty lay dying. He seemed to be sleeping. "Murty, Murty," called the Soggarth, like a general commanding his soldiers, "Honor Malone is here. Speak, man: speak before ye die."

Then the drawn, dying face looked up, and told me all. 'Twas he deceived me, your Honour; 'Twas he that pretended to be Martin's spirit, to get a little money off me. Sure himself never owed anything at all, at all—and it he slew my Maura—the pearl of my eye—the only sunbeam that God left me in my first great sorrow. And I thought of her, my golden-haired, blue-eyed jewel, and her scream came back to me with all its piercing horror. And 'Twas to forgive him they brought me—and I was going to have my revenge, when a white moth fluttered by me—and raisin' my eyes I saw the uplifted cross, with the crucified Christ, in the

Soggarth's hand—and the pleadin' eyes were on me. Murty was dying. Well, God was his judge—not me.

"I forgive ye, Murty," I cried: "and may God forgive ye too."—and, God rest his soul, he lay back in the Soggarth's arms—dead.

THE SWORD

Rachel Swete Macnamara

Published in The Sketch, 28 October 1917

Rachel Swete Macnamara (1869/70–1947) was an Irish and popular author whose many novels included either an Egyptian theme or a super-natural connection which ran throughout. Titles such as *The Trance* (her first novel, published in 1908), *White Witch*, *Dragon Tree*, *The Awakening* and *Strange Encounter*, to name but a few, nailed her genre colours to the mast. In the only interview she ever gave in 1935, Rachel stated that she began to write before she could write at all, at the age of four she was tell-ing her stories to her sister who would transcribe them for her. By twelve she had written her first play, and all three main characters were dead by its end. As she grew older she felt that she had to leave morbidity behind and try to write in a "most refreshing and entertaining manner". "The Sword" *appears* to be her only short story, and it's a decidedly bleak one!

THE wind sobbed round the turret of the old castle. It seemed aeons since Daphne had heard the distant chime of eleven's half-hour. Her heart beat uncomfortably.

She was alone in the turret-chamber. Her Highland cousins had dared her to carry out the old Hallowe'en rite of laying a supper-table for two in an unused room and waiting alone until midnight, when the man she was to marry would come and share it with her.

She had accepted the challenge amid chaff and laughter; but broad daylight in company is far removed from solitary midnight. Her cousins had come with her to the turret-stair at half-past eleven. Long ago their gay laughter had died away. The words of old Elspeth, the nurse, came back eerily to her.

"'Tis ill to meddle wi' the Powers above," she had muttered darkly.

But this was no real meddling with the supernatural. Daphne strained her ears to listen. She felt sure that her cousins would play some trick on her. The tapping of an ivy-leaf against the window made her start. She wished herself back in pleasant, comfortable England. Then another sound smote her ear—the sound of steps ascending the stairs. Her heart-beats quickened suffocatingly. She clutched the back of a chair, frozen to stillness, waiting…

A tall man entered, dressed in full Highland regimentals. He was lean and brown, with a slight scar across his left eyebrow. She had never seen him before. Their eyes met; his smile held reassurance.

All terror left her as he came forward, drew out a chair, and motioned her to sit. Her lips moved as if to speak, but he laid his finger on his own and shook his head.

Before he sat, he unbuckled his sword and threw it on an old oak settle behind him.

In silence they broke bread together and ate. In silence he filled her glass and raised his in an unspoken toast. As in a dream, she responded.

He rose. She rose too. The candles in the silver sconce flickered golden flowers of flame between them. The tapping at the window sounded as if some straying spirit begged for entry. They drank, their eyes on each other. Before he turned to go, he took her hand and kissed it.

The touch of his lips lingered long after the sound of his departing footsteps had died away.

Daphne stood still, enrapt. Trick or no trick, this was the man for her. Sighing heavily, at last she turned to blow out the candles and go. As she did so, a gleam caught her eye. It was the sword on the settle.

Here was visible proof! She would face them all with it at breakfast tomorrow—no, today—and make them confess…! But the man—who was he? When and where would she meet him again?…

She went slowly down the turret-stair, the sword cradled in her arms. At the bottom a dark shape crouched, moved, spoke. Daphne almost screamed aloud before she realized that it was old Elspeth.

Her white mutch loomed ghostly in the dusk; her quavering tones held a thrill of awe as her gaze lit on the sword.

"Whaar gat ye yon sword, lassie?" she cried, peering.

"He left it behind him," Daphne answered dreamily.

The bent figure drew itself upright. Her whisper was tense with warning.

"Hide it as ye wad hide your inmost shame. Let nae mortal eye look on 't, or ye'll rue the day, puir bit English lassie."

Daphne felt a little thrill of fear. The old woman always seemed to her to possess uncanny powers.

"Mind what I say," old Elspeth warned. "Now rin to yer bed and sleep—gin ye can."

The phrase was significant. Dawn broke before Daphne fell into a troubled sleep.

At breakfast her cousins flung a cascade of questions at her. She parried them as best she could. She felt a strange aversion from telling them the real story.

"You played a trick on me," she insisted. "You know as much as I do about it."

"I swear we did not," cried Jean.

"No, honestly we didn't," echoed Margery.

"Will Alan swear?" asked Daphne, glancing at Jean's husband.

"On my honour," he returned gravely. "I was in bed and asleep before midnight struck."

"You connived at nothing?"

"There was nothing to connive at," came in chorus. "Do tell us what happened."

"The expected, of course!" Daphne forced a flippancy which she was far from feeling. "My future husband came and supped with me." Bright spots burned in her cheeks. Truth rang in her cousins' tones. The mystery deepened round the affair.

"Nonsense!"

"I don't believe you!"

"Look at the supper things, then," said Daphne, rising.

"You used two sets!"

"Please yourselves," Daphne said. It was the strangest thing that had ever happened in her young life.

Months passed, and Daphne had long since returned to England. She had her cousins' word that they had played no trick; but the sword remained as visible proof that no mere dream had deceived her. She showed it to no one, but hid it away in an old trunk when she went home. Gradually the sense of expectancy which at first had tinged her days faded, but the memory of her vigil lingered. Even yet she looked round every new assembly she entered, half-hoping, half-fearing to see a face which she knew would never fade from her mind.

When friends invited her to their house-party for the Dorcaster Hunt Ball, she accepted with pleasure. Hope revived. Perhaps here and now would her dream be fulfilled.

It was.

The first thing her eyes lit upon in the gaily decorated ballroom was the swing of a kilt. The man wearing it was lean and brown, and had a slight scar above his left eyebrow. Their eyes met. Admiration, swiftly quickened interest shone in his, rather than actual physical recognition. It was evident that she alone knew.

Her heart beat tumultuously. The room seemed to spin. When she recovered, someone was introducing Captain Alistair Fyfe, of the Green Gordons.

He asked for a dance, and bore her off. Their steps suited. She seemed to float in his arms. She felt no need for speech.

"I hate talking while dancing, don't you?" he asked.

She nodded. His voice matched his smile, she thought.

When they sat out together, he took her fan and began to fan her gently.

"Do you know, I have the oddest fancy that we have met before," he said. "It must have been in my dreams, because I should surely remembered it had it been in reality."

She looked at him wonderingly. Suddenly she found voice.

"Where were you on last Hallowe'en?"

He thought for a moment. "We were stationed in York then. Yes; I was at an awfully jolly party given by some people named Cranbourne. Why? Where were you?"

"In Scotland, staying with some cousins at Cromie Castle."

"The Douglases?"

"Yes. My cousin Jean is married to Alan Douglas."

"How strange! My mother was a Douglas. Cromie once belonged to her branch of the family; but, oddly enough, I've never been there. I wish they had asked me to stay last Hallowe'en."

She looked questioningly at him. His tone was heartfelt, but absolutely innocent of any but the obvious meaning. No recollection of that midnight meeting and pledging was to be read in the eyes that said so eloquently that she was the sweetest creature he had ever seen. What could it mean? Involuntarily, she glanced at his side. No sword hung there! Of course not, at a ball!… Perhaps some day she would ask him about it.

Her silence piqued him. "Are you glad they didn't?"

A vivid blush flamed in her face. "No—oh, no."

"That's all right. Still, it doesn't throw any light on where we met. It must have been in dreamland."

"What does it matter?" she smiled happily at him. "Perhaps it was in some other incarnation, when 'you were a King in Babylon and I was a Christian slave!'"

For a moment a sense of the uncanny enwrapt her; but, as before, fear vanished at the light in his eyes. Vision or reality, what did it matter? She had met her man at last…

The course of true love belied tradition. No dragons lurked in their path. "It was roses, roses all the way."

The honeymoon was spent in Paradise, which was the generic term for an oddly different assortment of names, such as Paris, Venice, Bellagio, Capri. When it ended, as honeymoons will, it did not really end at all, Mrs. Fyfe explained. It just translated itself into terms of ordinary life, and glorified the great commonplaces of every day. Hanging pictures was huge fun, thinking out dinners more fascinating than any jigsaw puzzle.

Daphne took a pride and delight in unpacking and arranging her own belongings, which had been sent on from home. All had been put away except one box containing books and other odds and ends.

At breakfast Alistair said suddenly—

"Who wrote that thing you once quoted to me about the King of Babylon and the Christian slave? Do you remember? It was the first time we met in this incarnation. Swinburne, was it?"

"No; Henley, I think," she answered.

"Are you sure?"

"Not absolutely. I can easily find out, though. There's a copy of Henley in my box upstairs." She ran out of the room.

The book was not in the top layer. She burrowed deeper. Suddenly her fingers struck something hard—something wrapped in brown paper. She drew it out—a long, narrow parcel—and slowly unwrapped it.

It was the sword.

She stood looking at it for a moment, thrilled by thronging memories of the wonders love had brought her since that unexplained night. She forgot old Elspeth's warning. She kissed the hilt half-shamefacedly, and ran downstairs again, taking it with her, the book forgotten.

"Alistair, darling," she cried, her face alight. "that was not the first time we met. Don't you remember—*this*?" She held out the sword.

He looked up. His face changed suddenly when he saw it. Youth seemed wiped from it as by a sponge. Its tan faded to greyness. His eyes were as the eyes of one who looks across great spaces terribly. His lips parted, but no sound came.

For a moment he gazed at her in silent anguish. Then he rose, as one in a trance, took the sword from her trembling hands, went out of the room, out of the house—out of her life.

From that day, Alistair Fyfe was never seen or heard of again.

COCKROW INN

Tod Robbins

Published in Who Wants a Green Bottle? and Other
Uneasy Tales (1926)

Clarence Aaron "Tod" Robbins (1888–1949) was an author given the rare
freedom to write without boundaries, due to an inheritance left to him to
be able to pursue life as he saw fit. He is best known today for his short
story "Spurs" that was turned into the notorious *Freaks* (directed by Tod
Browning, 1932). He was a student at the first private boys' schools in
Brooklyn, The Polytechnic Institute, and became a renowned boxer and
pole-vaulter. His first novel, *Mysterious Martin*, was published in 1912,
followed by *The Spirit of the Town*, a novel about a student who witnesses
a suicide that no-one seems bothered by. Robbins claimed exemption
from the Great War in 1917, on the basis that he was married with
two children. That year, his breakthrough novel, *The Unholy Three* was
published and this was followed by several short stories that featured in
All-Story Weekly magazine. These would be published in 1926 in *Silent,
White and Beautiful*, a collection that featured a "redux" version of his first
novel, now titled "For Art's Sake". He moved to France, and during this
time director Tod Browning was hard at work adapting *The Unholy Three*
for the big screen. Released in 1925, it was remade with sound in 1929 by
a different director.

It is claimed that Browning was inspired to create the film *Freaks* after
the diminutive star of *The Unholy Three*, Harry Earles, gave him a copy
of the collection *Who Wants a Green Bottle?*, in which Browning encoun-
tered "Spurs". The film was banned in the UK.

Tod was still living in France as war broke out in 1939 and it was
reported that he had an "open house and keeps moving from one end
of the Riviera to the other, looking into favourite bars, restaurants and

casinos for friends who never come back." He simply refused to leave. War didn't stop his books being published; in 1943 *Une Bouteille Verte*, a translation of *Who Wants a Green Bottle?*, was published by Jean Vigneau Editions. Tod was taken to Saint Denis concentration camp by the SS, and in a cruel twist of fate was imprisoned there with his son, John. After the war he wrote *To Hell and Home*, which became his final published novel. He died on 10 May 1949 at Saint-Jean-Cap-Ferrat.

One month after Robbins's death, and in a scenario as strange and as morbid as one of Tod's novels, his son John was arrested for the murder of Robert Duff who was found strangled in Duffy's Hotel on Fire Island in New York. John and Robert slept in the same room together and after a night of heavy drinking, John woke up to find Robert dead. He maintained that Robert had committed suicide, however Robbins's left eye was blackened and his lip cut when he was arrested. He was subsequently found guilty of manslaughter and sentenced to seven and a half years in prison, serving four.

COCKCROW Inn stands defiantly facing the sea. For countless years it has stood thus, holding at naught the greatest strength of wind and water, quite careless of the dazzling thunderstorms which on sultry summer evenings attack it as though with lifted sword-blades—a staunch old dwelling raised by hands long gone back into their native dust. And on wild winter nights, when the waves thunder out their war-song on the beach, when the wind screams its challenge to the sky, when all nature's resources seem bent on destruction, the windows of this hostelry twinkle cheerily for lonely travelers by land or sea. It feeds the hungry and warms the cold; and only once in all its ten-score years has it failed to ward off the spirits of darkness which, if the villagers are to be believed, infest the moaning caves of Wishbone Point.

But I must let Ben Tibbit tell you the story as he told it to me, hunched up before his fireside like a shriveled old boot put there to dry—Ben Tibbit with the long, wizened neck and ferret eyes.

I was new to that country then, coming straight from the city. Death had been rapping on my office door in town. What I needed was a breath of salt air and a place to stretch my legs. Wishbone Point soon made me into a new man.

But the Tibbits! There's a tribe for you—all cut in one mold, like Noah and his family out of my nephew's ark. You can't mistake a Tibbit. There's little Archibald, just learning to crawl, like a baby rattler; and there are Mother and Aunt Tibbit, fat women both—yet get a peep at them through the tap-room window on their way to church of a Sunday; see the swing of their long, thin necks like Strasburg geese about to be fed, and you straightway know them for Tibbits; and, last of all, there's old Ben himself in his chimney corner, snuffling sin out through his nose over the Bible—a Tibbit every inch of him, well-seasoned by fourscore years and ten—a bent twig of the devil's briarbush which caught in his grandmother's skirts, as he'll tell you himself after a hot toddy. What a neck the man has—long and lean as a swan's, with an odd Adam's Apple peeping through like a half-swallowed frog on its way to the gullet! What a slim, sly neck, twisting this way and that, for all it's so wrinkled and yellow—what a neck to smother a hiccough!

Now when I first took up my quarters at Cockcrow Inn, what from the condition of my nerves, which were all of a snarl like macaroni in a bowl of soup, I couldn't do the Tibbit family justice. It seemed to me that there were too many of them, and all too much alike. I took a violent dislike to the breed. But this silly dislike soon turned to pity when I learned the truth of the matter.

I think that wild Hallowe'en night, when old Ben first opened his heart to me, marked the turning of the tide. What man could have withheld his sympathy? Poor old doddering chap, he had been marked at birth for the devil's fruit; he and his son and his grandson. Could he help what had befallen Nancy Greer, that wild slip of a lass who had once served a strange guest at Cockcrow Inn in the days when the country was new? No, nor could she, for that matter—although she might have attended the burning of Anna Mulvane, and thus cheated the devil. But I must begin at the beginning.

As I have said, it was a wild Hallowe'en. All day it had been blowing hard; now the waves came crashing down on the beach like falling towers. A venomous wind was abroad—a frantic, tearing wind which charged at Cockcrow Inn, shaking the solid doors on their hinges, bellowing down the great chimney and slipping through each crack and cranny. And the outer night was filled with wandering voices. It held them all like an ebony cup—laughter and tears, joy and sorrow.

"Bad weather," said Ben Tibbit, laying his Bible aside with a sigh. "All the praying in the world won't alter it. It's Hallowe'en."

"Hallowe'en, eh?" said I. "I suppose the witches will be riding their broomsticks."

"Aye, that they will," he muttered, uncoiling his neck and squinting up at the oak-paneled ceiling. "And there should be many to ride, for it's not like it was in my grandfather's day. In those good old times they couldn't go trapesing about just as they pleased. No, sir. Just let them cast a spell over man or beast, woman or fowl, and they had short shrift of it. But now, how is it? Why, folks are only too pleased to have them for neighbors. There's Witch Cabbot, who lives over by Bloody Creek. To my knowledge she cured little Archibald of warts by just a wave of her wand, and yet no one puts a lighted torch to her skirts. There's no religion left in the land, Mr. Tremain."

"But it was different in your grandfather's day?" I suggested.

"It was so," said he, with a solemn roll of his head. "Men were men then. They didn't let the devil have it all his own way. They met fire with fire. Fourteen witches my grandfather helped to drag to the stake; seventeen pirates he saw hanged by the neck. There was enough hanging and burning then in these parts to keep a good Christian satisfied. I remember my sister's first skip-rope came off the gallows-tree—a well-tarred bit of hemp if ever there was one."

"Can you remember your grandfather?" I asked.

"And could I be forgetting him, sir, when there was not another such in all this countryside? Big and red he was, with a mane like a lion. A mighty man once his blood was up. Why, I've seen him take two sizable lads by the scruff of the neck and knock their heads together till they were silly from it, and he over eighty at the time with a back bowed by years! There never was a stronger man than my grandfather, though since his day the Tibbits have dwindled. You see, sir, the family tree has withered root and branch from consorting with ghosts and the like of that."

"Ghosts?" said I, sniffing a story.

"Aye, ghosts—red-handed, black-bearded ghosts! Scum of the high seas who had made their own graves too hot to hold them! Ghosts with cutlasses in their hands and murder in their hearts! Damned souls that the devil himself would be glad to be rid of!"

"Spin me the yarn, Mr. Tibbit."

"Gladly," said he. "But first I must be asking you a question. You've been staying at Cockcrow Inn now for over a week, and you've seen every mother's son of us. Now, Mr. Tremain, have you noticed anything unwholesome? A peculiar family resemblance that—A sort of—" He paused, and I saw his red-rimmed eyes glimmer out at me from the chimney-seat. "A kind of a—"

"You mean your necks, Mr. Tibbit?" I said, helping him out as best I could. "You've all got long, graceful necks like swans."

"Swans be damned, sir!" he cried with a sudden heat, strange to come from a man who lived so close to his Bible. "To Hell's fire with your swans!"

"I was meaning you no offence, Mr. Tibbit," I hastened to add. "Perhaps you have an aversion to swans. I should rather say—" I was about to mention geese, but thought better of it.

"Never mind what our necks look like," he said with a bitter smile. "We Tibbits are all cursed with them. For five generations not one of us has got off scot free. We've prayed and we've fasted, we've worn out the knees of our breeches and the very patience of God. See Archibald there, the poor little toad!"

I looked to where he pointed and saw that child of misfortune trying patiently to hang his white kitten with a piece of curtain cord. But before I could interfere, it squirmed out of his hands and was off to the attic, leaving Archibald on his back, squalling.

"The poor little toad!" Ben Tibbit continued with a shake of his grizzled head. "Look how he lies, like a turtle!"

"You were about to tell me your story," I ventured.

"Well, then, to begin," said he, "you must know that the country was wild in my grandfather's youth. And if the country was wild, the sea was wilder. Black-hearted gentry there were afloat who swore by the Jolly Roger. Many a brave ship's crew walked the plank not five miles off Wishbone Point—many a corpse has bumped up on the sand like a bag of grain after the rats are through with it. What from pirates and witches, a body couldn't sleep safe in his bed at night for fear he'd wake up with a slit throat in the morning or maybe as mad as a hatter.

"Now, of all the pirates off our coast, there was none the country-folk feared as much as Whitechapel Willie. He was a Londoner born, was Willie—smooth as oil and fond of the lassies. The girls hereabouts used to quake in their beds, for he was not always content with his luck on the sea, but would come scudding in on cloudy nights, a dozen hairy lads to bear him company. Then he'd creep up to some lonely farmer's house and snatch a maid from her bed or the good wife herself, were she comely. It was a crying shame, and the neighborhood was fair sick of it.

"It happened that my grandfather was courting Nancy Greer at the time—and Cockcrow Inn, in a manner of speaking. She was the only daughter of Anthony Greer, landlord here then. The girl was a fair catch, and my grandfather was not the lad to let a good alehouse slip through his fingers once he gripped it. Besides all this, as I've often heard him say, Nancy was a comely lass with a way about her to make men follow at her heels like dogs after a butcher wagon. Not that she gave any of them favors, for my grandfather was jealous to a fault, and quick tempered with rivals."

"And Whitechapel Willie?" I asked.

"Well, Willie was different," said Ben Tibbit reminiscently. "I'll not say that he didn't worry my grandfather when his black bark was seen off the Point. You see, he had the name on the high seas of being of close kin to the devil—a reputation he fostered by chewing mouthfuls of glass like they were no more than plugs of tobacco, picking up live coals between finger and thumb to drop down the necks of his crew, and swallowing sword-blades, which he claimed sharpened his wits. From one thing and another, my grandfather did not fancy him much as a rival. And so, when Willie was finally caught and hanged on the beach, he lent a hand to the business with a grin on his face."

"So Whitechapel Willie was caught and hanged?" I said a trifle regretfully.

"He was so. And my grandfather, who was appointed hangman that year, slipped the halter about his neck as pleased as Punch—the more especial as Nancy Greer was looking on and Whitechapel Willie was rolling his wicked black eyes at her. Here was this bloody-minded pirate on the brink of the grave, about to be hung up for his sins like the Tibbits' wash on a Monday, and him rolling his wicked black eyes at our Nancy and dancing at her like a bear on the end of a chain! It was a sight to make your blood run cold, Mr. Tremain.

"'Think on your sins, wretched man!' says my grandfather, very stern, giving the halter a jerk to cut off a ribald rhyme in the making. 'Say your prayers, unhappy sinner!'

"So he swung him up as high as a kite to dance out his life in the air, and the country-folk took a long breath of relief and went about their business. My grandfather and Nancy Greer were the last to go, for there was not a man so religious as he, nor one who took more joy in a burning or a hanging. But Nancy was trembling from it, and he had to throw his greatcoat about her.

"'One pirate the less, Heaven be praised!' says my grandfather in a voice like a deacon.

"But Nancy Greer didn't answer him at all, just stared up at Willie, who was still jigging a bit on the gallows-tree. So strange a look she had on her face, and such a wild eye along with it, that he straightway began to look about for a witch. And lucky it was for Bess Cabbot that she hadn't been born yet to pick up driftwood on the beach, for as like as not she'd have been burned with her own faggots.

"Well, Mr. Tremain, the hanging of Whitechapel Willie kept my grandfather in good spirits for upward of a month. In those days the

Tibbit family had built themselves a house on the other side of Wishbone Point, where they did all the hanging; and he had but to cross his own doorsill to see Willie hanging as neat as a turkey-cock in Butcher Flint's window. Those were the times when the country-folk hereabouts let a pirate swing for a space till the red-handed gentry offshore got a sniff of him, which was sure to be good for their morals. A fine lesson it was to the lads and lassies, and a sure sign to strangers that Christianity had taken deep root in the land.

"As I have said, my grandfather was pleased to see Whitechapel Willie hanging there. Not that he was puffed up with pride over his handiwork, for he was modest as hangmen go; but just because he took an honest delight in having strung up with his own hands one of the devil's kin. Pleased and merry he was to see Willie jigging against the sunset till one Hallowe'en, a hundred and fifty years ago tonight—a black Hallowe'en for the Tibbits if ever there was one.

"It was another such evening as this, Mr. Tremain—a howling wind for the witches to ride on, black as the mouth of hell, with never a star a-quiver. It was no night to be out, but my grandfather was not the man to be turned aside from his duty. You see, they were burning Anna Mulvane, the witch of Whittington Common, beside the old Court House; and he had promised to take Nancy Greer on the pillion behind him, thinking that the sight might put the fear of God in her. So he saddled and bridled his nag, Queen Bess, and set off for Cockcrow Inn.

"It chanced, Mr. Tremain, that he rode along the beach, which was a short cut, although a bad one to follow on such a night. He had to pass under the gallows-tree before he was ten minutes in the saddle. Now, what from it being Hallowe'en, and so black that you couldn't see hand before face, another man might have thought twice before taking the beach-road. But not so my grandfather. On he went, singing a snatch of a hymn, not from fear, but just because he was partial to holy music, thinking no doubt of the good fire where he could warm his cold hands at the expense of Anna Mulvane, when all of a sudden

Queen Bess planted all four feet deep in the sand and let out a snort like a dragon.

"Now he was taken quite by surprise and came within an ace of losing his grip of the saddle; yet he steadied himself after a bit and gave Queen Bess a taste of his heels. But she wouldn't move an inch, just stood with her ears laid back and shook all over. Well, being a quick-tempered man, my grandfather was about to draw his sabre and give her the flat of it as a lesson in manners, when, all of a sudden, there came a flash of lightning which showed him a hair-raising sight."

"What was it?" I asked breathlessly.

Ben Tibbit took a long pull at his pipe before he answered me. His face was all working with excitement and his eyes glowed like a cat's in the dark. "What was it?" said he very slowly. "Why, I'll tell you, Mr. Tremain. My grandfather had ridden up to the gallows, never knowing it at all; and that flash of lightning, like a torch out of heaven, had showed him a mighty strange thing."

"What?" I demanded.

"Why, Whitechapel Willie had gone."

"Gone?"

"Aye, there he had been hanging to my grandfather's knowledge for a good three weeks or more, as dead as a herring, swinging back and forth like a pendulum of that clock yonder, a plaything for the birds and the wind and the rain—and now, come Hallowe'en, he wasn't there anymore."

"Perhaps some of his friends landed and cut him down," I suggested.

"That's what my grandfather was thinking after he'd rubbed his eyes for a bit. And hot anger rose up in the man. He had hanged Willie so neatly and all to no purpose. So he drew out his Bible and swore a great oath on it that he'd have the heart of this snatcher of bodies before the year had run out. But after a time the wind cooled him off a bit; and, knowing that nothing more could be made of the matter, he beat his nag forward with the flat of his sword, riding on with a heavy weight of curses behind his closed lips.

"Queen Bess trotted forward bravely enough once she had passed the gallows-tree till she came up alongside a tall, dark shape of a man striding along the beach like one in a hurry. Now my grandfather drew rein, perhaps feeling the need of companionship, or maybe just to break the news about Whitechapel Willie. And the moon peeped out for a bit, like a timid bride from behind a lace curtain, and showed him that the man had his chin on his breast. Tall and thin he was; and he didn't cast any shadow, though the light was bright enough.

"And my grandfather fell to wondering who it could be, knowing most of the men in the village whom he had thrown about like rag dolls in his day. Was it Red Tim, the blacksmith? No, Tim was shorter and broader. Was it Richard Bell, the barber? No, Bell had more of a stoop to his shoulders. Now wasn't it Parson Peabody's wild young brother—him who was said to be mad when the moon was full? He was just such a figure of a man, silent and moody—a bad companion, but better than none on a wild Hallowe'en.

"'God be with you, friend,' said my grandfather through his nose like a parson. 'Mayhap you're on your way to the burning?'

"'I am cold,' said the wayfarer then in a voice shrill as a crowing cock. 'Think you, good hangman, that it will be cheerful there as in the devil's kitchen?'

"'That it will,' my grandfather answered, not relishing mention of the devil's name on such a night, but making allowances for the parson's brother. 'They've planned a great fire by the Court House.'

"'Good!' cried the wayfarer with a shiver. 'Think you it would warm me, Hangman Tibbit? The cold of many a black night has eaten into my bones like quicklime.'

"'It'll warm you,' says my grandfather. 'And there will be rare sport besides. Anna Mulvane will be squalling like a dozen cats once the fire touches her.'

"And then at these merry words the wayfarer let out a laugh shrill as a cock crowing in the dawn—an unwholesome laugh, Mr. Tremain, which

181

made Queen Bess rear up from sheer fright of it. 'He, he, he!' he cried with a wicked roll of his head, 'There's a cloven hoof peeping out from under the robe of the priest!'

"'What may you be meaning by that, friend?' my grandfather asked.

"'Never you trouble your head over the matter, Hangman Tibbit,' says the wayfarer with an ill-favored grin. 'Stick to your trade. There's a science to it you've not quite mastered. When all's said and done, what you hang up is as likely as not to come down and be treading a jig-step on a black Hallowe'en!'

"'If you're meaning the disappearance of Whitechapel Willie off the gallows-tree,' my grandfather cried in a towering passion, 'I'll have you know that some rogue in these parts cut him down. I've sworn to clip the ears of that man if I once lay eyes on him!'

"'A coward sprinkles threats on all sides of him like a pot shaking pepper,' says the wayfarer with a sneer. 'Spur on, Hangman Tibbit, for I'm wanting only my own company.'

"Now, Mr. Tremain, had it not been Hallowe'en and he late for the burning of Anna Mulvane, and had he not thought that this impudent rascal was own brother to Parson Peabody, there's no doubt at all in my mind but my grandfather would have made short work of him. But, as it was, he swallowed his righteous wrath like a dose of bitter medicine; and, wasting no more words on the matter, but just putting it down to the liquor which must be shaking up and down in the man's belly to make him so bold, he clapped his spurs into Queen Bess and was off like the wind.

"Well, it wasn't long before he rode up to Cockcrow Inn and stamped into this very tap-room. It was a cheery place then, as it is now. A great log was spluttering a bit on the hearthstone and the easy chairs were gathered cozy about it, as if they had tiptoed out from the corners to have a friendly chat in the firelight. But there wasn't a drinking man in the place—all having tramped over the hill to the burning.

"'Nancy Greer! Nancy Greer!' my grandfather bellows like a bull that is mating. 'Where have you got to, Nancy?'

"And in a little while she comes down the great stairs into his arms, and he gives her a squeeze fit to crack the ribs of a bear. But she, being a lusty lass, only giggles a bit and blushes a bit, and tells him that he shouldn't be carrying on so.

"And at that he takes a proud look around the room, like a man who feels he has the property in his pocket; and then he bends down and gives her a loud smack—a masterful kiss to smother an argument.

"'That's for you, my good wench,' says he very lordly, for there wasn't every girl who could boast of such favor. 'Is your father at home, Nancy?'

"'No, sir,' says she, dropping him a low curtsey. 'He's just stepped over the hill to the burning of Anna Mulvane.'

"'And so he should do,' said my grandfather then as though from the pulpit. ''Tis the duty of every Christian in the land. Get your bonnet and shawl, Nancy.'

"But she shakes her head at that and sets her mouth hard. 'I'm not going to the burning of Anna Mulvane, Mr. Tibbit,' says she very firm.

"'Not going!' cried my grandfather, quite taken aback. 'What ails you, lass? Why, the whole congregation will be there, and Parson Peabody is to light the faggots with his own hand! Come, get your bonnet and shawl!'

"'I'm not feeling so spry, Mr. Tibbit,' says she, looking down on the floor like a sinner. 'It'll be cold by the Court House. There's a bitter wind abroad, and I—'

"But my grandfather cut her short, having smelt out a lie. 'Tell me the truth, Nancy Greer,' said he. 'Out with it, girl. Why is it that you fear to go to the burning of Anna Mulvane?'

"And now she just blurted out the black truth like the silly wench that she was. 'I like Anna Mulvane!' she cried, in a voice all broken with sobs. 'I don't believe she's a witch! And even if she is, I don't care! I like her!'

"'Have a care, Nancy Greer!' says my grandfather right solemnly.

"But she went on for all that, words falling from her in a shower. 'Why must you be always taking me to hangings and burnings? I hate them, Mr. Tibbit—yes, hate them! There was the time you men of the church

183

burned poor old widow Penwin. Mind how her hair flamed up, Mr. Tibbit, and how she clawed it? I see her yet in my dreams!'

"'Nancy Greer,' my grandfather said very sternly, 'did I not know you for a good lass at heart, these wicked words might go hard with you. Mayhap you're bewitched. Come, I'll wrestle with the devil which possesses you. Nancy, bring me a bottle of wine and we'll sit ourselves down by the fireside and say a few prayers to break this enchantment.'"

"Now, Mr. Tremain, Nancy Greer calmed down in a jiffy, as is the habit of most lasses once they get their own way. She was quick to bring him a bottle of her father's very best wine, for it was a night when good spirits could do no harm. And my grandfather was nothing loath to make love and toast his toes a bit. Perhaps he had grown a trifle weary of burnings, like a man who has gone too much to the playhouse. Besides, if the worst came to the worst, he could still get to the Court House in time to pocket a handful of ashes for luck.

"Well, there he sat, Mr. Tremain, with Nancy on his knee, sipping Anthony Greer's rare old wine and thinking of the day when he'd be master of Cockcrow Inn, when all of a sudden there came such a loud peal of thunder that the whole house seemed to shake from it. And on its heels there followed a great blast of wind that rattled the window-panes in their sockets and blew open the oaken door as though the devil himself had put a shoulder to it.

"'God save us!' cried Nancy, jumping up in a fright. 'I'd best be bolting the doors and the windows!'

"But my grandfather answered nothing at all—just sat back, pop-eyed."

Ben Tibbit paused to light his long clay pipe, and I took advantage of his silence to stir the fire a bit. We were both needing the warmth and cheer of it.

"What ailed your grandfather?" I asked at length.

"Matter enough, sir," said he between puffs. "A strange guest had been blown into Cockcrow Inn. I say blown, Mr. Tremain, for it was like that. In he came, swirling from side to side like an autumn leaf caught in a gale. For all he was so long and lean and solemn, there was a strange, unwholesome gaiety about him, like a wreath of smoke hanging over a bonfire."

"What manner of man was he, Mr. Tibbit?" I asked.

"Well, at first it was hard to make out, for he was all wrapped up in a long black cloak. But after he had skipped up to the fire and stretched his arms over it, my grandfather caught a glimpse of his face.

"Long and lean it was, Mr. Tremain, with a great hooked nose poking out like a vulture's. And to make matters worse, he had but one eye, like a window-pane with fire shining through it. The other was just a hole in his head and as black as a rabbit's burrow. But more disturbing than all was the unhealthy pallor of his skin, all soggy with damp like a mushroom that has stood out too long in the wet.

"'God be with you, friend,' said my grandfather, not forgetting his manners. 'Are you cold?'

"'Aye, cold—cold!' said the stranger in a voice like a crowing cock. 'Think you, Hangman Tibbit, that a man can lie out for a round score nights, blowing this way and that to every stray puff of wind like a whirligig, without just becoming as damp as a towel in a tap-room? I'm needing a bed of red-hot coals to lie on, Hangman Tibbit!'

"All this time he had been bending so close over the fire that it was a wonder his cloak did not flare up from it; but now he took a step back and began to unwind a long muffler from about his neck. And my grandfather could see that this stranger's clothes were in a most shocking state. Were it not for his cloak, the man might as well have been naked. Tattered and torn were his breeches and jerkin as though by the claws of wild beasts; and through a rent in his hose his bare calf showed green and moldy. And in all, he was in no fit state to be in a lass's company; and my grandfather would have told him as much had it not been Hallowe'en.

"Now, as I have said, this scarecrow of a man was unwinding a woolen muffler which sat tight about his neck. Coil on coil he unwound, and, strange to tell, with each coil his head tilted more to one side, till at last he was grinning at my grandfather from his bony left shoulder. A most disquieting thing to see, Mr. Tremain.

"Next he sat himself down and drained my grandfather's flagon without so much as a by-your-leave. 'You do yourself proud, Hangman Tibbit,' said he. 'Young women and old wine—they betoken a man whether in Heaven or Hell. Now bring me a flagon, Nancy Greer, and we'll drink to your bonnie blue eyes.'

"My grandfather, a proud man when in liquor, was loath to drink with such ragged company; but it being Hallowe'en and no one about to mark him, he clinked glasses with this wind-tossed traveler out of the night as friendly as possible. And what from the good wine he had already drunk, and what from the bumpers that followed, it wasn't long before he and his guest were as lively as limpets. He even sent Nancy down to the cellar for another bottle—and she was loath to be going for fear she'd be missing some of the stranger's sallies. For it seems that this ragged fellow had a rare humor, once you forgot his wagging head and his ruby-red eye.

"The tales he told them, Mr. Tremain, would fairly make your sides split—about shiploads of people walking the plank like a flock of sheep on their way to the butcher's, about wild pranks played at sea when strong men were hanged up by their toes to the rigging, about how one Captain Shark had his own cook served up to the crew in the form of apple dumplings. And my poor grandfather tried to hold his own with him, telling of the humorous sights that he'd seen at the hangings and burnings hereabouts. But he couldn't make a go of it, for they all seemed like skimmed milk at the best. So he shook his head as the stranger's stories grew wilder and wilder, reflecting no doubt that this merry fellow's youth had not been without blemish. And also he began to think that his roving eye fell on his Nancy more than was seemly.

"'On your feet, Hangman Tibbit!' the stranger cried out at last with a flourish. 'On your feet, you lubberly swine, for I've a toast for you!'

"'I'll have you know—' my grandfather began in a towering passion. But he got no further with it, for this ragged stranger drowned him out

186

with small respect and less manners. The ditty he sang in his high crowing
voice ran something like this:

'Here's to Whitechapel Willie who sails the four seas,
He's known from Calcutta to Florida Keys.
With a puncheon of rum and a dirk in each hand,
In a snug little lugger a league from the land,
For wine and women and plenty of duff
He'd sink a whole fleet and not call it enough.
For he's Whitechapel Willie who sails the four seas,
Well known from Calcutta to Florida Keys.'

"'Whitechapel Willie!' my grandfather cried. 'Did you mention the name
of Whitechapel Willie?'

"'Aye, pumpkin head!' said the stranger. 'I did sing of Whitechapel
Willie. What then, pop-eyed hangman?'

"Now, Mr. Tremain, there's no doubt at all in my mind but that my
grandfather would there and then have slain this fellow had it not been
for a strange trick of memory which tormented him. He had even laid his
hand on his sword-hilt, so far had he gone in the matter, when something
familiar about this stranger's manner held his arm back. Where had he
seen that hooked nose before? He must find out before he slew him, or
else his curiosity might go begging through life. Thus he reasoned, and
once swallowed his anger.

"'I hanged Whitechapel Willie with my own hands not a month back,'
says he, rather proud.

"'And did you so, Hangman Tibbit?' cried the stranger then, with a
wink at Nancy. 'Blast your soul for a bungler! I was passing the gallows-
tree not an hour gone, and there was no fruit on it for bird or beast.
Mayhap Willie has slipped your halter come Hallowe'en?'

"'When I hang a man he stays hanged!' my grandfather bellowed. 'The
devil himself could not slip my noose!'

"'Is it so?' said the stranger with a sneer and a smile. 'Nancy, my dear, surely a dead man is of more worth to a lively lass than this hulking, hic-coughing homespun. Sit you down on my knee, girl, and I'll sing to you of Whitechapel Willie:

'Now Whitechapel Willie was wooing a wench,
Pipe up on your flutes and your fiddles;
He sat her down on a cobbler's bench,
Sing high, sing low, sing—'

"But now my grandfather drowned him out with a volley of oaths which would have done justice to any pirate. He was fair foaming with rage, for out of the corner of his eye he could see Nancy creeping over toward this stranger like a bird once the snake beckons it. Something had to be done to keep this rogue in his place, or it might very well be that he'd have Cockcrow Inn and the girl in his pocket.

"'Draw, you crowing cock of perdition!' cried my grandfather, over-turning the table just to show what manner of man he was. 'Sing your dirty gutter songs, will you!'

"And at that the stranger leaped to his feet. 'So that's your tune, Hangman Tibbit!' says he. 'Well, we'll both dance to it!'

"Now, Mr. Tremain, it wasn't longer than it would take a man to call for a bottle of Scotch before swords were out and sparks flying. Back and forth it went, blade crossing blade in thrust and parry—a great roaring of oaths from my grandfather and a smashing of chairs and tables that stood in his path. Up and down this very tap-room they fought—the swords all a-quiver to be killing and the black night peeping in through the lattice.

"My grandfather was a grand swordsman, as he's told me himself in this very chimney corner. Few there were who'd faced his sabre and lived to tell of the matter. But tonight—what from it being Hallowe'en, when devils are strong and saints are weak—he was far from having his own way of it. This scarecrow of a man was like smoke to prick with a sword-point. Light he was as thistle-down, short at one moment and tall at the next, leaping about as nimble as a goat and with no sign of tiring. And now cold suspicion of the truth flowed into my grandfather's brain. Surely if this man were of flesh and blood he'd have been stretched on the floor long since. Perhaps it was Satan himself; or, at least, his lieutenant.

"But the Tibbit family are not easily daunted. Blinded with sweat he was, and shaking; but he fought on gallantly for all that, crying loudly on God to protect him. And then, as though in answer to his prayers, the point of the stranger's sword wavered; and my grandfather, thrusting forward with a hymn of praise on his lips, saw the point of his sword slip into the rascal as though he were made of green cheese—saw it slip in like a skewer in mutton and saw it come out again, all bright and shining.

"Now, being a man of quick perception, he knew for certain that something was amiss. Here was the blade of his sabre as clean as a whistle when it should have been red and dripping; and here was this ragged wisp of a swordsman hopping about as gay as a canary. It was enough to put the fear of the devil in a man, Mr. Tremain.

"Well, my grandfather staggered back against the wall from the fright of it, and all the wine went out of his head. So this was what came of sitting snug in a tap-room when he should have attended the burning of Anna Mulvane. Well, he was in for it now, and no dodging the issue. If only he could get the holy Bible out of his pocket to ward off this fiend from the pit.

"But there was no time for that now, Mr. Tremain, for the stranger was at him again like a cat on a mouse. Up and down the tap-room it went, swords rattling like the devil's dice-box, and my grandfather put to it to keep on his feet. Lucky it was for him that the hilt of his sabre was fashioned like a cross, which guarded him against the devilry afoot. Had it not been, he would have met death with his boots on, and not like a Christian in bed. But as it was, his head was swimming from the sweating fatigue of it, and his knees were clicking together like castanets, and his breath was whistling in his throat like the wind down this chimney. All in all, he was in no fit state for fence.

"Well, matters went on from bad to worse. Soon my grandfather got wandering a bit in his head. It seemed to him that the room was spinning around like a top. Faster and faster it went: and then, all of a sudden a great gust of wind pushed the tap-room door open and out of the night came a wild, wind-tossed company. Black, hairy lads were these, all dressed in silks and laces, marching in with a swing and a swagger—wild lads who had sailed the Spanish main, stained to the eyes with blood and treasure—rollicking bucks who would cut a throat for a bottle of grog or play a prank on a parson. In they marched, two by two, and formed a solemn ring about him—a ring of faces like you see in dreams, bearded all, with eyes red as coals in the gloaming.

"And as he fought wearily on, with hope of Heaven fast fading, the tattered swordsman before him burst out into song which the others soon raised to a roaring chorus. And now my grandfather felt that he, too, was singing, in spite of himself, and against all reason:

'Here's to Whitechapel Willie who sails the four seas,
He's known from Calcutta to Florida Keys.
With a puncheon of rum and a dirk in each hand,
In a snug little lugger a league from the land,
For wine and women and plenty of duff
He'd sink a whole fleet and not call it enough.
For he's Whitechapel Willie who sails the four seas,
Well known from Calcutta to Florida Keys.'

"And now he knew for certain with whom he had crossed swords on this black Hallowe'en, and all hope flickered out of him. Also he recognized two or three of the hairy lads who looked on—gentlemen of fortune these whom he had strung up right gaily at one time or another. And now that he felt that the devil had his own way with him, that it was useless to struggle further, he leaped back and snapped the blade of his sabre across his bent knee. What was left of it was but the hilt, made into the likeness of a cross as I have told you, Mr. Tremain. This he managed to clasp to his breast before he fell on the floor in a swoon."

Ben Tibbit broke off to throw another log of wood on the fire, which was dying down to red ashes. His neck lengthened incredibly for an instant as he bent forward to warm his wrinkled old hands.

"And who was this rollicking swordsman out of the night?" I asked. "Surely it was not Whitechapel Willie?"

"Aye, so my grandfather was thinking," said Ben Tibbit with a shake of his head. "Whitechapel Willie come down from the gallows-tree on a black Hallowe'en. But hear me out first, Mr. Tremain, and then you can be judging the matter.

"As I have told you, my grandfather had dropped in his tracks from fear or fatigue. How long he lay in a swoon on this tap-room floor he never knew; but, when he opened his eyes again, the place was as black as a pit. Not a candle glimmered, and the log in the fireplace had sputtered out, leaving the room as damp as a cellar.

"'Nancy!' he cried, sitting up in a fright. 'Nancy!'

"But there was no answer at all, just the whimper of the wind in the fireplace and the sad sigh of the waves on the beach. So he climbed to his feet and lighted one of the candles. Ghastly it was and silent, with broken furniture lying all about; but with no sign of woman or devil. My grandfather was fair sweating with fear.

"But he tramped from attic to cellar, stopping every now and then like a child in the dark to bellow 'Nancy! Nancy!' And then out he went into the night, which was graying with the first pallor of dawn. Long spirals of mist stole up from the grass and went creeping away in the dark; the stars were still bright overhead and winking; the wind had died down to a breath which just wagged the leaves on the birches.

"Giving no thought to Queen Bess, he tramped down to the beach where the waves were like weary sinners confessing. And standing there, his feet buried deep in the sand, he bellowed 'Nancy! Nancy!' over the breast of the sea.

"But there was no answer at all—just the sad waves confessing to the wickedness done out there beyond, and once the mournful cry of a gull. Lonely it was and drear, with the morning not born yet; and he was glad to turn way before his voice was quite gone.

"He plodded down the beach, still fuddled in his head from the night's devilry and not thinking or caring over-much where he might be going, when, all of a sudden, he heard a strange sound coming out of the mist far ahead. It was a shrill crowing sound like a cock makes on a dunghill, only louder and with a quaver to it which turned it into a wicked laugh most unpleasant to hear."

"Whitechapel Willie!" I broke in.

"So my grandfather was thinking, and he began to run. For now with the promise of dawn in the air, and Hallowe'en about spent, he was brave enough to face man or devil. On he ran with that wild laugh still stinging his ears, till soon he saw the gallows-tree looming up black through the mist—the gallows-tree and something that dangled there, jigging a bit on the heels of the wind."

"Whitechapel Willie?" I asked.

"Sure enough, Mr. Tremain—Whitechapel Willie. There he was, strung up for the world to see, a ball of dried meat that the birds might peck at, the same as he had been before Hallowe'en.

"But my grandfather had spied something else which made the hair on his head ruffle up. There, at the foot of the gallows, dim as a dream in the pallid dawn, was a queer shape all wrapped up in an old black cloak. Swinging back and forth like a gate in the wind, it crouched there in the dust. Forlorn and broken it was, like an old woman come to grieve on the graves of her dead; and it was only after he had stepped up to it that he knew it for Nancy.

"'My lass,' said he, severe as a judge of the land, 'why sit you here beneath the gallows-tree?'

"But she made him no answer—just stared up with wild eyes and broke out into a snatch of a song which ran something like this:

'The devil he put on the robe of a priest,
Sing high, sing low, my lasses;
So Willie and I sat long at the feast,
Sing high, sing low, my lasses.'

"'What ails you, Nancy?' cried my grandfather in a fright. 'Are you bewitched?'

"But still she made him no answer—just stared up, wild-eyed, at the gallows-tree and sang another snatch of her ribald ditty:

'Now Willie was merry as he could be,
Sing high, sing low, my lasses;
But the devil was rude to wink at me,
Sing high, sing low, my lasses.'

"Well, my grandfather clapped his great hand over her mouth, for he saw that all sense had been bewitched out of the girl, and feared she might sing something which she might have to burn for later. So he bottled up her music here and then and, picking her up in his arms, carried her back to Cockcrow Inn. And that about ends my story, Mr. Tremain."

"But how long was it before she regained her reason?" I asked, not at all satisfied.

"Never, rightly speaking. She was always breaking out into songs about Whitechapel Willie—some of them scandalous. I remember one time when I was a mite of a lad in church with her, and she piped up on a ditty which made the congregation stare, I can tell you."

"And your grandfather was willing to marry a mad woman?"

"He was so, Mr. Tremain. He was wont to say that his Nancy was better than a watchdog the way she'd pipe up if anyone stirred beneath stairs of a night. And then there was Cockcrow Inn to be considered. Was he going to let that slip through his fingers just because Nancy Greer wasn't as sensible as some?"

"Did he ever find out what had happened to her?" I asked.

Ben Tibbit flushed and shook his head. "Yes and no," said he. "Of course there were times when he had to close his ears to her pipings. There were ditties of hers that—well, the least said about them the better, Mr. Tremain. She's in her grave now, poor woman. Like a cackling goose she went about Cockcrow Inn in my childhood, mad as a hatter and merry—a handsome old dame despite her wild eyes and wilder music. There was the savor of the sea in her, Mr. Tremain—a wild, rollicking spirit which has hanged many a man, but which is rare to find in a woman. A chap could hear her from the attic to the cellar when she came out full blast with one of her ditties—all about rum and murder and pieces of eight."

"But the curse laid on your family?" I broke in. "Your necks? How did you come by them?"

Ben Tibbit made me no answer. Rising painfully to his feet, he began to blow out the candles which were guttering in their sockets. Picking up little Archibald by the belt and holding him at arm's length as though he were a large snapping turtle, he turned on the threshold for a last word.

"All the families have their skeletons," said he. "Well sir, I let ours out of the closet tonight to dance a bit for your pleasure, it being black Hallowe'en, when men grow talkative by the fireside. But I don't want you to be thinking that I'd throw mud at my own grandmother. No, sir. Nancy Greer was an honest lass; and, had she gone to the burning of Anna Mulvane, all this would not have happened. It was a slip that cost her dear and the Tibbits dearer. A good evening to you, Mr. Tremain."

WHEN HELL LAUGHED

Flavia Richardson

Published in Gruesome Cargoes *(1928)*

Flavia Richardson was the pseudonym of Christine Campbell Thomson (1897–1985), a British horror author, editor and literary agent. The daughter of Dr. Herbert Campbell Thomson, the nerve specialist, she found herself thrown into being a literary agent at an early age. Her first novels were *The Noble Army* and *Bourgoyne of Goyne* (both published by J. Bale & Co, 1921). By 1925 she was married to Oscar Cook, an Assistant District Officer who served in British North Borneo from 1911–1919, and had edited an anthology titled *Not at Night* (Selwyn and Blount). It would be the start of a landmark series, redefining what horror was and what could be achieved within the genre. CCT would go on to edit eleven original anthologies and one omnibus edition, with her and her husband both writing for them.

M. R. James wasn't a fan of the *Not at Night* series. In an essay entitled "Ghosts, Treat Them Gently" (*Evening News*, 17 April 1931), he remarked:

"On the whole, then, I say you must have horror and also malevolence. Not less necessary, however, is reticence. There is a series of books I have read, I think American in origin, called *Not at Night* (and with other like titles), which sin glaringly against this law [...] Of course, all writers of ghost stories do desire to make their readers' flesh creep; but these are shameless in their attempts. They are unbelievably crude and sudden, and they wallow in corruption. And if there is a theme that ought to be kept out of the ghost story, it is that of the charnel house. That and sex, wherein I do not say that these *Not at Night* books deal, but certainly other recent writers do, and in so doing spoil the whole business."

Thomson and Cook divorced in 1938; Cook's heavy drinking was the catalyst for their separation. Her autobiography, *I am a Literary Agent* (Sampson Low, 1951) barely touched upon her horror career. All of her short stories, bar one, were written under the "Flavia Richardson" name. *The Pan Book of Horror Stories* editor Herbert van Thal persuaded CCT to put pen to paper one last time with "Message to Margie" in *The Fifth Pan Book of Horror Stories*, a tale she described to anthologist Mike Ashley as her personal favourite. Although her ex-husband Oscar Cook died in 1952, she still managed his estate until her death, arranging reprints of his stories for a new generation to enjoy in the Pan Horror series—including his most celebrated tale, "Boomerang" (which was also adapted as an episode of Rod Serling's *Night Gallery*). Other pseudonyms used by CCT were Christine Hartley (for non-fiction occult titles *The Western Mystery Tradition* (1968) and *A Case for Reincarnation* (1972)), Dair Alexander (*Penelope's Daughter* (1975)), and, according to James A. Rock's *Who Goes There: A Bibliographic Dictionary* (1979), juvenile titles under the name Molly Campbell.

Christine Campbell Thomson died of natural causes on 29 September 1985.

CHESTER Warren crossed to the window, pulled up the blind and stared out into the garden. The night was wild and stormy; a watery moon rode high in the sky, obscured by dark clouds that hurried across her face and then passed on, jostled by their followers. The rose bush against the side of the house had come unfastened from the scraps of cloth that held it to the wall; long, loose tendrils flapped against the window panes, their wet tips on the wet glass making a squeaking noise.

The sight of the desolation outside made Chester Warren rub his hands with delight; it was what he had hoped for that evening. The ruin in the garden pleased him more than if he had seen it in the glory of the spring sunshine; the melancholy little lead figure in the fountain basin, dripping with water, was to him far more attractive than it had been a few days before when the fountain was playing and the spray from it watering immaculate turf.

Within the room all was warm and comfortable. A big blue chester-field had been drawn up in front of the fire and shaded copper lamps shed a soft light over the whole place.

As Chester turned back from the window, almost licking his lips and purring with excitement, a girl, stretched lazily on a white bear-skin before the hearth, raised herself on one elbow.

"How goes it?" she asked in a deep rich voice that seemed strangely ill-assorted with her small, slender body.

"Excellent. Couldn't be better," he replied, and again the voice struck a wrong note. It was as if they had changed tones, for while the girl's rich contralto would have suited the rather slight, pale man, his was a broken alto ruined by singing in his school choir as a boy after it should have been stopped.

The girl pulled herself further up on her elbow at the words and looked at him more closely. There was a curious, quizzical smile on her lips and a hint of almost fear in her eyes.

"You mean to try tonight?" she said, half hesitating.

"Certainly." He came over to the chesterfield as he spoke and let himself down on to the soft cushions with consummate care. All his movements had a hint of stealth about them; he gave an outsider the impression of walking like a huge Persian cat. As he sat there the light caught his high forehead and pointed ears; as a shadow flickered across from a falling log, Estelle, sitting on the rug, could have vowed that here was no man, but a faun, a satyr from the woods that bordered the garden.

She had felt the same uncanniness before when with him—yet she had promised to be his wife—why, no one knew. Some people said that Chester Warren had bewitched her; that he was not safe to be with after dark; that strange, uncanny things took place in his small, luxurious house thirty miles from London. But to all these innuendoes both Estelle and Chester himself turned deaf ears; yet she would have found it hard to explain the undeniable fascination he held for her.

The mere fact of her being in the house with him, alone, for the servants had all gone out, on All Hallows E'en was a proof of the thrall in which she was held. Normally rather super-conventional and old-fashioned, she had accepted his strange invitation without demur.

"We must wait a little longer," he said after a pause, and glancing at the clock as he spoke. "They won't be ready yet."

Estell shivered at the words.

"They?" she questioned.

"The spirits of the night," he retorted a little impatiently.

Outside the storm grew louder; they could hear the wind in the boughs of the shrubs and trees near by. Presently there was a terrific crash and the house seemed to shake. Estelle gave a terrible cry, but unheeding her Chester ran to the window.

"It's the great elm at the side of the lawn," he announced as he came back to the fire. "I thought it must be rotting inside."

For a few minutes he sat still again, contemplating his long, carefully tended finger-nails. Every now and then his eyes sought the clock. He was at ease and yet he was impatient. Estelle was growing more and more nervous. She began to wish she had not come that night. When he had asked her, had told her that he wanted for the first time to try a great experiment, to call up the Devil on All Hallows E'en, she had been half amused, half curious. Now she was becoming wholly frightened. That which had seemed an interesting experiment in which she scarcely believed, had now come to be a terrible undertaking fraught with horror.

At last the clock chimed half-past eleven, its mellow notes striking the air with a friendly, homely sound. Yet the mere suddenness of it caused Estelle to jump where she lay on the rug.

Chester laughed at her. "It is no good growing afraid," he said, and under the banter there was a hint of steel. "You said you'd like to help me in this, and I'm not going to let you off."

He got up as he spoke and pushed the chesterfield away from the fire and back against the wall. Estelle scrambled to her feet and helped him to roll up the bear-skin. The other rugs on the polished wooden floor were kicked aside. Going to a small cupboard, Chester fetched some white chalk and began to draw circles on the parquet. Three in all, with a broad space between each, which he sub-divided into small compartments.

"That's the beginning," he said, as Estelle watched him. "Now I've got to fill those compartments with the names of the Angels of the day and hour, of the Spirits guarding the season."

"Is that for protection?" she asked, as he fetched a small book from the cupboard and turned over the pages.

He nodded. "We'll want all the help we can get tonight," he said, marking a page with his finger. "It's the strongest night of the whole year, and if I'm calling up His Satanic Majesty I don't want to run too many riks. Listen to the wind! How it shrieks in the trees. It's a splendid night. Can't you feel the evil abroad and the witches riding in the high heavens?"

His high-pitched voice rose as he spoke, and Estelle shuddered.

"Must-must we go through with it tonight?" she whispered. "Wouldn't it be better, be safer to wait till another evening?"

Chester shook his head decidedly.

"Tonight!" he said in a tone so final that she did not dare open the subject again.

Having found the pages he needed in the book, he stooped once more to the circles of chalk and began to fill them in as directed, paying great attention to the instructions set down. Estelle did not say anything until he had finished.

"What happens next?" she asked, when he straightened himself again and slipped the ends of the chalk into the pocket of his coat.

"The incense. It's in the laboratory. Come and help me."

He stood aside for her to pass first into the hall, then preceded her again and unlocked the door opposite the sitting-room. The room on to which it gave was small and square, lighted by a large skylight, at that moment shrouded by a dark blind. Round two sides of the room ran a trestle table, heavily laden with retorts, crucibles and other chemical apparatus. The other two walls were composed of built-in cupboard. On a tripod over a small fire was a saucepan, from which issues a strange smell.

Instinctively Estelle drew back and sniffed the air as she crossed the threshold. The herbs in the saucepan made the place odorous like a church; the closed skylight rendered it stuffy.

"You've never been in here before?" asked Chester. "Of course I always keep it locked. It wouldn't do for the servants to come prowling round." And he gave a little falsetto laugh. "Strange things have been seen and heard in this room!"

Estelle shuddered. "I don't like it," she said. "Can't we go back to the sitting-room? Do you want that saucepan?"

"That, and several other things," he replied, going to one of the cupboards. "Look, here's my magic wand," he said, taking it from a shelf and holding it out to her. "A lovely thing, isn't it? It took me a long time to make that and render it powerful. I shall need it tonight. On that shelf is my crystal. One day I will read it for you and see the future that lies for us both."

Estelle was edging towards the door. The room had become more and more horrible; she was sure that it was full of unhealthy things, of spirits and ghouls, of eyes that watched and fingers that crept. She put one hand to her skirt and drew it closely round her, fearful lest something should catch hold of it.

Chester smiled, showing his white pointed teeth. Since he came into the laboratory he seemed to have changed a little. His ears had grown more pointed, his lips redder, his eyes narrower. He was more than ever like a coloured statue of a faun; there was something uncanny in the way he handled his magic properties. At last he had secured all that he thought necessary, and carrying the saucepan of boiling herbs with the utmost care, he let Estelle go back into the sitting-room, himself pausing to lock the door.

When he rejoined her, he found she was standing with her back to the dying fire, well out of the magic circles, eyes dilated.

"There is nothing to be afraid of, at any rate at present," he purred. "By-and-by you may see things that will be alarming. But if you obey my directions there will be not a scrap of danger. You and I are going to stand in the inmost circle, you holding me, and I holding the sacred pentacle which is under this cloth in my hand. Then no evil spirit, not even Satan, can have power over us. On the contrary, it will have to obey me in all things."

Estelle nodded. "What happens now?" she asked, trying to speak normally. Why had she ever come to the house that night?

"I am going to sprinkle the room with incense," he replied, putting a sprinkler into the strange liquid and scattering it over the room.

Everything in turn he touched, door, window, threshold, floor, reserving the greatest libations for the chalked circles.

Outside, the wind still shrieked and the rose tendrils tapped against the panes. It seemed to Estelle as if they were the fingers of spirits tapping at the glass, imploring entrance. She shivered as she saw Chester sprinkle the last drops of incense.

"Now," he said, "we are ready to begin. Estelle, come into the middle circle with me, and whatever you may see or hear, do not cry out and do not let go of my coat, or I may not be able to save you. If I accomplish what I am setting out to do, you will see a thing tonight that few people have succeeded in bringing up."

White to the lips, but mastered by his dominating personality and afraid to disobey, she staggered towards him and found herself in the middle of the sacred rings. Blindly she clung to him.

Filled with unholy joy and zeal, Chester raised his wand and began the incantation that should call up the spirits. Estelle, vaguely aware of the words, could make neither head nor tail of them; what she could understand seemed to be blasphemous, but for the most part the rites were carried on in an unknown tongue.

Higher and higher rose Chester's cracked alto, more and more emphatic became his words, more and more wild the waving of the magic wand. At last he ceased and for a moment there was silence.

"He's failed," thought Estelle to herself, and knew a great relief. She was about to say something when fear held her chained. On the outside of the third and largest circle, looking at them, was a strange being. He was twice the normal size, gold and green, with piercing eyes and what seemed long trails of hair.

But this was not what Chester wanted. With a stern command he caused this subsidiary spirit to disappear and again lifted up his voice in strenuous incantation. Suddenly the fire died out in the hearth, though a moment before it had been burning brightly. The lights had been extinguished before the beginning of the ceremonies, and the room was now in almost complete darkness. A grey light filtered in through the rain-washed window.

Chester waved the wand and exhorted again, and Estelle, sick with horror, could hear noises, voices, outside the window. Dark shadows fled across the grey panes, an ominous sound of tapping began on the glass as though someone desired admittance.

"Don't worry," Chester whispered swiftly. "They are only the advance guard; the spirits that are abroad tonight because it is All Hallows E'en. This is a wonderful night; we are getting on far better than I had dared to hope. Be brave, Estelle. I shall succeed this time, I think," he added, abruptly breaking off as a large grey cat appeared on the edge of the second circle.

It sat up before them, eyeing them curiously, then raised its back and spat violently seven times. The spittle reached the chalk line of the third circle but did not encroach over it. Then with a sound between a wail and an agonized cat-cry, the ghostly animal disappeared. At that moment, still retaining her hold of Chester's coat sleeve, Estelle quietly fainted.

She was fortunate to be spared the sights and sounds that came quickly afterwards. Careless of her plight, too far advanced to be able to stop, even had he wished to do so, Chester started the third portion of the incantation, working himself up to a frenzy of excitement, shrieking his words, foaming wildly.

Of a sudden the room was full of beings, grey, ghastly beings called up by his will. They flocked from every side, advancing to the edge of the third circle, mowing and gibbering, stretching out bony hands to clutch him but unable to lay hold. For a moment or two he watched them, wrapped in wonder and admiration at what he had been able to do. On the outside of the second circle was a strange great dog, that bayed dismally each moment, adding still more horror to the scene.

All at once a strange and awful silence fell upon that terrible company. A chill breath as of a charnel house passed through the room; even the dog ceased to bay. There was an unholy awful stillness as of the approach of some Supreme Being, foully, unutterably evil, before which these vile things were nothing.

Chester felt it coming; with all his might he held on to his wits; he had called it; he would be its master; by the power given to him through years of study he could control it; he would not fail himself and his highest ambition at this dread moment.

Bracing himself on his heels he stood still, awed by the strange silence, prepared for whatever he might see. The many shapes before his eyes melted into thin air, leaving the room clear of their filthy presence. But over and above all persisted that foul smell of death, and Chester was aware that he and Estelle were not alone. Something was coming, something was materializing.

Straining his eyes, he focussed on a certain spot on the outermost circle where the shadows seemed to be thickest. As he watched they seemed to assume a shape, and as the shape gathered in density and form, an awful clangour started round about, a noise of laughter born in hell, of tortured souls and fiends' delight.

The shape grew larger and larger, and he began to define it. In the centre of the smoke-clouds a figure began to appear, a figure in black and gold, with burning, red-hot eyes, a glance from which seemed to sear his eyeballs and penetrate to the brain.

"Sathanas!" cried Chester, waving his wand in the air.

The figure advanced to the edge of the third circle and put out a hand that shone like newly minted gold.

Suddenly Chester knew fear, and worse than fear, blind panic. What was this he had called up to do his bidding? Who was he to demand tribute from the King of Hell? He had thrown himself and Estelle into the hands of the Power of Darkness by his own will. The figure loomed larger and nearer; he was safe, he knew, inside the third circle with the mystic signs at his feet, but only so long as he could control his own soul, master his own emotions.

Half blind with terror he put out his hands, one holding the wand, the other the sacred pentacle. At the sight of it the figure swayed and drew back a pace, while the smoke clouds around him grew dimmer and the hellish noises less. Leaning forward, Chester stretched out his arm with the pentacle, and again the figure swayed and withdrew another pace, though this time the noises increased, as though Hell raged to see its master defied.

The fumes from the incense were rising up from the floor. Chester felt himself slipping; he struggled to regain his strength, knowing that one false move while that terrible thing was before him would mean his destruction. The noises above redoubled in fury, and it seemed to him now as if there were a triumphant note amid the laughter, a note of raucous, filthy joy. Overcome with sudden lassitude, he staggered and dropped the pentacle!

The servants, returning early next morning from the friends who had put them up after a late dance at a fair, found the house open but the sitting-room door locked. When they went round to the garden window they found the grass beneath it scorched and blackened.

Within the room, in the middle of three chalk circles, lay the body of Chester Warren, seared and charred as if he had been struck by lightning, while in the corner of the room, cowering behind the chesterfield was a white-haired, gibbering girl, who shrieked and screamed and babbled of things it was not good to hear.

ALL SOULS'

Edith Wharton

Published in Ghosts, *1937*

Edith Wharton (1862–1937) was an American writer whose best-known works are *The House of Mirth* (1905) and *The Age of Innocence* (1920), for which Edith won the Pulitzer Prize, becoming the first woman ever to do so. Edith (née Edith Newbold Jones) was born into extreme wealth, with some theorizing that the phrase "keeping up with the Joneses" began as a reference to her family name. Her early work was published anonymously or under pseudonyms since her family looked down on writing as an unworthy endeavour. As well as writing novels, she wrote over eighty short stories and published the celebrated collections of uncanny stories *Tales of Men and Ghosts* (1910) and *Xingu and Other Stories* (1916), among others.

"All Souls'" was one of the last tales that Edith Wharton wrote, included alongside the author's personal selection of her favourite stories in *Ghosts,* published in October 1937 following Wharton's death on 11 August of the same year. The collection bore the dedication: "I entrust my spectral strap-hangers in gratitude and admiration to Walter de la Mare".

QUEER and inexplicable as the business was, on the surface it appeared fairly simple—at the time, at least; but with the passing of years, and owing to there not having been a single witness of what happened except Sara Clayburn herself, the stories about it have become so exaggerated, and often so ridiculously inaccurate, that it seems necessary that some one connected with the affair, though not actually present—I repeat that when it happened my cousin was (or thought she was) quite alone in her house—should record the few facts actually known.

In those days I was often at Whitegates (as the place had always been called)—I was there, in fact, not long before, and almost immediately after, the strange happenings of those thirty-six hours. Jim Clayburn and his widow were both my cousins, and because of that, and of my intimacy with them, both families think I am more likely than anybody else to be able to get at the facts, as far as they can be called facts, and as anybody can get at them. So I have written down, as clearly as I could, the gist of the various talks I had with cousin Sara, when she could be got to talk—it wasn't often—about what occurred during that mysterious week-end.

I read the other day in a book by a fashionable essayist that ghosts went out when electric light came in. What nonsense! The writer, though he is fond of dabbling, in a literary way, in the supernatural, hasn't even reached the threshold of his subject. As between turreted castles patrolled by headless victims with clanking chains, and the comfortable suburban house with a refrigerator and central heating where you feel, as soon as you're in it, *that there's something wrong*, give me the latter for sending a chill down the spine! And, by the way, haven't you noticed that it's generally not the high-strung and imaginative who see ghosts, but the calm matter-of-fact people who don't believe in them, and are sure they wouldn't mind if they did see one? Well, that was the case with Sara Clayburn and her house. The house, in spite of its age—it was built, I believe, about 1780—was open, airy, high-ceilinged, with electricity, central heating and all the modern appliances; and its mistress was—well, very much like her house. And, anyhow, this isn't exactly a ghost-story, and I've dragged in the analogy only as a way of showing you what kind of woman my cousin was, and how unlikely it would have seemed that what happened at Whitegates should have happened just there—or to her.

When Jim Clayburn died the family all thought that, as the couple had no children, his widow would give up Whitegates and move either to New York or Boston—for being of good Colonial stock, with many relatives and friends, she would have found a place ready for her in either. But Sally Clayburn seldom did what other people expected, and in this case she did exactly the contrary: she stayed at Whitegates.

"What, turn my back on the old house—tear up all the family roots, and go and hang myself up in a birdcage flat in one of those new skyscrapers in Lexington Avenue, with a bunch of chickweed and a cuttle-fish to replace my good Connecticut mutton? No, thank you. Here I belong, and here I stay till my executors hand the place over to Jim's next of kin— that stupid fat Presley boy… Well, don't let's talk about him. But I tell you what—I'll keep him out of here as long as I can." And she did—for being still in the early fifties when her husband died, and a muscular, resolute figure of a woman, she was more than a match for the fat Presley boy, and attended his funeral a few years ago, in correct mourning, with a faint smile under her veil.

Whitegates was a pleasant hospitable-looking house, on a height overlooking the stately windings of the Connecticut river; but it was five or six miles from Norrington, the nearest town, and its situation would certainly have seemed remote and lonely to modern servants. Luckily, however, Sara Clayburn had inherited from her mother-in-law two or three old stand-bys who seemed as much a part of the family tradition as the roof they lived under; and I never heard of her having any trouble in her domestic arrangements.

The house, in Colonial days, had been four-square, with four spacious rooms on the ground-floor, an oak-floored hall dividing them, the usual kitchen-extension at the back, and a good attic under the roof. But Jim's grand-parents, when interest in the "Colonial" began to revive, in the early 'eighties, had added two wings, at right angles to the south front, so that the old "circle" before the front door became a grassy court, enclosed on three sides, with a big elm in the middle. Thus the house was turned into a roomy dwelling, in which the last three generations of Clayburns had exercised a large hospitality; but the architect had respected the character of the old house, and the enlargement made it more comfortable without lessening its simplicity. There was a lot of land about it, and Jim Clayburn, like his fathers before him, farmed it, not without profit, and played a considerable and respected part in state politics. The Clayburns were always spoken of as a "good influence" in the county, and the townspeople were glad when they learned that Sara did not mean to desert the place— "though it must be lonesome, winters, living all alone up there atop of that hill," they remarked as the days shortened, and the first snow began to pile up under the quadruple row of elms along the common.

Well, if I've given you a sufficiently clear idea of Whitegates and the Clayburns—who shared with their old house a sort of reassuring order-liness and dignity—I'll efface myself, and tell the tale, not in my cousin's words, for they were too confused and fragmentary, but as I built it up gradually out of her half-avowals and nervous reticences. If the thing happened at all—and I must leave you to judge of that—I think it must have happened in this way...

I

The morning had been bitter, with a driving sleet—though it was only the last day of October—but after lunch a watery sun showed for a while through banked-up woolly clouds, and tempted Sara Clayburn out. She was an energetic walker, and given, at that season, to tramping three or four miles along the valley road, and coming back by way of Shaker's wood. She had made her usual round, and was following the main drive to the house when she overtook a plainly dressed woman walking in the same direction. If the scene had not been so lonely—the way to Whitegates at the end of an autumn day was not a frequented one—Mrs. Clayburn might not have paid any attention to the woman, for she was in no way noticeable; but when she caught up with the intruder my cousin was surprised to find that she was a stranger—for the mistress of Whitegates prided herself on knowing, at least by sight, most of her country neighbours. It was almost dark, and the woman's face was hardly visible; but Mrs. Clayburn told me she recalled her as middle-aged, plain and rather pale.

Mrs. Clayburn greeted her, and then added: "You're going to the house?"

"Yes, ma'am," the woman answered, in a voice that the Connecticut valley in old days would have called "foreign," but that would have been unnoticed by ears used to the modern multiplicity of tongues. "No, I couldn't say where she came from," Sara always said. "What struck me as queer was that I didn't know her."

She asked the woman, politely, what she wanted, and the woman answered: "Only to see one of the girls." The answer was natural enough, and Mrs. Clayburn nodded and turned off from the drive to the lower part of the gardens, so that she saw no more of the visitor then or afterward. And, in fact, a half hour later something happened which put the stranger entirely out of her mind. The brisk and light-footed Mrs. Clayburn, as she approached the house, slipped on a frozen puddle, turned her ankle and lay suddenly helpless.

*

Price, the butler, and Agnes, the dour old Scottish maid whom Sara had inherited from her mother-in-law, of course knew exactly what to do. In no time they had their mistress stretched out on a lounge, and Dr. Selgrove had been called up from Norrington. When he arrived, he ordered Mrs. Clayburn to bed, did the necessary examining and bandaging, and shook his head over her ankle, which he feared was fractured. He thought, however, that if she would swear not to get up, or even shift the position of her leg, he could spare her the discomfort of putting it in plaster. Mrs. Clayburn agreed, the more promptly as the doctor warned her that any rash movement would prolong her immobility. Her quick imperious nature made the prospect trying, and she was annoyed with herself for having been so clumsy. But the mischief was done, and she immediately thought what an opportunity she would have for going over her accounts and catching up with her correspondence. So she settled down resignedly in her bed.

"And you won't miss much, you know, if you have to stay there a few days. It's beginning to snow, and it looks as if we were in for a good spell of it," the doctor remarked, glancing through the window as he gathered up his implements. "Well, we don't often get snow here as early as this; but winter's got to begin sometime," he concluded philosophically. At the door he stopped to add: "You don't want me to send up a nurse from Norrington? Not to nurse you, you know; there's nothing much to do till I see you again. But this is a pretty lonely place when the snow begins, and I thought maybe—"

Sara Clayburn laughed. "Lonely? With my old servants? You forget how many winters I've spent here alone with them. Two of them were with me in my mother-in-law's time."

"That's so," Dr. Selgrove agreed. "You're a good deal luckier than most people, that way. Well, let me see; this is Saturday. We'll have to let the inflammation go down before we can X-ray you. Monday morning, first thing, I'll be here with the X-ray man. If you want me sooner, call me up." And he was gone.

The foot, at first, had not been very painful; but toward the small hours Mrs. Clayburn began to suffer. She was a bad patient, like most healthy and active people. Not being used to pain she did not know how to bear it; and the hours of wakefulness and immobility seemed endless. Agnes, before leaving her, had made everything as comfortable as possible. She had put a jug of lemonade within reach, and had even (Mrs. Clayburn thought it odd afterward) insisted on bringing in a tray with sandwiches and a thermos of tea. "In case you're hungry in the night, madam."

"Thank you; but I'm never hungry in the night. And I certainly shan't be tonight—only thirsty. I think I'm feverish."

"Well, there's the lemonade, madam."

"That will do. Take the other things away, please." (Sara had always hated the sight of unwanted food "messing about" in her room.)

"Very well, madam. Only you might—"

"Please take it away," Mrs. Clayburn repeated irritably.

"Very good, madam." But as Agnes went out, her mistress heard her set the tray down softly on a table behind the screen which shut off the door.

"Obstinate old goose!" she thought, rather touched by the old woman's insistence.

Sleep, once it had gone, would not return, and the long black hours moved more and more slowly. How late the dawn came in November! "If only I could move my leg," she grumbled.

She lay still and strained her ears for the first steps of the servants. Whitegates was an early house, its mistress setting the example; it would surely not be long now before one of the women came. She was tempted to ring for Agnes, but refrained. The woman had been up late, and this was Sunday morning, when the household was always allowed a little extra time. Mrs. Clayburn reflected restlessly: "I was a fool not to let her leave the tea beside the bed, as she wanted to. I wonder if I could get up and get it?" But she remembered the doctor's warning, and dared not move. Anything rather than risk prolonging her imprisonment…

Ah, there was the stable-clock striking. How loud it sounded in the snowy stillness! One—two—three—four—five…

What? Only five? Three hours and a quarter more before she could hope to hear the door-handle turned… After a while she dozed off again, uncomfortably.

Another sound aroused her. Again the stable-clock. She listened. But the room was still in deep darkness, and only six strokes fell… She thought of reciting something to put her to sleep; but she seldom read poetry, and being naturally a good sleeper, she could not remember any of the usual devices against insomnia. The whole of her leg felt like lead now. The bandages had grown terribly tight—her ankle must have swollen… She lay staring at the dark windows, watching for the first glimmer of dawn. At last she saw a pale filter of daylight through the shutters. One by one the objects between the bed and the window recovered first their out-line, then their bulk, and seemed to be stealthily re-grouping themselves, after goodness knows what secret displacements during the night. Who that has lived in an old house could possibly believe that the furniture in it stays still all night? Mrs. Clayburn almost fancied she saw one little slender-legged table slipping hastily back into its place.

"It knows Agnes is coming, and it's afraid," she thought whimsically. Her bad night must have made her imaginative, for such nonsense as that about the furniture had never occurred to her before…

At length, after hours more, as it seemed, the stable-clock struck eight. Only another quarter of an hour. She watched the hand moving slowly across the face of the little clock beside her bed… Ten minutes… five… only five! Agnes was as punctual as destiny… in two minutes now she would come. The two minutes passed, and she did not come. Poor Agnes—she had looked pale and tired the night before. She had overslept herself, no doubt—or perhaps she felt ill, and would send the housemaid to replace her. Mrs. Clayburn waited.

She waited half an hour; then she reached up to the bell at the head of the bed. Poor old Agnes—her mistress felt guilty about waking her. But Agnes did not appear—and after a considerable interval Mrs. Clayburn, now with a certain impatience, rang again. She rang once; twice; three times—but still no one came.

Once more she waited; then she said to herself: "There must be something wrong with the electricity." Well—she could find out by switching on the bed-lamp at her elbow (how admirably the room was equipped with every practical appliance!). She switched it on—but no light came. Electric current cut off; and it was Sunday, and nothing could be done about it till the next morning. Unless it turned out to be just a burnt-out fuse, which Price could remedy. Well, in a moment now some one would surely come to her door.

It was nine o'clock before she admitted to herself that something uncommonly strange must have happened in the house. She began to feel a nervous apprehension; but she was not the woman to encourage it. If only she had had the telephone put in her room, instead of out on the landing! She measured mentally the distance to be travelled, remembered Dr. Selgrove's admonition, and wondered if her broken ankle would carry her there. She dreaded the prospect of being put in plaster, but she had to get to the telephone, whatever happened.

She wrapped herself in her dressing-gown, found a walking stick, and resting heavily on it, dragged herself to the door. In her bedroom the careful Agnes had closed and fastened the shutters, so that it was not much lighter there than at dawn; but outside in the corridor the cold whiteness of the snowy morning seemed almost reassuring. Mysterious things—dreadful things—were associated with darkness; and here was the wholesome prosaic daylight come again to banish them. Mrs. Clayburn looked about her and listened. Silence. A deep nocturnal silence in that day-lit house, in which five people were presumably coming and going about their work. It was certainly strange… She looked out of the window, hoping to see some one crossing the court or coming along the drive.

But no one was in sight, and the snow seemed to have the place to itself: a quiet steady snow. It was still falling, with a business-like regularity, muffling the outer world in layers on layers of thick white velvet, and intensifying the silence within. A noiseless world—were people so sure that absence of noise was what they wanted? Let them first try a lonely country-house in a November snow-storm!

She dragged herself along the passage to the telephone. When she unhooked the receiver she noticed that her hand trembled.

She rang up the pantry—no answer. She rang again. Silence—more silence! It seemed to be piling itself up like the snow on the roof and in the gutters. Silence. How many people that she knew had any idea what silence was—and how loud it sounded when you really listened to it?

Again she waited; then she rang up "Central." No answer. She tried three times. After that she tried the pantry again... The telephone was cut off, then; like the electric current. Who was at work downstairs, isolating her thus from the world? Her heart began to hammer. Luckily there was a chair near the telephone, and she sat down to recover her strength—or was it her courage?

Agnes and the housemaid slept in the nearest wing. She would certainly get as far as that when she had pulled herself together. Had she the courage—? Yes; of course she had. She had always been regarded as a plucky woman; and had so regarded herself. But this silence—

It occurred to her that by looking from the window of a neighbouring bathroom she could see the kitchen chimney. There ought to be smoke coming from it at that hour; and if there were she thought she would be less afraid to go on. She got as far as the bathroom and looking through the window saw that no smoke came from the chimney. Her sense of loneliness grew more acute. Whatever had happened below stairs must have happened before the morning's work had begun. The cook had not had time to light the fire, the other servants had not yet begun their round. She sank down on the nearest chair, struggling against her fears. What next would she discover if she carried on her investigations?

The pain in her ankle made progress difficult; but she was aware of it now only as an obstacle to haste. No matter what it cost her in physical suffering, she must find out what was happening below stairs—or had happened. But first she would go to the maid's room. And if that were empty—well, somehow she would have to get herself downstairs.

She limped along the passage, and on the way steadied herself by resting her hand on a radiator. It was stone-cold. Yet in that well-ordered house in winter the central heating, though damped down at night, was never allowed to go out, and by eight in the morning a mellow warmth pervaded the rooms. The icy chill of the pipes startled her. It was the chauffeur who looked after the heating—so he too was involved in the mystery, whatever it was, as well as the house-servants. But this only deepened the problem.

III

At Agnes's door Mrs. Clayburn paused and knocked. She expected no answer, and there was none. She opened the door and went in. The room was dark and very cold. She went to the window and flung back the shutters; then she looked slowly around, vaguely apprehensive of what she might see. The room was empty; but what frightened her was not so much its emptiness as its air of scrupulous and undisturbed order. There was no sign of any one having lately dressed in it—or undressed the night before. And the bed had not been slept in.

Mrs. Clayburn leaned against the wall for a moment; then she crossed the floor and opened the cupboard. That was where Agnes kept her dresses; and the dresses were there, neatly hanging in a row. On the shelf above were Agnes's few and unfashionable hats, rearrangements of her mistress's old ones. Mrs. Clayburn, who knew them all, looked at the shelf, and saw that one was missing. And so was also the warm winter coat she had given to Agnes the previous winter.

The woman was out, then; had gone out, no doubt, the night before, since the bed was unslept in, the dressing and washing appliances untouched. Agnes, who never set foot out of the house after dark, who despised the movies as much as she did the wireless, and could never be persuaded that a little innocent amusement was a necessary element in life, had deserted the house on a snowy winter night, while her mistress lay upstairs, suffering and helpless! Why had she gone, and where had she gone? When she was undressing Mrs. Clayburn the night before, taking her orders, trying to make her more comfortable, was she already planning this mysterious nocturnal escape? Or had something—the mysterious and dreadful Something for the clue of which Mrs. Clayburn was still groping—occurred later in the evening, sending the maid downstairs and out of doors into the bitter night? Perhaps one of the men at the garage— where the chauffeur and gardener lived—had been suddenly taken ill, and some one had run up to the house for Agnes. Yes—that must be the explanation… Yet how much it left unexplained.

Next to Agnes's room was the linen-room; beyond that was the house-maid's door. Mrs. Clayburn went to it and knocked. "Mary!" No one answered, and she went in. The room was in the same immaculate order as her maid's, and here too the bed was unslept in, and there were no signs of dressing or undressing. The two women had no doubt gone out together—gone where?

More and more the cold unanswering silence of the house weighed down on Mrs. Clayburn. She had never thought of it as a big house, but now, in this snowy winter light, it seemed immense, and full of ominous corners around which one dared not look.

Beyond the housemaid's room were the back-stairs. It was the nearest way down, and every step that Mrs. Clayburn took was increasingly pain-ful; but she decided to walk slowly back, the whole length of the passage, and go down by the front stairs. She did not know why she did this; but she felt that at the moment she was past reasoning, and had better obey her instinct.

More than once she had explored the ground-floor alone in the small hours, in search of unwonted midnight noises; but now it was not the idea of noises that frightened her, but that inexorable and hostile silence, the sense that the house had retained in full daylight its nocturnal mystery, and was watching her as she was watching it; that in entering those empty orderly rooms she might be disturbing some unseen confabulation on which beings of flesh-and-blood had better not intrude.

The broad oak stairs were beautifully polished, and so slippery that she had to cling to the rail and let herself down tread by tread. And as she descended, the silence descended with her—heavier, denser, more absolute. She seemed to feel its steps just behind her, softly keeping time with hers. It had a quality she had never been aware of in any other silence, as though it were not merely an absence of sound, a thin barrier between the ear and the surging murmur of life just beyond, but an impenetrable substance made out of the worldwide cessation of all life and all movement.

Yes, that was what laid a chill on her: the feeling that there was no limit to this silence, no outer margin, nothing beyond it. By this time she had reached the foot of the stairs and was limping across the hall to the drawing-room. Whatever she found there, she was sure, would be mute and lifeless; but what would it be? The bodies of her dead servants, mown down by some homicidal maniac? And what if it were her turn next—if he were waiting for her behind the heavy curtains of the room she was about to enter? Well, she must find out—she must face whatever lay in wait. Not impelled by bravery—the last drop of courage had oozed out of her—but because anything, anything was better than to remain shut up in that snow-bound house without knowing whether she was alone in it or not. "I must find that out, I must find that out," she repeated to herself in a sort of meaningless sing-song.

The cold outer light flooded the drawing-room. The shutters had not been closed, nor the curtains drawn. She looked about her. The room was empty, and every chair in its usual place. Her armchair was pushed up by the chimney, and the cold hearth was piled with the ashes of the fire at which she had warmed herself before starting on her ill-fated walk. Even her empty coffee cup stood on a table near the armchair. It was evident that the servants had not been in the room since she had left it the day before after luncheon. And suddenly the conviction entered into her that, as she found the drawing-room, so she would find the rest of the house: cold, orderly—and empty. She would find nothing, she would find no one. She no longer felt any dread of ordinary human dangers lurking in those dumb spaces ahead of her. She knew she was utterly alone under her own roof. She sat down to rest her aching ankle, and looked slowly about her.

There were the other rooms to be visited, and she was determined to go through them all—but she knew in advance that they would give no answer to her question. She knew it, seemingly, from the quality of the silence which enveloped her. There was no break, no thinnest crack in it anywhere. It had the cold continuity of the snow which was still falling steadily outside.

She had no idea how long she waited before nerving herself to continue her inspection. She no longer felt the pain in her ankle, but was only conscious that she must not bear her weight on it, and therefore moved very slowly, supporting herself on each piece of furniture in her path. On the ground-floor no shutter had been closed, no curtain drawn, and she progressed without difficulty from room to room: the library, her morning-room, the dining-room. In each of them, every piece of furniture was in its usual place. In the dining-room, the table had been laid for her dinner of the previous evening, and the candelabra, with candles unlit, stood reflected in the dark mahogany. She was not the kind of woman to nibble a poached egg on a tray when she was alone, but always came down to the dining-room, and had what she called a civilized meal.

The back premises remained to be visited. From the dining-room she entered the pantry, and there too everything was in irreproachable order. She opened the door and looked down the back passage with its neat linoleum floor-covering. The deep silence accompanied her; she still felt it moving watchfully at her side, as though she were its prisoner and it might throw itself upon her if she attempted to escape. She limped on toward the kitchen. That of course would be empty too, and immaculate. But she must see it.

She leaned a minute in the embrasure of a window in the passage. "It's like the Mary Celeste—a Mary Celeste on *terra firma*," she thought, recalling the unsolved sea-mystery of her childhood. "No one ever knew what happened on board the Mary Celeste. And perhaps no one will ever know what has happened here. Even I shan't know."

At the thought her latent fear seemed to take on a new quality. It was like an icy liquid running through every vein, and lying in a pool about her heart. She understood now that she had never before known what fear was, and that most of the people she had met had probably never known either. For this sensation was something quite different…

It absorbed her so completely that she was not aware how long she remained leaning there. But suddenly a new impulse pushed her forward, and she walked on toward the scullery. She went there first because there was a service-slide in the wall, through which she might peep into the kitchen without being seen; and some indefinable instinct told her that the kitchen held the clue to the mystery. She still felt strongly that what-ever had happened in the house must have its source and centre in the kitchen.

In the scullery, as she had expected, everything was clean and tidy. Whatever had happened, no one in the house appeared to have been taken by surprise; there was nowhere any sign of confusion or disorder. "It looks as if they'd known beforehand, and put everything straight," she thought. She glanced at the wall facing the door, and saw that the slide was open. And then, as she was approaching it, the silence was broken. A voice was speaking in the kitchen—a man's voice, low but emphatic, and which she had never heard before.

She stood still, cold with fear. But this fear was again a different one. Her previous terrors had been speculative, conjectural, a ghostly ema-nation of the surrounding silence. This was a plain every-day dread of evil-doers. Oh, God, why had she not remembered her husband's revolver, which ever since his death had lain in a drawer in her room?

She turned to retreat across the smooth slippery floor but half-way her stick slipped from her, and crashed down on the tiles. The noise seemed to echo on and on through the emptiness, and she stood still, aghast. Now that she had betrayed her presence, flight was useless. Whoever was beyond the kitchen door would be upon her in a second...

But to her astonishment the voice went on speaking. It was as though neither the speaker nor his listeners had heard her. The invisible stranger spoke so low that she could not make out what he was saying, but the tone was passionately earnest, almost threatening. The next moment she realized that he was speaking in a foreign language, a language unknown to her. Once more her terror was surmounted by the urgent desire to know what was going on, so close to her yet unseen. She crept to the slide, peered cautiously through into the kitchen, and saw that it was as orderly and empty as the other rooms. But in the middle of the carefully scoured table stood a portable wireless, and the voice she heard came out of it...

She must have fainted then, she supposed; at any rate she felt so weak and dizzy that her memory of what next happened remained indistinct. But in the course of time she groped her way back to the pantry, and there found a bottle of spirits—brandy or whisky, she could not remember which. She found a glass, poured herself a stiff drink, and while it was flushing through her veins, managed, she never knew with how many shuddering delays, to drag herself through the deserted ground-floor, up the stairs, and down the corridor to her own room. There, apparently, she fell across the threshold, again unconscious...

When she came to, she remembered, her first care had been to lock herself in; then to recover her husband's revolver. It was not loaded, but she found some cartridges, and succeeded in loading it. Then she remembered that Agnes, on leaving her the evening before, had refused to carry away the tray with the tea and sandwiches, and she fell on them with a sudden hunger. She recalled also noticing that a flask of brandy had been put beside the thermos, and being vaguely surprised. Agnes's departure, then, had been deliberately planned, and she had known that her mistress, who never touched spirits, might have need of a stimulant before she returned. Mrs. Clayburn poured some of the brandy into her tea, and swallowed it greedily.

After that (she told me later) she remembered that she had managed to start a fire in her grate, and after warming herself, had got back into her bed, piling on it all the coverings she could find. The afternoon passed in a haze of pain, out of which there emerged now and then a dim shape of fear—the fear that she might lie there alone and untended till she died of cold, and of the terror of her solitude. For she was sure by this time that the house was empty—completely empty, from garret to cellar. She knew it was so, she could not tell why; but again she felt that it must be because of the peculiar quality of the silence—the silence which had dogged her steps wherever she went, and was now folded down on her like a pall. She was sure that the nearness of any other human being, however dumb and secret, would have made a faint crack in the texture of that silence, flawed it as a sheet of glass is flawed by a pebble thrown against it…

I V

"Is that easier?" the doctor asked, lifting himself from bending over her ankle. He shook his head disapprovingly. "Looks to me as if you'd disobeyed orders—eh? Been moving about, haven't you? And I guess Dr. Selgrove told you to keep quiet till he saw you again, didn't he?"

The speaker was a stranger, whom Mrs. Clayburn knew only by name. Her own doctor had been called away that morning to the bedside of an old patient in Baltimore, and had asked this young man, who was beginning to be known at Norrington, to replace him. The newcomer was shy, and somewhat familiar, as the shy often are, and Mrs. Clayburn decided that she did not much like him. But before she could convey this by the tone of her reply (and she was past-mistress of the shades of disapproval) she heard Agnes speaking—yes, Agnes, the same, the usual Agnes, standing behind the doctor, neat and stern-looking as ever. "Mrs. Clayburn must have got up and walked about in the night instead of ringing for me, as she'd ought to," Agnes intervened severely.

This was too much! In spite of the pain, which was now exquisite, Mrs. Clayburn laughed. "Ringing for you? How could I, with the electricity cut off?"

"The electricity cut off?" Agnes's surprise was masterly. "Why, when was it cut off?" She pressed her finger on the bell beside the bed, and the call tinkled through the quiet room. "I tried that bell before I left you last night, madam, because if there'd been anything wrong with it I'd have come and slept in the dressing-room sooner than leave you here alone."

Mrs. Clayburn lay speechless, staring up at her. "Last night? But last night I was all alone in the house."

Agnes's firm features did not alter. She folded her hands resignedly across her trim apron. "Perhaps the pain's made you a little confused, madam." She looked at the doctor, who nodded.

"The pain in your foot must have been pretty bad," he said.

"It was," Mrs. Clayburn replied. "But it was nothing to the horror of being left alone in this empty house since the day before yesterday, with the heat and the electricity cut off, and the telephone not working."

The doctor was looking at her in evident wonder. Agnes's sallow face flushed slightly, but only as if in indignation at an unjust charge. "But, madam, I made up your fire with my own hands last night—and look, it's smouldering still. I was getting ready to start it again just now, when the doctor came."

"That's so. She was down on her knees before it," the doctor corroborated.

Again Mrs. Clayburn laughed. Ingeniously as the tissue of lies was being woven about her, she felt she could still break through it. "I made up the fire myself yesterday—there was no one else to do it," she said, addressing the doctor, but keeping her eyes on her maid. "I got up twice to put on more coal, because the house was like a sepulchre. The central heating must have been out since Saturday afternoon."

At this incredible statement Agnes's face expressed only a polite distress; but the new doctor was evidently embarrassed at being drawn into an unintelligible controversy with which he had no time to deal. He said he had brought the X-ray photographer with him, but that the ankle was too much swollen to be photographed at present. He asked Mrs. Clayburn to excuse his haste, as he had all Dr. Selgrove's patients to visit besides his own, and promised to come back that evening to decide whether she could be X-rayed then, and whether, as he evidently feared, the ankle would have to be put in plaster. Then, handing his prescriptions to Agnes, he departed.

Mrs. Clayburn spent a feverish and suffering day. She did not feel well enough to carry on the discussion with Agnes; she did not ask to see the other servants. She grew drowsy, and understood that her mind was confused with fever. Agnes and the housemaid waited on her as attentively as usual, and by the time the doctor returned in the evening her temperature had fallen; but she decided not to speak of what was on her mind until Dr. Selgrove reappeared. He was to be back the following evening, and the new doctor preferred to wait for him before deciding to put the ankle in plaster—though he feared this was now inevitable.

v

That afternoon Mrs. Clayburn had me summoned by telephone, and I arrived at Whitegates the following day. My cousin, who looked pale and nervous, merely pointed to her foot, which had been put in plaster, and thanked me for coming to keep her company. She explained that Dr. Selgrove had been taken suddenly ill in Baltimore, and would not be back for several days, but that the young man who replaced him seemed fairly competent. She made no allusion to the strange incidents I have set down, but I felt at once that she had received a shock which her accident, however painful, could not explain.

Finally, one evening, she told me the story of her strange week-end, as it had presented itself to her unusually clear and accurate mind, and as I have recorded it above. She did not tell me this till several weeks after my arrival; but she was still upstairs at the time, and obliged to divide her days between her bed and a lounge. During those endless intervening weeks, she told me, she had thought the whole matter over: and though the events of the mysterious thirty-six hours were still vivid to her, they had already lost something of their haunting terror, and she had finally decided not to re-open the question with Agnes, or to touch on it in speaking to the other servants. Dr. Selgrove's illness had been not only serious but prolonged. He had not yet returned, and it was reported that as soon as he was well enough he would go on a West Indian cruise, and not resume his practice at Norrington till the spring. Dr. Selgrove, as my cousin was perfectly aware, was the only person who could prove that thirty-six hours had elapsed between his visit and that of his successor; and the latter, a shy young man, burdened by the heavy additional practice suddenly thrown on his shoulders, told me (when I risked a little private talk with him) that in the haste of Dr. Selgrove's departure the only instructions he had given about Mrs. Clayburn were summed up in the brief memorandum: "Broken ankle. Have X-rayed."

Knowing my cousin's authoritative character, I was surprised at her decision not to speak to the servants of what had happened; but on thinking it over I concluded she was right. They were all exactly as they had been before that unexplained episode: efficient, devoted, respectful and respectable. She was dependent on them and felt at home with them, and she evidently preferred to put the whole matter out of her mind, as far as she could. She was absolutely certain that something strange had happened in her house, and I was more than ever convinced that she had received a shock which the accident of a broken ankle was not sufficient to account for; but in the end I agreed that nothing was to be gained by cross-questioning the servants or the new doctor.

I was at Whitegates off and on that winter and during the following summer, and when I went home to New York for good early in October I left my cousin in her old health and spirits. Dr. Selgrove had been ordered to Switzerland for the summer, and this further postponement of his return to his practice seemed to have put the happenings of the strange week-end out of her mind. Her life was going on as peacefully and normally as usual, and I left her without anxiety, and indeed without a thought of the mystery, which was now nearly a year old.

I was living then in a small flat in New York by myself, and I had hardly settled into it when, very late one evening—on the last day of October—I heard my bell ring. As it was my maid's evening out, and I was alone, I went to the door myself, and on the threshold, to my amazement, I saw Sara Clayburn. She was wrapped in a fur cloak, with a hat drawn down over her forehead, and a face so pale and haggard that I saw something dreadful must have happened to her. "Sara," I gasped, not knowing what I was saying, "where in the world have you come from at this hour?"

"From Whitegates. I missed the last train and came by car." She came in and sat down on the bench near the door. I saw that she could hardly stand, and sat down beside her, putting my arm about her. "For heaven's sake, tell me what's happened."

She looked at me without seeming to see me. "I telephoned to Nixon's and hired a car. It took me five hours and a quarter to get here." She looked about her. "Can you take me in for the night? I've left my luggage downstairs."

"For as many nights as you like. But you look so ill—"

She shook her head. "No; I'm not ill. I'm only frightened—deathly frightened," she repeated in a whisper.

Her voice was so strange, and the hands I was pressing between mine were so cold, that I drew her to her feet and led her straight to my little guest-room. My flat was in an old-fashioned building, not many stories high, and I was on more human terms with the staff than is possible in one of the modern Babels. I telephoned down to have my cousin's bags brought up, and meanwhile I filled a hot water bottle, warmed the bed, and got her into it as quickly as I could. I had never seen her as unquestioning and submissive, and that alarmed me even more than her pallor. She was not the woman to let herself be undressed and put to bed like a baby; but she submitted without a word, as though aware that she had reached the end of her tether.

"It's good to be here," she said in a quieter tone, as I tucked her up and smoothed the pillows. "Don't leave me yet, will you—not just yet."

"I'm not going to leave you for more than a minute—just to get you a cup of tea," I reassured her; and she lay still. I left the door open, so that she could hear me stirring about in the little pantry across the passage, and when I brought her the tea she swallowed it gratefully, and a little colour came into her face. I sat with her in silence for some time, but at last she began: "You see it's exactly a year—"

I should have preferred to have her put off till the next morning whatever she had to tell me; but I saw from her burning eyes that she was determined to rid her mind of what was burdening it, and that until she had done so it would be useless to proffer the sleeping-draught I had ready.

"A year since what?" I asked stupidly, not yet associating her precipitate arrival with the mysterious occurrences of the previous year at Whitegates.

She looked at me in surprise. "A year since I met that woman. Don't you remember—the strange woman who was coming up the drive the afternoon when I broke my ankle? I didn't think of it at the time, but it was on All Souls' eve that I met her."

Yes, I said, I remembered that it was.

"Well—and this is All Souls' eve, isn't it? I'm not as good as you are on Church dates, but I thought it was."

"Yes. This is All Souls' eve."

"I thought so… Well, this afternoon I went out for my usual walk. I'd been writing letters, and paying bills, and didn't start till late; not till it was nearly dusk. But it was a lovely clear evening. And as I got near the gate, there was the woman coming in—the same woman… going toward the house…"

I pressed my cousin's hand, which was hot and feverish now. "If it was dusk, could you be perfectly sure it was the same woman?" I asked.

"Oh, perfectly sure; the evening was so clear. I knew her and she knew me; and I could see she was angry at meeting me. I stopped her and asked: 'Where are you going?' just as I had asked her last year. And she said, in the same queer half-foreign voice: 'Only to see one of the girls,' as she had before. Then I felt angry all of a sudden, and I said: 'You shan't set foot in my house again. Do you hear me? I order you to leave.' And she laughed; yes, she laughed—very low, but distinctly. By that time it had got quite dark, as if a sudden storm was sweeping up over the sky, so that though she was so near me I could hardly see her. We were standing by the clump of hemlocks at the turn of the drive, and as I went up to her, furious at her impertinence, she passed behind the hemlocks, and when I followed her she wasn't there… No; I swear to you she wasn't there… And in the darkness I hurried back to the house, afraid that she would slip by me and get there first. And the queer thing was that as I reached the door the black cloud vanished, and there was the transparent twilight again. In the house everything seemed as usual, and the servants were busy about their work; but I couldn't get it out of my head that the woman, under the shadow of that cloud, had somehow got there before me." She paused for breath, and began again: "In the hall I stopped at the telephone and rang up Nixon, and told him to send me a car at once to go to New York, with a man he knew to drive me. And Nixon came with the car himself…"

Her head sank back on the pillow, and she looked at me like a frightened child. "It was good of Nixon," she said.

"Yes; it was very good of him. But when they saw you leaving—the servants I mean…"

"Yes. Well, when I got upstairs to my room I rang for Agnes. She came, looking just as cool and quiet as usual. And when I told her I was starting for New York in half an hour—I said it was on account of a sudden business call—well, then her presence of mind failed her for the first time. She forgot to look surprised, she even forgot to make an objection—and you know what an objector Agnes is. And as I watched her I could see a little secret spark of relief in her eyes, though she was so on her guard. And she just said: 'Very well, madam,' and asked me what I wanted to take with me. Just as if I were in the habit of dashing off to New York after dark on an autumn night to meet a business engagement! No, she made a mistake not to show any surprise—and not even to ask me why I didn't take my own car. And her losing her head in that way frightened me more than anything else. For I saw she was so thankful I was going that she hardly dared speak, for fear she should betray herself, or I should change my mind."

After that Mrs. Clayburn lay a long while silent, breathing less unrestfully; and at last she closed her eyes, as though she felt more at ease now that she had spoken, and wanted to sleep. As I got up quietly to leave her, she turned her head a little and murmured: "I shall never go back to Whitegates again." Then she shut her eyes, and I saw that she was falling asleep.

I have set down above, I hope without omitting anything essential, the record of my cousin's strange experience as she told it to me. Of what happened at Whitegates that is all I can personally vouch for. The rest—and of course there is a rest—is pure conjecture, and I give it only as such.

My cousin's maid, Agnes, was from the isle of Skye, and the Hebrides, as everyone knows, are full of the supernatural—whether in the shape of ghostly presences, or the almost ghostlier sense of unseen watchers peopling the long nights of those stormy solitudes. My cousin, at any rate, always regarded Agnes as the—perhaps unconscious, at any rate irresponsible—channel through which communications from the other side of the veil reached the submissive household at Whitegates. Though Agnes had been with Mrs. Clayburn for a long time without any peculiar incident revealing this affinity with the unknown forces, the power to communicate with them may all the while have been latent in the woman, only awaiting a kindred touch; and that touch may have been given by the unknown visitor whom my cousin, two years in succession, had met coming up the drive at Whitegates on the eve of All Souls'. Certainly the date bears out my hypothesis; for I suppose that, even in this unimaginative age, a few people still remember that All Souls' eve is the night when the dead can walk—and when, by the same token, other spirits, piteous or malevolent, are also freed from the restrictions which secure the earth to the living on the other days of the year.

If the recurrence of this date is more than a coincidence—and for my part I think it is—then I take it that the strange woman who twice came up the drive at Whitegates on All Souls' eve was either a "fetch," or else, more probably, and more alarmingly, a living woman inhabited by a witch. The history of witchcraft, as is well known, abounds in such cases, and such a messenger might well have been delegated by the powers who rule in these matters to summon Agnes and her fellow-servants to a midnight "Coven" in some neighbouring solitude. To learn what happens at Covens, and the reason of the irresistible fascination they exercise over the timorous and superstitious, one need only address oneself to the immense body of literature dealing with these mysterious rites. Anyone who has once felt the faintest curiosity to assist at a Coven apparently soon finds the curiosity increase to desire, the desire to an uncontrollable longing, which, when the opportunity presents itself, breaks down all inhibitions; for those who have once taken part in a Coven will move heaven and earth to take part again.

Such is my—conjectural—explanation of the strange happenings at Whitegates. My cousin always said she could not believe that incidents which might fit into the desolate landscape of the Hebrides could occur in the cheerful and populous Connecticut valley; but if she did not believe, she at least feared—such moral paradoxes are not uncommon—and though she insisted that there must be some natural explanation of the mystery, she never returned to investigate it.

"No, no," she said with a little shiver, whenever I touched on the subject of her going back to Whitegates, "I don't want ever to risk seeing that woman again..." And she never went back.

MOONLIGHT-STARLIGHT

Virginia Layefsky

Published in When Evil Wakes, *edited by August Derleth,*
1963

Virginia Layefsky, née Farmer (1927–2019), was an author and a student at Julliard, born of Scots/English descent. As a teenager, she would play piano at weddings. She met her husband, the noted violinist Godfrey Layefsky, when he was playing with the Metropolitan Opera Orchestra as its lead. They married in 1951 and moved from Seattle to Pittsburgh and Virginia gave up piano playing and turned her hand to writing. Constantly travelling with her husband's work, she would write and send out stories. "Moonlight-Starlight" was written in 1959 and published in August Derleth's *When Evil Wakes* in 1963. Moments of solace were spent in the British Virgin Islands where they had a three bedroom house with a huge sundeck only five minutes away from seven unspoiled beaches.

It took six weeks and five drafts of "Moonlight-Starlight" before Virginia was satisfied with the finished result. A naturally happy and outgoing person, she found solace in writing melancholic stories, but most of them would be returned by magazine editors because they were "too sad". Apart from "Moonlight-Starlight", a ghost story, Virginia only wrote non-genre tales, and these were published in *Ellery Queen's Mystery Magazine* ("Statement of The Accused", "This Place Belongs To You"), *Alfred Hitchcock's Mystery Magazine* ("Cat Dance"), *The Virginia Quarterly Review* ("Jennifer"), *Ladies Home Journal* ("The Last Wish"), *Chatelaine* and *Woman's Day*. A novel aimed at teenagers, *Impossible Things* (Marshall Cavendish) was published in 1998. Layefsky died of natural causes in Point Breeze, Philadelphia, age 91.

THE genesis of the idea for the party was in an old Holloween costume Anne Carey found packed in a box in the attic. It had been made thirty years ago for a seven-year-old Anne by her mother. She had been a woman who threw nothing away.

After Anne inherited the large Victorian spaces her mother had swept and garnished most of her life, she often came upon pieces of her own life—up until her marriage at least—neatly labelled and stored here or there. She was apt to find them on those first days of her husband's occasional absences when she used house cleaning as a balm for initial loneliness.

The costume she found that day was so beautifully sewn and carefully packed that its state of preservation was remarkable. When she shook out its folds, the coins which her mother had sewn individually on the bodice long ago clinked with a special sound that set up a painful little echo of disappointment in her forgetful heart. Though she remembered clearly then the smell of chrysanthemums and sewing-machine oil in her mother's room the day the costume was fitted, she could not have said why the sound of the coins oppressed her with such a profound sense of loss.

It had to do with the party she had lost, of course. It was to have been her very own. The games had been planned and the decorations made. Invitations had already been sent when, due to the death by drowning of two small cousins in upstate New York, the party was cancelled. The accident had happened the day before they were to leave to visit Anne. She had been broken-hearted, not for the cousins whom she had never seen but for the party which was cancelled. In time she was able to forget everything about it but the sense of loss, which persisted unacknowledged up today when she opened the box to find the costume still waiting there.

And that was the reason why Halloween became the occasion for the only really large children's party Anne Carey ever gave. She made a costume, less carefully done, for her nine-year-old son and dressed her daughter in the gypsy outfit she herself was to have worn long ago.

The party was a resounding success. Children, remembering it, asked her for months afterwards to give another, but she never did. Nor did she tell the reasons why it became the last children's party of any kind that she ever gave...

The arrangements seemed so simple at first. She told her son Bobby he could invite the entire fourth grade with all its younger brothers and sisters.

Games and refreshments were no problem. Now that Anne thought of it, she remembered the entire programme of the beautiful party planned long ago. The bobbing for apples, followed by pin the tail on the donkey and musical chairs, marched through her mind in a succession almost as orderly and magical now as then. There would be none of the professional entertainment that had figured recently in some of the more ambitious neighbourhood parties. What she wanted was a real, old-fashioned Halloween party.

It was something she was to repeat often during the week to the friends who called her with warnings and advice.

Had she a first-aid kit? She would probably need one. And be sure to omit the booby prizes—children who won them were apt to weep, considering them a disgrace.

The warnings began to include, unpleasantly often, the names of the Usher children. Everyone hoped they had not been invited, although on being questioned no one seemed able to tell Anne more than that they were considered strange, the rather menacing unknown quantity in the local algebra of human relationships. They were not much liked by other children.

And then, everyone knew how strange the parents were, living off by themselves as they did, never associating with anyone.

Had she seen the father's work? Gruesome decadent stuff that no one who hadn't a morbid streak would think of painting. And according to rumours, it was just as well they did keep to themselves. It seemed Usher had a sense of humour that, to say the least, was sardonic. It could be, they had heard, very ugly at times.

By that time, however, it was too late. The older child—the girl—was in the fourth grade. She and her brother had been invited along with the rest.

On Halloween Anne with her two children stood in the golden porch light welcoming their guests. The children, in various disguises, began to come shortly after dark. They all seemed to arrive at the same time, coming out of the gloomy, old-fashioned lane like a small army of faceless grotesques. Every child was masked.

For an instant Anne felt invaded by a force of nameless, not necessarily friendly strangers. Only the shadows of parents coming from the obscurity into familiarity assured her that beneath the grinning skull or monstrous face was a dimple or a freckled nose she knew.

The party had become a reality at last. Each adult whispered instructions of various sorts to each small mystery at his side before setting it free to join its wriggling, hopping contemporaries. As they took leave of Anne with compliments and thanks, there was an unmistakable look of relief on most of their departing faces. She had said she could manage alone, even with her husband absent on business for his firm.

By eight o'clock, when the party hats had been passed out, and the last parent had gone, almost everyone who had been invited was there.

The party began in good order. They all pinned the tail on the donkey. Waiting patiently, good-children-all-in-a-line, each child was blindfolded and sent with cardboard tail in hand towards the donkey on the wall. Only one very young black cat—anonymous to Anne—cried because it had pinned its particular tail to the donkey's nose. It was quite easily comforted.

The second game passed gaily, even hilariously. The children unmasked as they went to the big tin washbowl full of apples floating on top of the water that filled it. At the sight of laughter on small faces freed so recently from the horrors which had hidden them from sight, Anne was charmed with a sudden feeling of felicity.

The children, hands held behind their backs, bobbed for the apples. She watched them, holding to her moment with the sweet satisfaction of fulfillment.

Down to the last detail, from the sound of the children's shrill, excited voices to the orange-and-black crepe paper and balloons, the festive smell of candle wax heating the pulpy pumpkins, she had her party at last.

It was well that she held to the moment, listening to the laughter, seeing the children's warm cheeks and tender, perspiring necks, her own daughter's thrilled awareness of her multicoloured petticoats. For shortly after that the party began to change.

It started during the next game, which was musical chairs, and at first it was almost imperceptible. Perhaps because it was the third rather strenuous game of the evening, Anne noticed some of the children show-ing signs of being overtired. Some of the smaller ones' cheeks were too flushed or pale.

They had put the chairs in a row themselves, working rather wildly with some petty wrangling. There were quarrels in the air before they even started. And at the same time, something else, an odd feeling of restless-ness and distraction as though their minds were somewhere else.

Watching them march around the chairs, and the way each scrambled for a place once the music stopped, Anne decided she never had liked the game. It demanded a ruthlessness in the end that she found unpleasant, disliking the ultimate winner.

She was glad when it was over and she had settled the children to making funny men and animals out of the marshmallows, gumdrops and toothpicks she had set out on card tables.

A drooping rabbit's ear, a cat's tail hanging from its owner down the back of a chair, a worn sneaker sticking out beneath a ghost's shroud seemed charming to her still. And yet, she felt less delighted than before.

The room became quiet enough for her to hear the children's laboured breathing as they concentrated on their efforts. As they reached for the coloured candies to fit them awkwardly on the toothpicks, Anne was not able to get rid of the slight depression settling over her. There was that furtive, restless quality creeping about the room as though all the small figures bending over their nonsense were less intent than they pretended to be. There was a sense of shifting, of lifting the head to listen, though no child did these things.

In the near silence she heard the wind rising outside. It was then, too, that she heard the front gate creak as it opened.

No child looked up. As Anne listened for the footsteps which should have sounded on the porch afterward, each child seemed to concentrate more obliviously than before.

When Anne crossed the room to the entrance hall, she felt she was being watched. It was such a strong feeling she turned to look back. No one had even seen her go.

Nothing but the wind, rushing into the hall like some belated guest, met her at the open door. Behind it, in darkness that crept away from the porch light, she could see no one.

It was when her eyes searched the old garden at the side of the house that she saw them. They were standing by a small stone sundial Anne's grandfather had set there years ago. A boy and a girl, hand in hand, they stood looking at her, motionless as it was.

Not until she called to them inviting them inside did they move forward. As they came through the dark, up the porch steps, Anne felt at last how truly starless the night was, how like these particular parents to send them out alone.

They passed in silence through the door she held open for them. Once inside the hall, they waited, making no move towards the living-room, standing always together in their peculiar stillness. Anne, for some reason unknown, not only closed but bolted the door.

They were staring wordlessly up at her when she turned back to them. She found herself struggling with a feeling of aversion for them, since now that they had arrived she realized how relieved she had been earlier at their absence.

The girl was a head taller than her brother, though both were identically costumed. Neither of them was masked, yet it was only one face that both turned to her, the boy's being simply a smaller version of the girl's.

To Anne they had the look of having been drawn by their father instead of procreated in the usual way. She thought she even recognized Usher's personal style in the deliberate exaggeration of line and the faintly corrupt, half-graceful proportions of that face with its twofold glance.

The eyes, in particular, were as overly large as the ones he painted. They were a flat, tobacco brown. It was to the expression in them that she owed her feeling of aversion. For both pairs held a fixed, impersonal intentness that was less unchildlike, she thought, than inhuman.

Still, they were only children, just come to a strange house. Anne, feeling slightly guilty, pointed the way to the living-room,

They walked ahead of her, docilely enough, not seeming to notice when Anne, following them, suddenly stopped still. She had noticed at last what they were wearing. She felt a sense of affront, of somehow being publicly insulted. If friends had called Usher's humour unpleasant and sardonic, she had not known up until then what those words could mean. For even to Anne, no authority on such matters, it was obvious he had sent them dressed in costumes representing the grave-clothes of children of a past generation. Both wore on their heads wreaths of stiff formal leaves, and were dressed in folds of white cloth from shoulder to foot. The costumes were draped delicately and, from a distance at least, looked as beautifully sewn as her own child's dress. That each detail had the stamp of conscious artistic effect only added to the cynical horror of the idea.

Though the other children looked up as they entered the room, they remained sitting at their tables. Anne, sensing the general withdrawal on their part, came closer to her new guests, intending to reassure them. Close enough to the boy, in fact, to feel she had seen the worst, ultimate point of the joke. For the material of their costumes had the limp suppleness of age. The hand-sewn lace on them was yellow.

After their initial drawing back the children began to speak again, to laugh, get up from the tables and show her what they had made.

They began a game of blindman's buff. It was not one of the games planned for the evening, but Anne took advantage of it to go away to privacy for a few moments.

She stood alone in the gaily decorated dining-room with its rows of shining, waiting plates. She frowned, moving her lips slightly like a child over a mathematics problem, wondering uneasily how the children of such a father might be expected to behave. A need to see what was happening, as urgent as the need for privacy had been a few minutes before, sent her to the door of the room.

What she saw reassured her. The two children, along with the others, crouched, hiding from the blindfolded child who groped after them with outstretched hands. She saw the boy shrink away in his turn from the blindman, giggling softly. His eyes were shining childishly. She reproached herself.

Yet the party was changed. The mood of it began to resemble more nearly the wild "play-outs" of her childhood's summer nights, when the long, soft dusk encouraged a feeling of lawlessness, of perilous emotions, a sort of childish debauch. There was a feverish, tense look on some of their faces.

Anne had gone to the kitchen before the party went out of control. The children had begun to choose their own games by that time, and had been playing a comparatively quiet one when she left the room. It was an ancient game, a sort of ritual she remembered having played herself, known as old witch.

"I'm going downtown to smoke my pipe
And I won't be back till Saturday night
And if you dare let the old witch in
I'll beat you red—white—and blue!"

A small voice chanted the words behind her as she entered the kitchen. For a time she busied herself pouring cider, warming plates, mentally counting heads, as she concentrated on her own activities.

Until the lights went out.

The entire house was suddenly dark. Someone, she knew, had pulled a switch. When she called out anxiously she was answered by her son's cheerful voice.

They had decided, he called, to play moonlight-starlight.

The name, heard aloud, made a chill run over Anne. She hadn't thought of it for years. As a child it had been the only game she had feared and hated. She felt intolerable anxiety as she wondered, while knowing at once, who had suggested it. The party was out of hand.

She groped across the kitchen to the drawer that held her husband's flashlight, disguising her unreasonable fear with irritation at her son for pulling the switch without permission.

Someone had taken and forgotten to return the flashlight. As she turned away, trying to think where she had put candles, she was remembering against her will the way the game was played.

For moonlight-starlight was an outdoor game, another part of the summer nights. Children played it only after dark.

Anne remembered it well. The child who was "it," the ghost, hid in some dark and secret place. Each child, separate and alone, had to wander in search of it. On finding it they, too, became ghosts. Until at last only one child was left to wander alone, watched by all the secret ghosts, who would, in the end, pounce upon it.

There were no candles. She set out in darkness.

The switch box was located across the living-room in an alcove which had been built as a small conservatory with french doors opening into the garden. Even in the blackness of the hall, Anne knew exactly where it was.

The house, except for small sounds and sudden scamperings, was silent. It seemed to take a long time to walk the length of the hall. In darkness the house grew larger, as large as she had thought it as a child. And now, more nearly child than adult, she walked forward with dread.

At any time now "it," changed from the familiar playmate to some nameless horror, could jump suddenly upon her from its hiding place. For, like it or not, she, too, was a player now.

Her hand touched the living-room wall and she groped forward, angry with herself for the way she shrank against it. She had reached the doors leading to the conservatory before she heard the whispering. It came from inside the room and there was a quality in it that froze her motionless, hardly breathing.

For a few seconds her faculties were turned inward on her own pounding heart. It was only gradually, as she realized she had not been noticed, that she calmed somewhat. She found she was able to see dimly the three small figures standing inside. The white garments of two of them even shone slightly, though so little light came from the night which waited outside in the garden.

When she was able to hear something besides her own pulse she listened to the phrase the two in white whispered again and again, distinguishing, at last, the words.

"Come out... come out into the dark... come with us..."

They whispered it together, excited, persuasive, with an urgent, secret sibilance that held an increasing seductiveness at each repetition.

The third child, so enticed, whimpered once and stood quiet between them after that. It had been the small sound of an animal so full of fear as to be beyond outcry.

It released Anne from the fear that held her. For the voice had been her daughter's.

Though she leaped forward she made no attempt to reach her child. Her urge was the primitive, overwhelming one for light to chase away the darkness. The hands that had fumbled so often before moved with the speed and sureness of fear which is beyond panic.

And if the taller of the two, the girl, swayed gently towards her with smiling teeth at the same second lights blazed throughout the house and her own child was in her arms.

They stood alone in the glass-enclosed room. Other players who had been wandering about downstairs blinked their eyes in the sudden light, calling reproachful questions.

Every child had come back into the living-room before Anne, with trembling hands, shut the french doors which had been swinging open in the wind from the garden. No child asked where two of the guests had gone.

No one mentioned them at all through the final stages of the party. Anne, having had to choose between illness and anger, chose rightly. It was anger that sustained her through the refreshments, the collecting of coats and the arrival, thanks and goodbyes of parents.

It was faithful through the night. She went to bed angry and it was with her when she woke the next morning. She guarded it carefully as she planned the call she would make to Usher that day, since if she lost it she feared what might take its place.

In the end, it was Mrs. Usher who called Anne first. She had a pleasant voice, crisp and courteous though rather impersonal sounding.

She called, she said, to explain why her children had not been able to attend the party. They had had fever all day and she believed it might be developing into a light case of chicken pox. Both she, and they, had been so disappointed. She had made their costumes herself; they were to have gone as a cat and a mouse.

The voice seemed to fade out on the next few sentences. At the first words Anne heard there had been a slight, sickening wrench some-where inside her. It was a relatively mild one, considering that it was the displacement of whatever held her being secure in its particular place in the universe.

The voice wanted to know if most of the other children had been able to make it. Some of them, it knew, had had to come a long way.

The invitations had been on orange paper. She remembered them. Her mother had let her cut out and address them herself, guiding her hand as it made fat wavering letters on the envelopes. She had been so proud that they were to go all the way to upstate New York.

Anne's voice, when she answered, was steadier than the room, still wheeling crazily around herself and the telephone.

Yes, she said, some of the children had had to come a very long way.

Children would do almost anything not to miss a party, the voice said.

Yes, Anne said. All the children had come.

THE NEW HOUSE

Elizabeth Walter

Published in Snowfall and Other Chilling Events, *1965*

Elizabeth Walter (1927–2006) was born in London to parents who were both teachers. She was educated at Hereford High School for Girls and graduated in English Language and Literature. Early jobs saw her work in technical journalism and bookselling before working with Jonathan Cape. Her first novel, *The More Deceived*, was published by Jonathan Cape in 1960. In 1961 she became the editor of Collins Crime Club, overseeing forty-eight books a year until she retired in 1993, when the series was brought to an end. From 1965–1979 she wrote five collections of supernatural tales, *Snowfall and Other Chilling Events* (1965), *The Sin-Eater and Other Scientific Impossibilities* (1967), *Davy Jones's Tale and Other Supernatural Stories* (1971), *Come and Get Me and Other Uncanny Invitations* (1973) and *Dead Woman and Other Haunting Experiences* (1975), all published by Harvill Press (founded by Manya Harari and Marjorie Villiers in 1946). A collection of her best work was published by Arkham House as *In the Mist and Other Uncanny Encounters* (1979).

Walter also saw broadcasts of several of her works; Rod Serling's *Night Gallery* took her tale "The Spider" and turned it into *A Fear of Spiders* (S2/ep4) starring Patrick O'Neil and Kim Stanley. The anthology series *Ghost Story* (then changed to *Circle of Fear*), created by Richard Matheson, used four of her tales, with the pilot episode an adaptation of "The New House". The following story is a neglected folk horror classic, which suggests that it's probably wise that you do your homework and check out the history of the land the house is on before you move into that new build.

THE footsteps were coming very slowly up the stairs. Eileen Travis shifted cautiously in bed and raised herself on her elbow. At that moment a stair creaked. It was the fourth from the top, and she and John had commented on it irritably, for surely such things should not be in a new house? But the stair only creaked if trodden on. There was someone coming up the stairs.

Eileen looked at her husband, sleeping beside her the heavy sleep of a man who has done a hard day's digging in a new garden. Obviously he had heard nothing, and indeed, the sound was so faint that she had at first attributed it to her imagination, or thought that her ears were playing tricks. The sound would certainly not have awakened her had she slept, but now that her first pregnancy was well advanced, discomfort and heaviness kept her wakeful. And there was someone coming up the stairs.

Urgently she shook John's shoulder. He stirred, mumbled, and was suddenly wide awake, as though her fear had transmitted itself by touch.

"What is it? Are you all right?"

"Shh-hh! Listen: we've got burglars."

They were both sitting bolt upright in bed. The footsteps reached the top of the stairs and, more muffled on the solidity of the landing, began to come quietly towards the door.

The telephone was on John's side of the bed. In a single movement he had slid out of bed and into his slippers and handed the telephone to his wife.

"Dial the police. Be as quiet as you can."

"Where are you going?" Eileen asked.

"I'm going to see our intruder off the premises."

"Darling, be careful."

"I'll be that all right."

As he spoke, John picked up an ornamental candlestick with a heavy metal base. The footsteps had stopped on the landing and the silence was complete. On the other side of the door the intruder waited, was perhaps bending down to peer through the keyhole—but for what? "What the burglar saw" would be darkness, as on the landing. They had only the March moon shining through the window for light.

With the spring of a man who is young, athletic and in training, John wrenched open the door and snapped on both bedroom and landing lights. A gust of cold air rushed in from some opened downstairs window. The footsteps retreated with what seemed phenomenal speed. The landing was already abandoned; by the time John reached the head of the stairs, the intruder had gone.

Shakily Eileen replaced the telephone receiver, thankful none the less that a police-car was on its way. She pressed her hands to her heart to still its thudding, assuring herself that she was safe and the child within her was safe. Downstairs she could hear John blundering about furiously, opening doors in a frenzy of relief and rage. She slid cautiously out of bed and huddled her dressing-gown around her. She must be in some sort of state to be questioned by the police.

On the landing a frightening thought struck her. Suppose the intruder had not gone downstairs but had merely slipped into the spare room, soon to be the nursery, or the airing-cupboard, the bathroom, the box-room? Fearfully she opened each door and peered around it; in each case the room was empty and undisturbed. It was not here that they must seek for their housebreaker. Clutching the banisters, she began to go downstairs.

Again the coldness and dankness of the stairs and landing struck her. She could have believed herself transported underground. Could the new house be showing signs of damp already? Her common sense protested it could not.

As she reached the bottom step, John came into the hall.

"Sweetheart, you shouldn't have come down. Why didn't you stay upstairs in bed, in the warm?"

"I'd rather be with you," Eileen said matter-of-factly. She was ashamed of her fears, for nothing had happened, after all.

"Has anything been taken?" she murmured.

"Not that I can see," John said. "In fact, it's a mystery to me how he entered. All the doors and windows seem fast. I haven't examined them minutely, but there's nothing left gaping wide, although there obviously must have been to let so much cold air in. We're dealing with a jolly fast thief—to get down those stairs and through a window and latch it behind him, and still get clear away."

"If he has got away," Eileen whispered.

"You can see for yourself he has. There's no one in the house except the two of us—"

He was interrupted by a low, gurgling laugh.

It was impossible to say where it came from, except that it was somewhere very close at hand. The Travises swung round, eyes staring. And then a car braked, footsteps sounded, and a thunderous rat-tat-tatting shook the door.

Outside stood a sergeant and two constables.

"The burglar's still in the house," John gasped.

The sergeant turned to give instructions to the men behind him, one of whom promptly went round to the back. The other two thrust into the hallway.

"You'd best get back upstairs, ma'am," the sergeant said.

He was already investigating the living-room, while the constable waited in the hall. After that came the kitchen, every cupboard, the downstairs cloakroom, the larder—every door.

"Nothing there," he announced grimly, emerging backwards from the cupboard under the stairs. "We'll have a look upstairs, if you don't mind, sir, just in case he's hiding there."

"I've looked," Eileen informed him from the top step. "And in any case, our burglar is a she."

The sergeant looked at her in astonishment. "Lady burglars? That's something new." He turned enquiringly to John for confirmation. "I take it you saw her, sir?"

"We heard her," John said. "Both my wife and I heard her quite distinctly. It was just as you arrived. She laughed."

"She won't laugh if I lay my hands on her." The sergeant started purposefully up the stairs.

His search of the upstairs rooms revealed nothing. Eileen was hardly surprised. Muttering a little with frustration, the sergeant began a tour of doors and window-frames, testing the catches, seeking for marks where tools might have been used. The constable, a helpful supernumerary, announced after each inspection, "Everything's O.K. there."

"Beats me how the fellow got into the house," the sergeant muttered. "There's not a sign of anything being touched. Are you sure, sir, you didn't automatically close a window or snap back some faulty catch?"

"I touched nothing," John assured him. "I couldn't see myself how the hell a burglar had got in. I said so, didn't I, darling?"

Eileen nodded. "And then we heard her laugh."

"Well, she's not in the house now," the sergeant said firmly. "Perhaps it was the wind you heard."

Eileen's eyes turned towards the window. In the moonlight, the trees were still.

As if to cover up the asininity of his suggestion, the sergeant turned to the constable at his side. "Go and give Jim a hand with the garden and the out-houses. When you've finished 'em, come back in. There might be someone lurking on the premises," he explained needlessly. "After all, you're the last house on the hill."

Its isolated position was one of the points which had made the Travises eager to buy the house. It was at the top of a gentle slope known as Pleasant Hill, which had been developed as a housing estate of small, ultra modern, detached-houses, described by the agent as "suitable for young professional and executive households". Much emphasis was laid on the accessibility of a railway station, and the frequent fast train service to Waterloo. From the front bedroom, Hindhead was visible in the distance. The back garden sloped down to open country, on which no planning permission to build could be obtained. This combination of rural solitude and urban amenities had appealed to the Travises, and the milieu of "young professional and executive households" seemed to them exactly right. John being an advertising executive and Eileen, until she gave up work because of the baby, a freelance dress-designer. In the six months since they had bought the house, they had seen the Pleasant Hill Estate fill up, which merely underlined the satisfaction they felt with their purchase, whose position made it much the most desirable of the lot.

Now for the first time they began to wonder if its position were such an advantage. The sergeant's words had disquieted them both. If tramps and gipsies were likely to make the surrounding country their headquarters, they might regret their choice.

A heavy stamping in the hall heralded the return of the search-party. "Nothing in the garden, sir," the senior constable announced. "Not a sign of any disturbance. The whole place is quiet as the grave. In fact, if you'll pardon me saying so, I don't think anyone got in at all. Not unless he could have slid in under the door or something, for the doors and windows haven't been touched outside. I'll swear to that."

"How do you know?" John demanded.

"Your doors are mortice-locked; they'd be difficult to tamper with, and no burglar in his senses would risk it while you were both in the house. That leaves the windows, which are fairly easily opened despite catches, which incidentally are fast. But to get to the windows you'd have to tread on the flower-beds, which are soft and recently dug. There isn't a footmark anywhere—I've examined. So no one came in from outside."

"She might have stepped over the flower-beds," John suggested.

"No, sir, they're much too wide. And there's not much outer sill to give purchase, let alone foothold. Even if a window had been left wide open on purpose, anyone getting in would have had to pull himself up from the ground."

"But a window *was* open," Eileen protested. "We could feel the cold air coming in from outside."

The sergeant shrugged and tried too late to suppress it. "A draught," he suggested, avoiding Eileen's eyes.

"How about the laugh?" John asked bluntly.

"Oh, I don't deny you heard the laugh, sir. There are half a dozen acceptable explanations for that. An owl, now—owls can make a noise very much like a woman laughing. Low and soft—a sort of chuckle it is."

"It was not an owl. I am certain. Besides, it was here in the house."

"Yes, ma'am, but there's nobody here now to make it. And no one got in from outside. Those newly-dug flower-beds make that absolutely certain. I take it you're a keen gardener, sir?"

"Beginning to be," John admitted, accepting the deliberate change of subject. "But it's back-breaking work up here."

"New ground," the sergeant said sympathetically. "It's always a terror to dig. And so much rubbish gets thrown around these days, apart from the heather roots! I expect you've dug up some odd things in your patch, sir? A gentleman down the hill dug up a scythe in his."

"I haven't found anything of interest," John murmured. "Just the usual debris of our society—bits of china, tin cans, rusty nails. Nothing worth putting in a glass case."

For some reason which he did not analyse, he said nothing about the skull. Not that it was a matter for the police in any case. A skull as old as that could never be Exhibit A. It was more likely to interest a zoologist than a policeman, for it must be an animal's skull, John assured himself anxiously, despite the human appearance of the teeth. But it was old, yellow and brittle, the bone reduced to honeycomb; his spade had smashed through it at the bottom of the garden as if it were an imitation, plastic-thin. It was already broken into pieces when he first saw it; only the teeth and lower jaw were still intact. They had lain there grinning at him in the earth a mere two spade-depths down. John, hypnotized but disgusted, had gazed unsmilingly back. Unwillingly he bent down to touch the jaw-bone; he was loath to pick it up. When he did, the teeth fell out with a rattle. It looked less human now. The jaw-bone he was holding might be any animal's jaw-bone; the fragments in the earth were not a human skull.

Nevertheless, he dug the surrounding area carefully, finding occasional traces of similarly rotting bone, but too destroyed, too disordered to reveal any relationship. They could have come from several different beasts. Collecting his findings together, John dug another hole and buried them deep.

He did not tell Eileen of the incident in case it should cause her distress, which in her condition was hardly advisable; and distressed she would surely be, for either they were animal bones (and Eileen was an animal-lover), or, if human, they had probably belonged to some tramp. It would not be a good idea to alert Eileen to the fact that tramps and vagabonds might have made the top of Pleasant Hill their headquarters, that one of them had even died in what was now their garden. And it would be useless to point out that it had probably happened in the last century and that no one living would either care or know. How long, John wondered, would it take for a bone to vanish in that light, dry, sandy soil? Rather longer, perhaps, than in water-logged London clay. It would be better to say nothing to anyone—a case of letting the sleeping dog lie. So long as it was literally a sleeping dog they need not worry. It was well worth giving it a try.

All the same, he had not expected to be questioned by the police, however innocently. He was relieved when they stood up to go. The sergeant promised to report the incident at the station, and if there was any further disturbances, the Travises were to call them at once.

257

"Though I don't think there will be," he reassured them. "If the burglar was real, he—or she—will have had a good fright. If she turns out to be a bit more insubstantial…"

He allowed the sentence to die discreetly away, and as they were leaving, sought to draw John to one side. "This your first child?" he asked, with a glance in Eileen's direction.

Surprised, John said it was.

"I thought so." The sergeant nodded sympathetically. "Women get some strange fancies at these times. My wife, now—even with her fourth—kept worrying, first one thing, then another. Couldn't stop her. Once the child arrived, she was as right as rain. She's a placid woman as a rule, too. Now, I don't mind betting your good lady was the first to hear these footsteps. She woke you, and you thought you heard them too."

John could not deny that this was exactly what had happened. It was a relief to believe it in a way—to attribute the whole thing to Eileen's disordered fancy, which by transference had then affected him. It gave him a slight sense of disloyalty towards her, for after all, he had thought he heard the footsteps too, but it was infinitely the most reassuring solution. He cautiously consented to agree.

The sergeant, misinterpreting his hesitation, hastened to put him at his ease. "Don't you worry, sir. There's nothing abnormal about it. And don't you worry about having called us out. It's only common sense to phone the police if you think you've got burglars, and it keeps us on our toes. Though it beats me what we can report about this one—" he grinned encouragingly at his men—"a lady burglar who can enter and leave without a sign of how she did it, and of whom no trace can be found."

"Only a ghost could have done it," the senior constable said.

Without knowing why, John answered unexpectedly sharply: "There are no ghosts in a new house."

They had no more trouble with burglars, but Eileen, John realized, had had a shock. By the end of a week she was pale and listless, tearful at any unexpected sound. In answer to John's enquiries, she shook her head wretchedly.

"It's this place. It's getting me down."

"What's the matter with the place?" John demanded, for with returning spring the country was becoming alive. There were hazel catkins in all the hedgerows. On sheltered banks the first primroses could be seen. It was the time of birth and new beginnings, yet Eileen, germinal as earth, did not respond. As for the house, she had been so keen on it. It was absurd to turn against it in this way. John repeated his question with an edge of sharpness: "What's the matter with the house?"

"It isn't ours any longer."

"What do you mean?"

"Oh, John, can't you feel it? Can't you feel how she's here all the time? She's so close I can almost touch her. Every time I go round a corner, I expect to see her there."

"I don't know what you're talking about," John said brusquely. "There's nobody here but ourselves."

"Yes, there is, John. You know it as well as I do. There's been somebody else in the house since that night."

"Look, darling," John said with all the patience he could muster, "we searched and the police searched and we didn't find a thing. There was no way anyone could get in from the outside. Whatever we thought we heard, it was imagination—creaking boards, wind in the chimney, something like that." He remembered the sergeant's words about pregnant women's fancies, and went on with a casualness that he hoped would conceal the direction of his thoughts, "Why don't you go and stay with your mother for a bit?"

He was both surprised and disturbed when Eileen promptly agreed. He had made the suggestion with the idea of ridicule, but her agreement indicated how seriously she was taking it. True, her mother lived only ten miles away at Guildford and Eileen was already booked into a nursing-home there. All the same, it was disquieting that she should prefer to spend the last month of her pregnancy with her mother, rather than in her own home with him.

Nevertheless, John accepted his wife's decision with a good grace. In his heart, he repeated the sergeant's comforting words. It was in the hope of obtaining some sort of further confirmation that he reported Eileen's fears to Mrs. Shaw. Mrs. Shaw came in twice weekly to do the cleaning. She had borne six children in one of the old cottages, survivors of the original village of Penfold, which clustered at the foot of Pleasant Hill. She had been prodigal of advice, which Eileen had not taken. If anyone were likely to be an expert on pregnant fancies, it was Mrs. Shaw.

As he had expected, Mrs. Shaw showed little surprise. Contrary to her voluble custom, she said nothing beyond an occasional "Poor lamb."

"I suppose it's not unusual for expectant mothers to get nervous fancies," John concluded, a note of interrogation in his voice.

Mrs. Shaw continued with some polishing. "I couldn't say, I'm sure."

"But you're not surprised my wife is fanciful?"

Mrs. Shaw pretended not to hear.

"Did you suffer with your nerves when you were expecting?" John persisted.

"I can't say as I ever did." Mrs. Shaw's stocky, chubby body did not look the sort to contain a single nerve. John was therefore all the more surprised when she gave him a curious sideways glance and added darkly, "But then, I didn't live on Pleasant Hill."

"What's that got to do with it?" John demanded. "Is the air supposed to be bad at the top of the hill?"

"I don't know as it's the air." Again that curious glance, half pitying, half condemning. "It ain't supposed to be healthy up here."

John burst out laughing. "What nonsense! It's some of the finest air in Surrey round here."

"I dare say, but there's some as found it fatal."

John crossed the room to confront her. "What is all this?"

Mrs. Shaw sat back on her haunches and looked up at him with round bright eyes. "Look, sir, you don't know much about this district, do you? How should you, being a Londoner? It's the same with all you young folks as has bought property up here—you none of you knew what you was buying. But you won't find anyone from the village living on what used to be known as Gibbet Hill."

"Gibbet Hill! Oh come, Mrs. Shaw, you're joking."

"I am not, sir. This place was Gibbet Hill afore the property company bought it. It was them as changed the name to Pleasant Hill. Pleasant!" She almost spat the word in disgust at its connotation. "It was very pleasant for them as hanged in chains up here."

"Do you mean there really was a gibbet?"

Mrs. Shaw looked at him in scorn. ""Course there was. My father said his father saw it. He wouldn't have come up here for anything after dark. Nor I wouldn't, nor my husband neither. We didn't do our courting *here*. It's only you young folks who know nothing about it that are prepared to live on Gibbet Hill."

"Was one of the fellows who was hanged in chains a notorious housebreaker?" John asked sceptically. "Are you trying to tell me we've got a ghost?"

"I'm not trying to tell you nothing, Mr. Travis. I don't know what poor souls was hanged up here. But I know I wouldn't live here if you paid me, and after this I don't want to work here any more."

All John's cajolings, bribes and blandishments were useless. Mrs. Shaw departed, resolutely refusing to return. John did not tell Eileen for fear it might distress her. Instead, he set about finding someone else, and suspecting that other local women would be equally shy of coming, he drove in to the nearest town to place an advertisement there. It was only three miles distant and he was willing to pay bus fares. The woman in the agency seemed hopeful she could send someone along.

John was on his way back to the car when he passed a small stone building with a notice saying "Public Library". On an impulse, he went in and asked for books on local history. The librarian seemed taken aback.

"I don't think we have much," he murmured. "You'd have to go to Guildford for that. I'm afraid there's not much interest in the subject. Was there something particular you had in mind?"

"Yes," John said. "I live at Pleasant Hill, on the way to Hindhead, and I've been told it used to be called Gibbet Hill. I wondered if it was true, and if you had any further information as to how the place came to be called Gibbet Hill."

"It's true all right," the librarian assured him. "I remember it was called that when I first came here. Very fine view from the top, but rather bare and windswept. I believe there was a gibbet there once."

"So I've been told, but I wanted some more information—how long ago, who was hanged there, and all that."

The librarian looked doubtful. "I don't think we've got anything. Or—wait a minute! There might be something in here."

He took down a leather-bound volume: *Rural Beauties in the County of Surrey: A Guide*. The date on the title-page was given in Roman figures, but John had time to work out that it was 1889.

"Here we are." The librarian consulted a brown-spotted page, and, leaning over his shoulder, John read: "From Penfold the road rises steeply towards the heather-clad slopes of Gibbet Hill. From here is obtained a magnificent panorama, reaching southward as far as Hindhead, and eastward over a tract of hilly country bisected by the London to Portsmouth road and the main-line railway. The haunt of highwaymen before the advent of the locomotive, this stretch of road was once the scene of armed robberies and every form of crime. The malefactors, when caught, were hanged, together with local murderers and criminals, on the gibbet from which Gibbet Hill takes its name. They were thus visible from the main road, and it is to be hoped their grisly warning served to deter those contemplating similar crimes. The practice has long been discontinued, but the gibbet itself was in existence until pulled down in 1872."

"You won't get much more than that," the librarian said as John finished reading, "unless you go over to Guildford and see what they've got there. Surrey was notorious for its hold-ups by highwaymen before the railway age arrived. A good many 'gentlemen of the road' must have taken their last sight of earth from what are now your sitting-room windows. There could be worse views to take with you into the next world."

"I'm sure there could be," John agreed. "This is all very interesting." But it did not help to explain the ghostly burglar, nor why the intruder should have had a woman's low, gurgling laugh.

He was about to go when the librarian said as though it were too obvious to need saying: "Of course, you could always apply to Dr. de Witt."

"Who's Dr. de Witt?" John asked, adding: "I'm sorry if I seem very ignorant of local personalities, but remember we've only lived here for the past six months."

"Dr. de Witt's a retired M.O.H.," the librarian told him. "He's over eighty and not too sure on his feet, but as strong as you or I in the upper storey. He came to live here about twenty years ago—before my time—and local history's his hobby. There's nothing about this part of Surrey he can't tell you. He ought to write a book—I'm always saying so. But he won't. Just keeps it all in his head and on his bookshelves. He's got a wonderful collection of books on his subject," he added wistfully. "We've nothing to compare with it, even at Guildford."

"Do you think he'd see a stranger?" John asked doubtfully.

"I'm sure he would. He loves talking about his hobby. If you like, I'll ask him. I could ring him up straight away."

Dr. de Witt was delighted to have a visitor. Within a very short time John was being shown into his study, which, after the darkness of the hallway, was unexpectedly bright. A jug of daffodils stood in the window, the walls were covered with old prints, and where there were no prints there were bookshelves filled with volumes of every degree of size and antiquity, arranged according to no discernible plan, and giving off the slightly musty smell that goes with closed windows, old leather-bound volumes, and old age.

Dr. de Witt had been a man of medium stature and good carriage, but his back was so bent that his head seemed to grow out of his chest. He walked with a stick clasped in a hand whose veins were like knotted silk cords, and when he looked up at John his head maintained a perpetual though almost imperceptible trembling that made his visitor momentarily suspect his own eyes. He was not reassured until, having settled the doctor in his own chair, which was easily recognizable from the rugs and shawls which half filled it, he was able to fix his eyes on some inanimate object whose outline remained unblurred.

The old man regarded him intently with bright, slightly rheumy eyes. "The librarian said you were a newcomer to the district," he remarked. "Are you a historian, by any chance?"

"Not at all. I'm very much a layman. That's why I was advised to come to you." This did not sound very flattering. John amended it by adding: "I understand you're an expert in the history of these parts."

The old man's gaze roved over his prints and bookshelves. "I wouldn't say that. It's a hobby. Like collecting stamps. One collects, sorts, classifies and collates, and at the end, there are sometimes rarities in the collection."

"You mean things that no one else knows about?"

"Only because they haven't looked for them, my boy. The past is very close to the present—always. It's in the things around us. It's in the language we speak and in our physical selves. Hereditary characteristics, you would call them. But what's heredity except the past in us?"

John murmured agreement.

"Are you married?"

"Yes."

"Any children?"

"We're expecting our first."

"Ah, you'll understand what I mean by and by. Our children are our claim to immortality. In a hundred years' time your nose and chin may still exist—but in another face. Nothing is wasted. Nothing changes. Nothing dies."

John said: "I'm not sure I like the sound of that."

"Why not?"

"Isn't it a rather fatalistic attitude—this inexorable linking with the past?"

"Not more so than our inexorable linking with the future. The link is there, but we don't have to repeat the past's mistakes."

"So you think you can escape from it?" John murmured.

"Suppose you tell me what it is you have in mind."

"I wanted to know something about Gibbet Hill," John answered. "Pleasant Hill they've renamed it now. About three miles out, on a side-road leading to Hindhead."

The old doctor interrupted him: "I know."

"There was a gibbet there until 1872," John continued. "I learnt that in the library today. The local people seem to hold the hill in horror. I wondered if you perhaps knew why."

He was careful to say nothing about their burglar. Dr. de Witt might think him some sort of crank. But the old man was far too engrossed to notice any constraint in his visitor's manner. He was leaning forward, his hands clasped on top of his stick.

"Surely oral tradition would account for it," he said slowly. "You must remember 1872 is not so long ago. My father, for instance, could have seen that gibbet. And a place associated with repeated death is always feared. Besides, the penalty then applied to so many crimes which today we should call misdemeanours, so that of those who were hanged a great many were regarded as innocent by those who knew them best. There were some bad men hanged there too, of course. Charles Cleeve, the highwayman, had seven murders laid at his door. I don't say he didn't deserve what he suffered, though he repented and made a very moving farewell speech. But the last person to be hanged on Gibbet Hill was a woman, who was hanged for stealing a loaf of bread."

"Good God!" John exclaimed. "You're inventing."

"No, my boy, I only wish I were. She was young and by all accounts very pretty, and she protested her innocence to the last."

"Who was she?"

"A certain Thomasina Sampson. She lived at Penfold in a cottage owned by a farmer named Jarvis—a tied cottage; her husband worked on Farmer Jarvis's land. There were never any complaints about Thomasina until one day her husband fell sick and could not work. Farmer Jarvis, who had an unsavoury reputation, evicted them and they were sent to the poor law institution, where, according to custom, they were separated even though man and wife. Shortly afterwards Michael Sampson died—probably of neglect. Thomasina, who was expecting a child, ran away. This was not allowed; the destitute could be re-arrested. Thomasina was therefore on the run. For weeks she lived a nomad-like existence. Then the weather turned suddenly cold. Almost starving, she stole a loaf of bread from a baker who had allowed her to sleep near his oven for warmth. But she was a bad thief—she had had no practice. She was arrested and sent for trial. And there she did a foolish thing and destroyed her chances. She decided to tell the magistrates the truth."

"Why was she foolish?" John interrupted, but the old man held up a trembling but imperious hand.

"Thomasina believed that her troubles had begun with the eviction. But for that, she would have had her husband and her home. She had pleaded very hard with Farmer Jarvis, and he had offered a bargain in return: they could stay in the cottage if she would become his mistress. Thomasina indignantly refused. Unfortunately for her, Mrs. Jarvis was a cousin of the presiding magistrate, before whom she appeared for trial. Whatever he may have known of Farmer Jarvis's evil reputation, he felt his family honour was impugned. Far from softening him, her story won her the maximum sentence, which happened to be sentence of death. Attempts were made to get it commuted to transportation, but they all bogged down in the mud of legal procedure. Thomasina Sampson, aged twenty-two, a widow and the mother of a stillborn child, was hanged on Gibbet Hill on March 2nd, 1827, in the presence of a sympathetic crowd.

"Possibly the business disquieted the authorities. At any rate, there were no more hangings on Gibbet Hill. In 1868, public executions were abolished, and in 1872 the gibbet, already rotting, was taken down."

"And about time too!" John declared roundly. "It makes one's flesh creep to think of that poor girl. I'm not surprised Gibbet Hill had an evil reputation, although of course it's very different now."

The old doctor regarded him thoughtfully, looking up at him from between his bowed shoulders. "It wasn't only the savagery of the sentence," he said slowly. "It was the character of Thomasina herself. She had the power to capture public imagination. Do you understand what I mean?"

"Yes, of course," John said. "I'm in advertising. She must have put her image across, all right. Today she'd need a public relations expert, but she evidently had a flair for do-it-yourself."

"Do you want to read a contemporary account of her?" Dr. de Witt enquired; and when John nodded: "Then pass me that book over there. No, no"—as John mistook the direction of his pointing finger—"the third from the left, bottom shelf."

The volume in question was a leather-bound folio of incredible dryness and age. The calf binding flaked, and the pages were brittle and crumbling. The gilt lettering had faded on the spine. It proved to contain bound numbers of a local broadsheet John did not know. The dates ranged from 1816 to 1847, but there were only three or four issues a year. Guided by Dr. de Witt, John turned to 1827, and there, together with an account of a visit by His Majesty King George IV to Portsmouth, was an item "Malefactor Hanged".

"On Saturday, March 2nd," ran the report, "at eleven o'clock in the forenoon, was hanged Thomasina Sampson, thief. The condemned woman being young and of a pleasing demeanour, the crowd assembled was unaccustomedly large, and His Majesty's officers were much impeded in their duties, many persons expressing sympathy with the condemned. How misplaced was the sentiment of pity was made manifest by the condemned woman herself, who had contumaciously maintained her innocence throughout her trial and imprisonment, and refused even at the foot of the gallows to acknowledge and ask pardon for her fault. Exhorted by the chaplain to prepare herself, the condemned woman replied that she would not pray, since prayer had availed her nothing, and while the Revd Mr. Venn implored God's mercy upon her blasphemy, she cried to the assembly that she went now to a final resting-place from which no unjust landlord could evict her. She died unrepentant."

"You can hardly blame her," John observed.

"No. One law for the rich and another for the poor was never more true than in the days of the Industrial Revolution. All the same, she won herself an evil name. Where ignorance and poverty are rampant, superstition also has its hold. It is not surprising that legends grew up around Thomasina."

"What legends?" John asked, conscious of a sudden unease.

"The legend of her beauty, for one thing. The chances are she was no more than an averagely good-looking girl, but in the course of a few years she became transmuted into one of the loveliest of living beings. Of course such loveliness could not be natural; it was the Devil's gift to Thomasina, so it was said."

"Are there any descriptions of her?" John interrupted.

"Yes, several, and remarkably consistent they are. She was very small, that was the first thing about her, and very dark and she had beautiful even teeth. Good teeth were a rarity in those days; they alone would have singled Thomasina out. But it was her voice that was her principal fascination: it was throaty and musical and she had a very pretty laugh."

John felt his mouth go suddenly dry and sandy. "What was it like?" he managed to ask at last.

"Her laugh? Her contemporaries described it as low and gurgling. One said it was like water rippling over pebble-stones." Dr. de Witt looked up at the young man from under incredibly shaggy eyebrows. "Thomasina interests you, doesn't she?"

"Yes," John said, adding a moment later: "Do you believe in ghosts, Dr. de Witt?"

"Why not?" the old man answered with amusement. "I shall be one myself very soon."

John felt uncomfortable and looked it, and the old man hastened to go on: "Do you believe that personality—the soul, the spirit—is automatically extinguished at death?"

"I don't know," John said. Like most people, he avoided thinking about such matters. He knew only that a frightful unease had possessed him ever since Dr. de Witt had mentioned that low, gurgling laugh. But why should Thomasina return to haunt him and Eileen? There was no previous record of her ghost. If there were, he was sure Dr. de Witt would have mentioned it. It would be part of the legend he described.

The old man was looking at him curiously. "Do you think you have seen Thomasina Sampson's ghost?"

"Not seen it, heard it," John said quickly. He told the doctor about the footsteps and the sound that could only be a laugh.

Dr. de Witt looked thoughtful, rather troubled. "I suppose it's possible," he said at last. "If she were ever evicted from her last resting-place, she threatened she would return to take revenge. It could be that that had happened when the foundations were excavated for the houses put up on Gibbet Hill."

"Do you mean she was buried there?" John asked, horrified.

"Yes, of course. She couldn't be buried in consecrated ground. There must be a regular cemetery on that hill-top. All the hanged were cut down and buried there. Most of them lie easy enough, God rest 'em. But Thomasina—well, I wouldn't like to disturb her bones."

Her bones. The bones in the garden. The hollow sound of a spade against a skull. Their smallness, and their desiccated, crumbling condition, which indicated that they were already very old. And the loosened teeth that rained down from the jaw-bone when he held it. Hadn't Dr. de Witt said something about beautiful teeth? The more he thought, the more convinced John became that the bones were Thomasina's.

"What do you think I should do?" he asked the Doctor. "Do you really think a ghost can take revenge?"

"I see no reason why a strong emotion shouldn't persist," the Doctor said slowly. "If Thomasina still wants revenge, then revenge she'll take."

"But there must be some way of appeasing her. In the twentieth century, there must be something we can do."

The old man looked at him a long time without speaking. "You don't understand these things," he said at last. "For that reason you'd do better not to meddle. My advice would be to sell the house and get out."

"Sell the house? That's impossible!" John protested. "Why, we've only been there six months."

Dr. de Witt shrugged—as near as his bowed shoulders would come to shrugging. "Then I don't think I can help you. But I'll give you a further piece of advice."

He rose with difficulty, and stood gazing up at John on the hearth-rug. Then he tapped the young man's chest with a stiffened, claw-like hand.

"If you'll listen to an old man who's very near the end of his existence, you'll find Thomasina a new house before she decides to find one for herself."

John had cause to remember the old doctor's words many times in succeeding months, but it was not the warning about Thomasina that recurred to him: it was the old man's definition of heredity. "The past in us", he had called it, adding: "Nothing changes. Nothing is wasted. Nothing dies." With the birth of his daughter in April, John had cause to recognize this.

The child, whom they named Sarah, was a beauty; everyone admitted as much. She was not noticeably like either parent, though John insisted that she had Eileen's brow. Eileen laughed and said Sarah was a changeling, and John wondered to what ancestor Sarah harked back. "The past in us", but from a distance; from across the generations, as it were.

John said nothing to Eileen about his visit to the old doctor, nor did he ever mention Thomasina Sampson's name. Eileen appeared to have forgotten the ghostly intruder, and John preferred it should be so. She was happy and busy with her daughter. Perhaps the police-sergeant had been right after all, and it was nothing more than a pregnant woman's fancy. John sincerely hoped this was the case. Thomasina—if Thomasina it was—gave no indication of her presence; there were no footsteps, no laughter, no sudden draughts. The sun shone, the summer was protracted and perfect, and in her parents' eyes Sarah grew bonnier every day. Not even the death of Dr. de Witt, which he saw announced in the local paper, could stir John to more than momentary regret; he had intended to go back and gather some more information, and now the old man himself was a ghost.

The weather did not break until October, but when it did, there was torrential rain. The river overflowed and flooded the water-meadows. One Thursday—the last day in October—John's train was forty minutes late from Waterloo.

It was already dark when he alighted at the station; the platforms gleamed wetly under the lamps. The wind, more noticeable here than in London, had risen to gale force. A gust swept round the corner of the booking-hall and nearly knocked John off his feet. He picked his way through the puddles in the car-park, holding his hat on his head.

He was unlocking the car when a policeman materialized at his elbow. "Going in the Hindhead direction, sir?"

"Yes, I am," John said, wondering what was the matter.

"Then I'm afraid you may not get very far." The policeman was apologetic, even regretful. "There's a tree blown down across the main Hindhead road. The road's impassable to all traffic and won't be open tonight."

"Is there an alternative route?" John asked, frowning.

"You'll have to go round through Rundlefold."

"That'll take hours," John objected.

"I know, sir. I'm sorry, but there it is. Going far?" the policeman asked sympathetically.

"Only to Pleasant Hill," John said.

"If you take my advice, sir, you'll walk it. It's only a couple of miles. And the rain's stopped sheeting down. It's only an occasional squall now," the policeman encouraged.

The advice was sensible and John took it. He managed to ring Eileen and allay her fears. Sarah, she assured him, was sleeping peacefully, undisturbed by either wind or rain.

By the time John left the station yard the rain had stopped completely. He strode out briskly, eager to reach his home. The wind alternately aided and impeded him, for it seemed to come from all quarters indiscriminately. It was as though a series of express trains rushed past in the air above him, barely managing not to collide. As each passed, he was flattened to a standstill, and while he struggled breathless in its wake, another would roar past coming from a different direction, and he would have to struggle all over again.

The trees also struggled to keep their balance, their branches flailing the sky. In places they had caught at the cloud-cover, which now showed ragged rents and an occasional star. The road was full of dead leaves, brittle twigs and broken branches. The hedges cowered against the wind and creaked and groaned. A rain of conkers like machine-gun bullets left John startled, and before he could recover a cold wet hand had slapped his face. Stifling a cry, which in that tumult would have been inaudible, John clawed at his face and removed a horse-chestnut leaf. Angry and sheepish at his own discomfiture, he endeavoured to quicken his pace.

He breasted a slight rise and saw before him lights, an ambulance, a police-car drawn into the side of the road. Beyond was a dark mass illuminated in the police-car's headlights: the fallen tree that was blocking the road. To one side and almost beneath it was the rear of a dark-green car.

The tree had landed squarely across it, and the front was a twisted mass of metal—aluminium foil crumpled by a hand. There was no sign of life but the ambulance men were working busily. John paused by the police-car to enquire.

"Dead," one of the occupants told him, not taking his eyes off the scene. "Take hours to get him out, what's left of him. Thanks for asking, but there's nothing anyone can do."

Slightly sickened, John stooped under the tree-trunk, which lay like a low bridge across the road. As he passed the wrecked car, he caught a glimpse of a dark and sluggish substance which was oozing out to join the rain.

Oil or blood, he did not stop to speculate. All he wanted was to get safely home. He was not prepared to admit to being frightened, but his nerves were certainly on edge. The policeman at the station should have mentioned the accident; it was not fair to let an unsuspecting pedestrian come upon it unawares. Curious the coincidence that had brought the tree crashing down upon the car—curious and somehow sinister, as though the impersonal elements were motivated tonight by some alien and hostile force.

The crashed tree now suggested a new danger. What had happened once could easily happen again. With each fresh gust John's ears were alert for the tell-tale creaking, while his eyes strained to discern the gathering flurry of branches against the sky. Once, in a sudden lull which seemed unnatural, he heard a strange metallic clank. He looked round; there was nothing to cause it—nothing but the houses of Pleasant Hill neatly tucked in for the night. He was evidently the last commuter making his way homewards. The metallic clank came again. It was as if some heavy object were swinging in the wind very slowly. A gate, a loose casement, John reassured himself; whatever it was, was out of sight. Of course a more highly strung homecomer who knew that this had once been Gibbet Hill might easily fancy he heard chains as the hanged swung back and forwards, but he was not like that. He was firmly rooted in the twentieth century; superstition, like slavery, was not for him. Nevertheless, he would have preferred not to remember the hill's associations. It was with distinct relief that he opened the door of his home.

Eileen came to meet him in the hallway. Her welcoming smile assured him all was well. When he went up to change, he peeped into Sarah's small bedroom. His daughter slept as though there were no gale at all. On her soft cheeks the lashes lay like shadows. Her lips, slightly parted, were soft and moist. As he watched, a bubble of saliva burst and the child stirred in her sleep, resettling her head upon her medically approved hard pillow, which like every other item of her equipment was text-book rec-ommended and correct. Even Sarah herself subscribed to text-book reg-ulations and was cutting her first tooth to time. This no doubt accounted for her restlessness and dribbling, whereas the wild night outside left her calm and unperturbed.

Just as well, John reflected, as the house reeled from another buffet, for on the crest of the hill they had no protection from the wind. From whichever direction it blew, it hurled itself four-square against the house. The rain, which had started again, beat on the windows like hail.

John was half way downstairs when he heard Eileen drop a pan in the kitchen and come running into the hall. A glance at her face was enough.

"What is it?" he asked quickly.

"Oh, darling, I heard it—that laugh."

John felt suddenly sick with apprehension. "What laugh?" he asked, pretending to forget.

"The one that we heard the night we had the police here. I've never heard it again until now. I thought she'd gone away and forgotten all about us. Since Sarah was born, I haven't felt her near at all."

"Felt who near? What are you talking about?"

"That woman, whoever she is." Eileen clutched her husband's arm in desperation. "Promise you won't let her in."

"I promise," John said mechanically. "But you know she got in before."

"Yes, I know. But this time it's different. She's outside. She was by the back door. I've fastened everything because of the rain and the way the wind was blowing. There isn't the smallest crack she can get through."

"Then there's nothing to worry about." John strove to sound reassuring. Next moment there was a thunderous knock at the front door.

He was moving instinctively to open it when Eileen flung herself in his path. "Are you mad? Do you want to invite her in? For God's sake don't open that door."

"But suppose it's someone else?" John protested. "I wouldn't leave a beast out on a night like this."

"There's no one there." Eileen was peering through a side window.

There was another tremendous rat-tat at the door.

"It's the wind," John said in an attempt at scientific explanation.

"Have you ever known the wind lift a knocker?"

"I haven't known a gale like this."

As if in mockery of his theory there came a ring at the bell.

"That's not the wind," Eileen insisted, half in fear, half in triumph.

"I'm going to open that door."

"You are not." She stood against it, arms held wide to prevent him.

"But supposing there's someone there? Someone may be lost, have had an accident." He thought fleetingly of the wrecked car. "It's inhuman to keep that door shut."

"I tell you there's nothing human there. See for yourself—through the window."

John looked out into the storm-blackened night. The porch-light illuminated silver rain-needles, but there was nothing else to be seen. Thomasina was not showing herself—if Thomasina it was. With sudden anxiety John remembered the old doctor's parting advice to him: "Find her a new house before she decides to find one for herself." And now Dr. de Witt was beyond reach of the longest long-distance telephone-call. He was no longer available to give advice. And Thomasina whom he, John, had evicted from her last resting-place, was clamouring for shelter without.

275

Eileen had begun to cry. "Oh, John, do something. We ought to have known she'd come tonight."

"Why tonight?" John asked, his mind a turmoil.

"Because it's Hallowe'en, of course. The night the ghosts are at large from sundown to sunrise, only I've never believed it until now."

Before John could reply another knock resounded, coming this time from the back door.

"She's a very practical ghost," he said, trying to speak lightly. "There's no answer at the front so she promptly goes round to the back."

"Don't answer it," Eileen implored him.

"I think we must. I don't believe this is a ghost."

"*I* believe it's a ghost," Eileen said fiercely. "For my sake, darling, don't go."

"I'll only open the outer door enough to make certain. The inner door behind me will stay shut."

A gust of wind shook the house. Eileen was trembling. "You couldn't hold any door against a gust like that."

"I can," John said stoutly. "Not to worry. I'd never forgive myself if there was someone outside in distress." Someone who had been evicted and sworn vengeance. Someone with small white teeth and an unforgettable laugh.

To his astonishment, Eileen flung herself on her knees before him. "John, I've never asked anything like this before. I may be a silly hysterical woman, but if you love me, then for my sake—Sarah's sake—promise me you won't open either door."

Her face was tight and strained with terror. There were tears like raindrops on her cheeks.

"If it means so much to you, then I promise." He was conscious of a sense of betrayal as he spoke.

Eileen subsided in a flood of thankfulness. "Thank God, thank God, I was so afraid you would. I know it's wrong to be so superstitious, but this storm is getting me down."

The wind seemed if anything to be rising. They could hear it gathering itself for another attack. Its sigh deepened into a roar and then to a blast-off which made preceding blasts like puffs of smoke. Its intensity was equalled by its duration. John and Eileen clung together in the hall, listening to what seemed like an express train roaring towards them and through them and around them in a mighty crash and the tinkle of broken glass.

The iciness of the incoming wind was breath-stopping. It seemed hours before the paralysis of fear would let them relax. The door between living-room and hall had been flung open, and from where they stood they could see the disaster plain enough. The big picture-window had blown inwards. The floor was covered with silver shards of glass. Wet leaves, twigs, a mud-splashed chrysanthemum, joined the glass to form a solid carpet. The curtains flapped horizontally from their poles. The rain, almost as horizontal, swept inwards. All small movable objects were thrown over, some broken. It was as if a tornado had devastated the room.

John spoke first. "Lucky nobody was in there." He indicated the wicked-looking jags of broken glass. "God knows how we're going to get this mess cleared up. I can't do much tonight."

He disengaged himself from Eileen and walked forwards. She said: "I must see if Sarah's all right."

"She will be," John assured her. "Good job she sleeps at the back. You can tell the noise hasn't even wakened her. She'd soon let us know if it had."

"That's true," Eileen admitted, her mother's ear on the alert. There was no sound from the bedroom where Sarah slept peacefully. John called out that he needed a broom.

For three-quarters of an hour they worked solidly. John managed to get the curtains down and some hardboard nailed across the lower part of the window, while Eileen set about clearing the floor. After that last tremendous gust, the wind had subsided. It still tossed the trees, but it seemed more distant, more subdued. By the time Eileen went upstairs to wash and peep at her daughter, it had spent the worst of its rage. The rain too had stopped; the clouds were breaking; behind them a pallid moon gleamed. When Eileen put her head into the nursery, the room was lit by one weak and trembling moonbeam.

His wife's scream was a more terrible sound than John had ever imagined could be uttered. Years afterwards in nightmares he was to hear that scream. Now he simply stood helpless among the living-room wreckage as Eileen's frantic feet pounded down the stairs.

"Get a doctor," she commanded him urgently. "*Any* doctor. But get one at once."

"What is it?" John asked her, already reaching for the phone. "What's happened?"

"It's Sarah. I think she's dead."

"But she can't be! I saw her. I watched her breathing…"

"She had the pillow over her face." Eileen wailed then, the long wail of a grief-stricken woman, and sank down, her child in her arms.

She was still cradling the inert, unresponsive little body when John turned round from the phone.

"I can't get through. That gust must have brought the wires down."

"Get the car," Eileen ordered, tight-lipped.

John recollected. "It's at the station. And besides, the road is closed."

Eileen never took her eyes off her daughter. "There must be *something* we can do."

"But how can it have happened?" John burst out, despair and grief flooding over him. "She can't have suffocated, they said a pillow like that was safe."

"I told you—it was over her face." Eileen didn't look at him. "It must have been put there."

"You mean deliberately? But we were both down here."

"Yes," Eileen said, still not looking at him. "As you say, we were both down here."

"It isn't possible!" John cried, overcome by horror.

For answer Eileen kissed the dead child's cheek.

What if she was right, John thought in anguish, and this was the vengeance of Thomasina—Thomasina evicted from her grave, knocking at the door in the wind and rain and darkness, bursting in through the window and up the unguarded stairs? "Find her a new house before she finds one for herself," Dr. de Witt had warned him. And he, fool that he was, had ignored the old man's advice. Now Thomasina had had her revenge and was presumably satisfied. Well might she have uttered her peculiar throaty laugh.

But now the house was curiously silent—John tried not to think "as silent as the grave". In the wrecked living-room his wife crouched over their daughter. In the hall he looked with loathing at the useless telephone.

"There must be something we can do," Eileen repeated; but her words were mechanical, spoken without hope. Again she bent to kiss the face before the life-blood faded, and again John felt the extent of his helplessness.

Suddenly his brain, which had moved so slowly that each second seemed like an aeon, began to work as though jolted by a high-voltage charge. A kiss could be the kiss of life. It was barely possible, but even the slimmest chance was worth a try.

"Give Sarah to me," he ordered.

Eileen clutched the child to her in fear. Her first thought was that her husband's mind had been affected, that he was temporarily insane from shock and grief. Sarah was past all harm, but Eileen's mother-instinct refused to let the little body go.

"Give her to me," John insisted. "I can save her. At least, I'm going to try."

When Eileen still offered resistance, he struck her a savage blow.

From the muddied floor where she had fallen, Eileen watched uncomprehendingly. Her husband must certainly be mad. The same evil power that had destroyed her daughter had deprived her husband of his wits. She was alone in the house with a madman, who was even now bending over the child, his lips seeking and finding—like a vampire's—the baby's pitiful mouth.

In—out. In—out. Never had John paid so much attention to breathing, never before regarded it as anything but a reflex physical act. In—out. Breathe deep and exhale more deeply, forcing the expelled air into the baby's lungs. Her body was still warm, her colour not yet faded. The vital functions might still be recalled to life. It was not possible that a woman dead more than a century should retain her, when her own father was breathing his breath into her lungs.

In—out. In—out. Eileen was sobbing quietly in a corner, a dreary, hopeless, misery-racked sound. But John dared not lift his head to explain what he was doing. The warmth, the regular rhythm, that was all. In—out. Even though it seemed quite hopeless; even though Sarah's life had gone beyond recall; even though Thomasina and all uneasy spirits were against him, he would go on breathing in to the unformed, unresisting, slackly open, colourless little mouth.

John could not have said how or when he first noticed the change in the body; he was only aware that it had taken place. The face, though pale, had lost its deathly pallor; the flesh was no longer chilling in the grip of death. He dared not stop, not even to call Eileen, but he worked now with a surge of hope that was almost more painful than despair.

In—out. Surely there was a faint vibration under the ribcage, as a cranked car may indicate that the engine will fire next time? John's hands on his daughter willed her to live, each fingertip speaking separately to her flesh. A tremor so slight that it might have been a shadow passed over her face and was gone. For an instant John held his own breath and watched her intently. Against his cheek he felt the faintest breeze, and just as he was abusing himself for his own credulity, the child's chest moved beneath his hand.

"Eileen," he called, "she's alive."

For a long second Eileen sat there, not daring to move. Her husband's insanity seemed to be becoming more dangerously delusional every minute as he leaned frantically over the child. He looked almost as though he were trying to devour her in some ritual cannibal act. When he raised his head for a moment, she was surprised his jaws were not dripping slaver and blood.

"Come here," he called urgently. "She's breathing."

Hesitantly Eileen crossed the debris of the room. The wind blew coldly through the shattered window. Light from the lamps and light from the moon combined. But not even their mingled yellow-and-silver brilliance could render Sarah as pale as she had been. Even as Eileen watched, the small chest rose and fell in a hurried respiration. After a pause that seemed unending, came the next. John was gently chafing the baby's hands. Eileen kissed her feet, finding them to her astonishment wet with her own unnoticed tears.

Sarah's breath was coming more naturally now, the rhythm of inhalation and exhalation had returned. She moved her head restlessly, like one about to wake, at the same time screwing her eyes up as if to shut out some unwelcome sight. Feeling himself suddenly weak with relief and reaction, John sank down beside his wife, who had tucked a hastily-fetched blanket around their daughter, whom otherwise she seemed reluctant to touch.

"Best leave her where she is for the moment," John whispered. "She'll come round in a minute or two."

As if she had heard and were anxious to anticipate his wishes, Sarah opened her dark-blue eyes. Two smiling faces leaned side by side towards her. She opened her mouth and breathed in for a cry.

And then the horrible happened—so horrible that neither John nor Eileen could believe it was anything but a bad dream. Sarah was looking at them without a hint of recognition, not even when Eileen held out her arms. From her lips, now rapidly regaining their colour and drawn back for a lusty infant bawl, came the most bloodcurdling sound John and Eileen had ever heard or believed existed: it was a woman's low, gurgling laugh.

THE GROVE

Mary Williams

Published in Chill Company: Ghost Stories from Cornwall,
1976

Mary Williams (1903–2000) was born in Leicestershire and went to
Collegiate School, Leicester. There she took an interest in art, history
and literature. When she left school, her first job was at the *Leicester
Chronicle*, where she reported on social events under the name "June"
and interviewed actors who appeared at the local theatre, such as Diana
Wynward and Laurence Olivier. She spent some time living on the canal
boat "Cressy" with L. T. C. Rolt and his first wife Angela during WWII,
broadcasting on behalf of the BBC from it. Her first novel, *Louise*, was
published in 1947 (London Sentinel) and marriage took her away from
Leicester—she moved to Wales and became "Jane" of *The Abergavenny
Chronicle*. She then moved to a studio home overlooking the harbour
in St. Ives, Cornwall and continued to write short stories, with Francis
Hyland becoming a champion of her work. She opened a gallery with
her husband at Porthmeor Beach where she would sell her paintings and
black and white illustrations. She kept her connection with Wales, with
several of her stories and illustrations featured on Welsh BBC children's
programmes.

She was invited to write a story ("The Lost Ones") for Denys Val
Baker's *Haunted Cornwall* (1973) and the story proved so popular with
readers that they flooded publisher William Kimber with letters asking
to read more of her work. This resulted in her first collection for Kimber,
The Dark Land: A Book of Cornish Stories (1975), prompting other pub-
lishers to advise Kimber against publishing a collection by a little-known
writer. Kimber was not to be dissuaded and the book sold well, especially
to libraries in the UK and also in the European market.

On her ghost stories she had this to say: "I'm very happy writing ghost stories because I know they give pleasure to so many people [...] living in Cornwall is ideal because it is so inspirational for a writer. The surrounding area is rather silvery in winter and very eerie on occasions, so it does help me with my imagination."

Mary died in 2000, aged 97.

I COULD see the hill from my bedroom window, rising gently from lush pasture land towards the crest of moors bordered on the skyline by a few stunted wind-blown trees. The vista, though not exactly dramatic, was interesting, because of the dark huddle of trees and furze in the centre of an otherwise large open field, where cattle grazed placidly in the grass under yellowish autumn skies.

My break from city life was late that year, following the unpleasant but necessary finalizing of divorce, which had entailed the usual tag-ends to be tied neatly and laid away like a parcel in a perfectly civilized manner.

Oh yes; Julia and I had behaved, I'm sure, in the manner expected of two rational and presumably intelligent members of society... parting as friends... outwardly anyway; although the small chore of resentment gnawed at me later when she took my hand saying, "Thanks, John. And all good luck darling."

It was then I knew, and actually had to accept, from the clear brittle voice and relief in her blue eyes, that she just didn't care a damn. Five years of marriage had meant no more to her than a prolonged affair gone sour. Being a practising medical psychotherapist of course, I should have been able to assess her potentialities considerably earlier. That I hadn't, was humiliating in the extreme.

"Good luck to you," I'd said, thinking, "and I hope you bloody well get ditched as you deserve." But of course she wouldn't be; because Lawrence had fallen for her hard in the same blind way I had in my time. And when the breaking point came *he* wouldn't be the one to force the issue.

I had come to know my beautiful Julia pretty well by then. No man could resist her... unless he married her... like me.

So when I went to Trengorse for a late holiday, I wasn't exactly broken-hearted. I didn't yearn for her any more. But I was bitter. Five years was quite a time to waste from a life. Time was precious. I had seen too many patients respond, eventually to mental treatment, with their youth gone… lost in the dark hinterland of prolonged psychopathic disturbance… not to realize that every day of living was a precious thing. And Julia had stolen so many of mine.

Not of course, that I blamed her entirely. In every broken marriage mutual shortcomings and errors were entitled. It was her casualness that rankled. Even her… gaiety almost.

Anyhow, there it was. I was away for a time in Cornwall, and during the first week was playing with the idea of throwing up my town practice and settling for the simple life; farming perhaps, in a modest way. Probably I knew deep down this was a mere pipe dream; but once established in my mind, it lingered, encouraged by the freedom of my surroundings… the wide stretch of countryside merging on the east into the rim of sea and sky, under hazily lifting mornings, and quiet twilights disturbed only by the cries of gulls and other muted sounds of nature.

The hotel, though not large, was well-run, standing on its own, two miles from Braggas, half-way up a slope, facing the hill with the dark grove on it. At night, when the moon came up, its humped shadows crept downwards towards the valley, giving a queer semblance of atavistic life, stimulating and slightly uncanny.

I was commenting on the fact to the manageress, a friendly Cornish woman one morning, mentioning that I was thinking of taking a walk there.

After a perceptible pause, she shrugged, and said ambiguously, "Yes; well, it *is* a bit of a curiosity I suppose. But there's really nothing to see there… just a broken circle of old oaks so tangled up with briars you can hardly get in. It's fenced round now, with a gate too… to keep the cattle and sheep from getting caught. Not that there's any need for it, with all that thick undergrowth. But a lamb *was* lost there once. So Mr. Thomas, the farmer likes to have access."

"Why doesn't he get it cleared?" I asked.

"Now *that* I can't say," she replied. "History perhaps. Those trees are very old... hundreds of years; and the ones before them... the old stumps... must've been there since the beginning of time almost."

My interest began to quicken.

"You referred to history. Do you mean there's a story attached? A legend perhaps?"

"Oh!..." She gave a short laugh. "Everything has a legend round here if you look for it. Miss Mellyn now... she'd be the one to ask about such things..." she glanced round... "Ah! you're lucky. Here she is. I expect you've met, haven't you?"

"We've seen each other at meal times," I answered, as a slim, tawny-haired girl in a blue trouser suit came into the hall from the lounge. "That's about all, I'm afraid."

After the usual introductory process, we chatted for a few moments, while I assessed the lady. She was about twenty-five, I guessed; sophisticated beneath her youthful exterior; very cool looking, with high cheekbones and a full sensuous mouth that belied her manner. Her eyes were a very light grey, slightly tilted and shrewd. Oh yes... she was no fool. I wondered what she was doing at Trengorse, and when Mrs. Pender had gone, as though sensing my thoughts, she told me.

"You're interested in old places, obviously. So am I. That's why I came here. To Cornwall I mean. I travel around a lot, and if I like a place I stay; if not I just move on somewhere else."

"I see. You're lucky."

She lit a cigarette, and offered me one, which I refused. "In a way I suppose I am," she agreed. "I don't have to be a hippy or scrounger to get around. I pay."

The way she said it mildly annoyed me.

"How convenient."

"Of course. I like my comforts. In other words I can afford to have them. Do you blame me?"

"Certainly not. Your life isn't my affair."

"No." After the brief statement she smiled, and looked quite beautiful. But I was unimpressed. Her type was not the sort I liked. Perhaps at that period no type was. I wasn't on the rebound to fall for any glamorous female who crossed my path, being "hipped" temporarily by the whole lot of them. All the same, from a purely medical angle something about her had me puzzled. I had the feeling that despite her underlying calculating quality… part of her wasn't with me at all. She would glance at me briefly, then look away as though her eyes couldn't focus for more than a few moments at a time. I suspected drugs, but couldn't be sure.

In any case I'd no intention of getting involved. As I'd pointed out, her life was her own affair. A statement that later was to prove ironic in the extreme; because of course I *did* get involved; not maybe in the way she'd expected, but by events so macabre that they register in my memory now more as some dark nightmare of the psyche rather than fact.

I was about to end the little interim with her in the hall, when she said casually, "I heard you talking to Mrs. Pender about the hill… the oak grove."

"Yes. I *was* enquiring. I thought it rather odd to see such a massed huddle of trees in the very centre of such a large field."

"Not really," she told me coolly. "In the past it was a sacred place… for the Druids you know. Cornwall's full of that sort of thing."

"Oh. So *that's* it."

"Of course the time to see it property's at night… if there's a moon." She paused, continuing with a light laugh, "Not that I advise it. It's a bit of a climb, and I expect you keep regular hours for sleeping."

In spite of myself I was irritated by the inference that I registered with her as some old fuddy-duddy of a city man who had to eat, sleep, and work to time-table, even on holiday.

"Thanks for the information," I said curtly.

"Don't mention it." She shrugged, went to the door, looked back once before going out, to say, almost slyly. "Why don't you take a peep tonight? You might learn something."

I had the feeling she was trying to taunt me... though whether I accepted the challenge or not didn't really matter to her one way or the other.

From mild dislike, my reactions became positively hostile. She was so damned sure of herself. Like a sleek cat peering contemptuously from some hidden corner, while a distracted owner jumped this way and that calling and searching in vain.

I did not see the delectable but distasteful Miss Mellyn again that day, and did not just then take my intended walk to the hill, thinking it quite possible she had gone along before me, contemplating a further encounter. Neither was she in for dinner.

"The poor young lady's gone to bed with migraine," I was told. "Been upstairs most of the day. Had no lunch or anything much to eat at all. A shame isn't it? On holiday too."

"Rather a waste," I agreed, wondering what kind of migraine the girl was suffering from.

Something in my voice, a touch of irony perhaps, brought a quick glance of curiosity from Mrs. Pender, followed by a probing remark, "I thought you and Jennet... I mean Miss Mellyn... might take that walk together to the hill...?"

"It wasn't as important to me as that," I answered casually, adding quickly, "Did you say her name was Jennet?"

"Yes. Pretty, isn't it?"

"Unusual," I retorted. "A supposed witch of that name was burned at the stake in the dark ages, I believe."

"*Witch!*" scornfully. "Savagery I call it. I didn't know *you* had an interest in that stuff and nonsense, Mr. Cave."

"Not personally," I assured her. "But references to such things occasionally crop up in my work."

"What are you then, sir? I thought you were a doctor."

"So I am. Of mental illness."

"I see."

She didn't, of course. She was extremely disapproving, and I sensed I had gone down in her estimation.

After this brief conversation I spent an hour reading, had a smoke, then took a stroll down the lane to The Boar's Head, on the outskirts of Braggas, where I chatted with one or two of the natives, farmers and fishermen mostly, who were quite amicable and forthcoming, now the influx of invading "furriners" during the holiday season had gone.

I didn't refer to the oak grove, having already decided to do just what Jennet had suggested… take a walk up there myself when the moon was up. My intention had nothing whatever to do with her taunts of "regular hours," although her allusions to Druid territory had admittedly heightened my curiosity.

The evening itself, somehow, was already inducive to mystery and exploration… fading from crimson sunset to a translucent greenish sky in which a first star hung, gem-like over the darkening line of moors.

When I left the inn, what slight wind there had been, had gone, leaving a curious stillness through which silvered mist crept insidiously from the damp earth, veiling shrubs and trees into uniformity, enclosing the dying vista of hills until earth and sky became one, lit only by the rising moon which crept gradually above the vaporous cloud, shedding its eerie light over the distorted landscape.

However, I had a good sense of locality, and if it took me a little longer than I'd anticipated in locating the grove, this provided no problem. Mrs. Pender's custom was to provide all her guests with a key, and I had mine with me. So if I wished I could spend the whole night away.

Not that I contemplated the idea. But the atmosphere of "place" was already affecting me, with its sinister implications of years long gone.

As I approached the copse, cutting up a mere thread of lane leading past the field, I noticed a reddish glow curdling the mist by the grouped trees. I climbed a fence, where a few cattle were huddled; but except for one long "moo…" they did not stir. It was as though they, too, were entranced and mystified by the magic and weird trance-like quality of the night.

I was half way across the field when I had a compelling impulse to turn and go back. That I didn't, was entirely due to self-pride... a reluctance to admit to any "compulsion" having no sane basis... a state of mind which through my professional capacity I'd had to deal with countless times in others.

So I went on, walking quickly over the soft grass, until I was on the verge of the grove itself.

The reddish light still lingered there, but not so brightly. It could have been, I told myself reasonably... a glow from a bonfire... or perhaps a distant moorland blaze which had died down or been effectively dealt with. The thickened air *did* seem to hold a distinct aroma of smoke; and yet from the trees themselves there was no crackle or sign of disturbance; only their odd static ancient shapes entangled at the roots by the hungry clutching company of thick furze, briars, and general undergrowth. The fence was undiscernible in parts, although it must have been circular, because the shape of the grove was distinct and almost black against the pale expanse of moon-washed grassland surrounding it. The gate, though entangled with growth and weed, was comparatively negotiable.

I pushed it open, and plunged through.

My first impression was of icy, intense cold; of having entered a secret place... tomb-like and hostile to humanity. The thick branches of the trees stretched and entwined each other overhead, making an arched roof through which, in parts, no semblance of light filtered.

The air was stagnant; the ground underfoot intensely dark, cloyed, and seeping with decay. I could at first distinguish no form or movement in the dank enclosure. But as my eyes grew accustomed to the gloom, I perceived a grey half-circle of broken stones which I thought to be the immense roots of oaks, until I touched one with my foot. Its granite surface seemed to shudder, disturbing the air momentarily from darkness into a faint lifting quiver of light. At the same time the mist formed, intermittently, into spiralling macabre shapes... wraith-like and somehow obscene, resembling spectral creatures risen from graves, in the rotting winding sheets of the dead.

I couldn't stir. I dare hardly breathe, although they seemed unconcerned, and unaware even of my presence. If I could have escaped at that moment I would have done; but all volition had gone from my rigid limbs, leaving me static and useless. I could not even close my eyes. It was as though through my own fool-hardy intrusion I was held prisoner, and unwilling witness to the foul scene that followed.

And foul indeed it was... an unhallowed ritual more debased and terrifying than any modern conception of black magic dealt with so frequently in current fiction and films. There was no symbolic goat... no sexual orgy... or phoney self-induced hypnotism... just a grey circle of slowly moving shapes with luminous hollow-eyed faces and bared jaws... chattering and grimacing... lifting their skeleton tattered arms in unison towards the ever-climbing moon, until in the lifting light, I saw something else. One immense standing stone at the far end of the grove, where a naked woman knelt, pale hair brushing the ground, slim neck bowed; arms raised in ancient obeisance to her own dark god.

There was no attempt from the macabre company to interfere or touch her; but when she stood up and turned, revealing her blossoming pale body in the curdling green light, they converged slightly upon her, still chattering soundlessly, sunken eyes and jaws greedy for living flesh and blood... for a taste of the sexual savagery they had once known in the far-off centuries of their earthly lives.

A surge of sickness rose in me. But I had no power to vomit or remonstrate; could only stare helplessly at Jennet... oh yes, I no longer doubted her identity... as she moved forward slowly, hips and breasts swaying, into the heart of the unholy throng, touching them one by one on their rotting shoulders, until at last she paused, and lifted her face to a gaunt cowled creature standing nearest to the gate. The hood fell back completely from its face, revealing in a flood of full moonlight, the lusting skull and fiery eye-sockets.

Jennet waited, smiling, as the bared strong-toothed jaws sought her lips, but failed; closing instead upon her right cheek.

She struck out, with a high shrill cry of rage. The creature backed and fell to the ground. I watched, petrified, as the woman's figure seemed to expand and grow to an immense height, in which every feature and line of her body was visible, even the curious scarlet triangle of her face where the bite of the dead had been.

Almost simultaneously, the throng began to disintegrate before my eyes. One by one I saw the ghastly shapes quiver, and shrink, to become finally sucked back into the stagnant earth of their corruption.

My heart then, began to hammer against my ribs. With an effort I turned from the unholy grove, and on heavy legs managed to push through the gates.

The field before me lay calm and pale, streaked with shadows from the ancient oaks. As I waited briefly struggling for composure, I caught a glimpse of a ghostly nude shape rushing ahead of me down the slope. I started after her, but before I was half way to the valley, cloud and mist obscured the landscape, taking the figure of the woman into the darkness of intense night; and at that moment a bell tolled from behind me... doom-like, as though heralding the return of corpses to their domain. I rested until the power of movement had returned properly to my limbs, then went on, not looking back, until at last I reached the fence, climbed it, and was lurching down the road towards the guest house.

What time it was when I got there, I don't know. I didn't even look at the clock. Exhaustion had swept every normal reaction into complete negation. I recall vaguely clutching the hand-rail of the stairs, and climbing automatically to my room, where I flung myself still fully dressed on to the bed.

Then I knew no more until the morning.

When I woke it was already past nine-thirty. I lay for a time until there was a knock at the door. "Yes?" I shouted curtly and unwelcomingly.

The girl entered, with the cup of tea she usually brought about an hour earlier.

"Sorry, sir," she apologized. "I *did* come before, but there wasn't an answer, so Mrs. Pender said to leave it until you were properly awake."

"That's all right. Thank you," I said. "I didn't mean to bark at you. Put it down there. As it's so late I won't bother with breakfast."

"Oh but it's ready. Cook's left it in the oven."

"Very well. I won't be long, but I doubt if I'll want anything except a bit of toast."

She left, satisfied. I drank the tea which revived me a little; washed, shaved, and dressed lethargically, then went down.

Mrs. Pender was in the dining room when I entered. Despite the slight concern on her face, curiosity was stronger.

"Well, Mr. Cave... I mean doctor, I hope you had a good night," she queried. "I was beginning to wonder if everything was all right with you."

"All right?" I echoed, with forced brightness, "Of course. I had a walk before turning in, and went further than I'd thought."

"A *walk?* Oh. I thought maybe you'd gone to Braggas. The Fair."

"I didn't know there was one," I answered, sitting down at the table.

"On Hallow's E'en?... No *party* or anything?" she laughed. "Oh we always have some 'goings on' then. In the Market square when it's fine... you know, the usual games, bobbing the apple... turnip lanterns with candles in them, and a dance for youngsters dressed as witches and such like. They wouldn't miss it for the world."

"Hallow's E'en." I echoed slowly. "Of *course*... 'All Souls'"... the time when the dead leave their graves, and phantoms walk..."

"Oh!" The exclamation was sharp. "I don't agree with *that* side of it. Just an old tale left over from pagan times. Not healthy. No-one believes in such things these days, except some of them hippies and layabouts with nothing better to do."

"Of course not," I said soothingly.

Mrs. Pender was about to leave, when I enquired, "Did *you* go to Braggas, Mrs. Pender?"

She turned at the door.

"No. I generally do; but that poor Miss Mellyn seemed so ill I thought I'd keep an eye on her. At one time she went off in a kind of faint; took some bringing round too. So I called in the doctor."

"I see," I said abruptly, trying to instil a note of sympathy into my voice, but failing utterly. "And what did the doctor say?"

"He couldn't quite make it out," she admitted. "Said she must be run-down, and left some tablets. But..."

"Yes?"

"Well, he *did* say she perhaps ought to see a specialist when she got back to town." She paused, adding almost immediately, "*Why*, Mr. Cave?... I mean doctor?... Forgive me, I keep forgetting you're a medical man... Why are you so interested?"

"Nothing," I said, "except that I agree with him. The thing is..."

"Yes, sir?"

"Are you *sure* she was in bed *all* the evening? You see, I thought I saw her in the distance when I was out."

"You couldn't have. Quite impossible," Mrs. Pender assured me uncompromisingly. "As I said, I was in and out all evening... as a matter of fact it was past twelve when I left her. That's why I knew *you* were out somewhere; I was all ears until the early hours. I felt kind of responsible, you see."

"Naturally."

She left me then, and went out, closing the door with a sharp click.

I toyed with the appetizing breakfast before me, but couldn't eat much. In the light of day it was impossible and unreasonable to doubt Mrs. Pender's statement. What then, was the explanation for the night's macabre events? There must be one. I had never before had reason to doubt the evidence and stability of my own senses.

At that point it *did* seem that I must have suffered some kind of hallucination... a state of mind induced, perhaps, by the shock of my sundered marriage, coupled with a deep fundamental desire for some erotic experience calculated to erase the unhappy culmination of my frustrated libido.

Experience had taught me how potent were the powers of a disordered psyche over the normal functioning of mind and body. It was therefore quite conceivable, though distinctly disturbing, that for once in my life I had reverted temporarily to the unfortunate position of needing medical and psychological therapy rather than having the capacity for administering it.

My instinctive dislike of the lovely Jennet herself, seemed to confirm the theory. As for the date, the legend of "All Souls,"'... this could be mere coincidence.

Reviewing myself from such an angle, however shattering, it appeared nevertheless, the only satisfactory conclusion, and one which I had to face squarely and accept. Otherwise, I knew, I would be of little use in dealing with patients suffering from similar disorders.

By then, of course, I had already decided, that the country life, for me, would be unthinkable. The idea in the first place had also been a divergence from the norm, and I had to recognize that my choice of a holiday retreat had not been the right one; all things considered.

I spent a few more days at Trengorse, during which time I saw Jennet Mellyn only briefly at meal times, or when we happened to meet in the lounge or hall. She seemed lethargic and withdrawn, appearing more delicate and colourless than when we first met. Her beauty had somehow diminished, leaving her face, though unlined, with no sign of a blemish, deadly pale and expressionless, having no provocative allure or charm.

I sensed that she was aware of it, which accounted probably for the hostile glance of her grey eyes... and the contrived way she managed to avoid me whenever possible.

I was more than ever convinced of her involvement with certain drugs, but as it was not my business, put the implications to the back of my mind, and wilfully forgot... for the time being.

I returned to London before the week-end, and there I imagined, the episode of Jennet Mellyn was over. For me, anyway.

But things did not work out like that.

The following week, when I happened to be walking along one of the main corridors of the hospital, a casualty from a street accident was brought in... a girl who was obviously dead on arrival. Although such cases were not in my line of work, something about the prone figure caused me to pause and follow the depressing little procession to the mortuary.

As I had thought, the girl was Jennet.

She had suffered multiple abdominal and pelvic injuries, although her face was untouched, showing nothing but a triangular curious red mark on her right cheek... a scar starkly vivid against the white skin.

The wound though comparatively recent, had not been inflicted that day.

The pathologist was puzzled.

"Strange," he said. "It's healed, but torn at the edges... looks like some kind of a bite. Queer."

"Yes," I thought, "and more than that." But I said nothing. What *could* be said, anyway, that would make sense? And how was it that a mark could appear, in death, that had not been apparent during my last few days at the guest house?

There was no answer. Neither did I look for one. Some things were best left in the dark unconscious regions of their conception where they belonged.

I had had enough of the dead. My business was with the living to which in future I meant to contribute whatever skill and commonsense I possessed.

ACKNOWLEDGEMENTS

First off, to my family—Lou, Marnie and Lilly. They all have to put up with me when I'm doing these books, so it's only fair they get thanked first!

Additional thanks to David Brzeski for all things Elizabeth Walter, to Jen Baker for alerting me to "'Twas the Night of All Hallows". Thanks also to Mike Ashley, James Machin, James Rockhill, Tommy Atkinson, Richard Wells and Roger Clarke for being sounding boards when I was putting this book together.

To the whole team at British Library Publishing—it's been a very difficult time for them as of late, what with the insidious cyber-attack upon that most august of institutions, but everyone kept the boat rowing. So, to Jonny, Gary, Cerys, John, Alison and Thomas (who has now moved onto another job)—I raise a glass, and here is to a much calmer future.

Finally, to everyone who has read *Celtic Weird* and *Scotland the Strange*. I've been given a truly marvellous gift—that of interacting and meeting some of you when I've been promoting the book. I hope you love this book as much as the previous ones, and here's to the next!

JOHNNY MAINS is an award-winning editor renowned for recovering lost stories from the archives. His books edited for the British Library include *Celtic Weird* (2022) and *Scotland the Strange* (2023). His latest book is *Bound in Blood* (Titan, 2024).